A Shift in Shadows

Lost Legacies
Book 1

Maddox Grey

GREYMALKIN
PRESS

Published by Greymalkin Press
www.greymalkinpress.com

Cover Design by Seventhstar Art

eBook ISBN: 978-1-7375381-0-3
Paperback ISBN: 978-1-7375381-5-8

The Lost Legacies Series

A Shift in Darkness*

A Shift in Shadows

A Shift in Fate

A Shift in Fortune

A Shift in Ashes

A Shift in Wings

A Shift in Death

A Shift in Tides

*A Shift in Darkness is available for free download at maddoxgreyauthor.com.

Quick Note From The Author

Hey there! I just wanted to chat real quick about what you can expect in this book. This is a fantasy novel that contains adult content and situations. If it was a movie, it would probably be rated "R" for violence, language, and sexual content. If you want to go into this book completely blind and prefer not to read content warnings, you can skip on ahead, my friend.

If there are certain topics that you need to avoid for the sake of your own mental health, or that you simply don't like, please take a look at the list below for some things you will find in this book.

- Emotionally abusive ex-lover with stalker tendencies
- References to physical torture (actual torture happens off page)
- Emotional death of loved ones including parental death and death of a lover by abusive ex-lover
- Drinking alcohol as a coping mechanism
- Depression & panic attacks related to grief/trauma
- Consensual explicit sex scene (there is no dub-con or non-con)

Also… quick little note on language. I am a strange, strange person, and I've lived a bit of an odd life. I was born and raised in California, but was mostly raised by my Canadian grandmother and was then unofficially adopted by an Irish family in my late teens. You might be wondering why I'm mentioning this, and the reason is that I have a bit of a magpie approach when it comes to the English language.

Sometimes I like the American English spelling… sometimes I'm really attached to that extra "u" and go for the non-American version. Variety is the spice of life y'all.

Bless the soul of my copy-editor because she just sighs heavily at the start of each manuscript and deals with my eccentricities. So if you're an American and looking at a word and thinking it's not spelt right… it is most likely the non-American version of the word.

To Cee for always making me the perfect cup of coffee.

Prologue

Darkness was never something I feared. Quite the opposite, actually. It was something I sought out for comfort. To feel safe. When I was young, I believed I was the creature to be feared by everything that went bump in the night.

I thought myself invincible.

Almost four centuries of living taught me just how wrong I was. But even after I realized there were things even I had to dread, I still harbored no fear of darkness itself.

Until *they* took me.

And shattered my soul.

The room that currently served as my prison was so devoid of light that even with my exceptional night vision, I saw nothing. No shapes. No outlines. No hints of anything. No windows and no clocks, making time infinite.

That was one of the many ways they tortured me. And there *were* many.

"Ah, good. You're awake," a pleasant voice said in the darkness.

A snap sounded, and soft light filled the room. I blinked

rapidly, trying to adjust my vision. Clear, light blue eyes met mine.

The warlock waited until I was focused on him. "How are you doing this beautiful evening, my love?"

"Fu-fu-fu—" Spasms ran through my cracked and dry throat before I could force the rest of my words out.

The vampires working for the warlock had already visited me for their nightly entertainment. One of their favorite games was to see how much pain I could handle before screams finally tore out of me. I'd choked down my cries as they shattered each finger bone. But I broke when they began crushing the bones in my legs.

My magic had healed the more serious injuries first, leaving my throat sore. Under normal circumstances, I would have healed myself within minutes, but my magic was running a bit low these days. The warlock sitting across from me made sure of that. In addition to the vampires essentially using me as a juice box, he had crafted a potion that made it hard for me to think and weakened my magic, all except for healing. He only wanted to break me, not kill me.

Sebastian always was a clever one.

When we'd been lovers, he'd used that cleverness to charm and entertain me. That had been so long ago; it was hard to remember a time when I had loved him instead of hating him with every piece of my broken soul.

It's amazing how much can change in a century. Now Sebastian uses his spells to torture me in an attempt to bend me to his will.

I was fairly certain my stubbornness would outlast his cleverness, but my mind wasn't exactly firing at all cylinders these days, so that might be wishful thinking.

Sebastian clucked his tongue and moved towards me. I tried to shift away, but they'd tied me too tightly to the metal table I currently laid on. Panic rose as I pulled against the ropes. Memories of being bound and powerless in my youth flooded my mind.

I reached for my magic even though I knew I would find nothing but emptiness. Sebastian gave me a small smile.

Gods, I hated that smile.

"I'm so sorry it had to play out like this," he murmured. His eyes looked me over sadly, and I wanted nothing more than to claw them out. "I would have preferred to keep things between us a private affair. You would have come back to me eventually, I'm sure of it. But things are changing, and my hands are tied."

He lifted a hand and stroked my cheek, fingers trailing down my jawline and brushing against my lips. I held perfectly still, biding my time.

"The others don't know you're here. They think I'm still looking for you. But I can't hide you forever. And they will do far worse to you once they have you." His thumb brushed gently over my bottom lip once more. "Agree to work with me, and this will all be over. I can protect you from them. You loved and trusted me once. We can put the past behind us and be as we once were. Together. Unstoppable."

I snapped my teeth. He yanked his hand back with a glower, but not before I drew some blood. My tongue flicked over my lips, and I savored the sweet, coppery taste.

"I will never come back to you." I sank every scrap of strength left in me into those words, my voice coming out strong and even.

Rage flashed across his features before the smooth, charming façade settled back into place. "I'll see you soon."

He snapped his fingers, and the lights went out.

I closed my eyes, not that it really mattered, and listened. Sebastian was gone, and my body relaxed as much as it could while bound this table. I had no idea when he'd be back. Sometimes he'd be gone for long stretches of time. He never participated with the vampires in their torturous games. But he was the one in charge, so he was responsible all the same. Sebastian had always preferred psychological torture over physical.

My ears picked up on a slight shuffling sound outside my door. The guards were probably bored. I don't know why they bothered; no one had come for me, and it seemed unlikely anyone would do so now.

I wasn't sure exactly how much time had passed, but Sebastian and his vampire cronies had kidnapped me on my last birthday. And he hadn't mentioned my birthday again. There was no way he wouldn't have brought it up and made some sort of perverse celebration around it. So, less than a year. My friends and family likely thought I was dead.

If only. Death would be a gift.

My heart ached every time I thought about them. They'd been so worried about me and my never-ending quest for revenge against Sebastian. They'd pleaded for me to stop, at least for a while, instead of continuing to throw my life away as I tried and failed to kill Sebastian for decades.

It was all for nothing. I had failed, and he had finally won.

All I could do now was continue to deny him until he finally lost his patience and killed me. Or until the vampires went too far and drained me dry in their games. I hoped Sebastian would at least leave my body somewhere to be found by my loved ones, but he was a vindictive enough asshole to deny them that.

I had started to drift off when I heard one of the guards gasp, followed by several thuds.

My eyes shot open. Bodies hitting the floor?

Two of the thuds sounded lighter than the others. I craned my neck to look in the direction of the door, even though I couldn't see anything. A few seconds later, the door swung open, and light filtered in from the hallway.

The scent of a cool rainy night drifted into the room, and I went completely still.

Impossible. There was no way he was here.

I had finally gone insane, and my memories were fucking with me. Or I had drifted off to sleep and Sebastian was using his ability to weave dreams to mess with me.

Despite my disbelief, I couldn't stop myself from inhaling that familiar scent. It'd been centuries since I'd smelled it, but I would never forget it.

"My apologies for taking so long, child," Magos whispered quietly while cutting me loose from the steel table.

I said nothing as I studied him quickly and efficiently cut me loose. Last I'd seen him, his hair had been long and contained in tight braids. Now it was shaved close to his scalp. Other than that, he appeared the same as he had the day I'd saved his life by being a nosy child with very little self-preservation instincts.

"Are you real?" I whispered as he helped me stand.

His copper eyes burned bright with anger, making them stand out even more against his dark brown skin. "Yes, I'm real. I'm sorry I didn't come sooner. Your family and friends have been looking for you. When I heard you were missing, I did my own investigating. Some old contacts claimed a shifter had been captured by a group of vampires aided by a warlock. I took a chance on it being you."

Maybe I'd finally lost it and was hallucinating this conversation. I rolled my shoulders back and shifted my weight, savoring the ability to move. It *felt* real.

Hesitantly, I reached out and touched his arm, trailing my fingers down towards his hand. He held a sword with a slight curve. Mist still clung to it.

The tentative hope I'd been feeling settled deep within my chest at the sight of the blade.

This was real. It had to be.

"I take it you can't shift or use magic?" His voice was gentle as he looked me up and down, but his face hardened the longer he looked at me. The torn-up tank top and underwear I wore left most of my flesh on display. There was no hiding the bite marks, cuts, and burns all in various stages of healing.

"No." I shook my head vehemently before stopping and forcing myself to focus on his question. "No magic. No shifting. They dose me with a potion every morning to block that." I licked my dry lips. "It clouds my thoughts, too."

"I'll get us out." With slow but urgent movements, he led me to the door and out into the hallway.

Pain flooded my still-healing body with each step, and I latched onto that to help push back the fog that settled over my mind. We stepped over the headless bodies of the guards and continued down the dimly lit hallway.

The vamps hadn't bothered to keep the house in any decent shape. The wood floor was worn, some lights were missing bulbs, and the '70s-style wallpaper was peeling or completely missing in some areas. Random statues and paintings decorated the hallway. They'd likely killed or turned the owners ages ago and used this as a feeding house. My nose wrinkled at the stench of rot leaking from some of the other rooms. Furious shouts came from somewhere deep within the house.

"Stay behind me. And stay close." Magos ran out the door and down the hallway.

I followed, trying to push away the questions bouncing around in my head. *How much time has passed? Why had he come by himself and not gone to my friends and family if they were looking for me? Are they okay?*

"Escape first. Ask questions later," I mumbled. I didn't have a clue where the exit was, but my intuition was adamant I should trust him.

Even if he *was* a vampire.

"Come on, Nemain! Move!" he called out in that melodious accent I'd never been able to place.

We soon reached the end of the hallway and turned around the corner, and my vampire rescuer shoved me to the side. I slammed into the wall. Magos was fast, but not fast enough. I bit back a scream as the blade that had been aimed at my heart buried itself in my shoulder instead. Pain erupted as it tore through flesh and bounced off bone, ripping free with more damage.

A growl rumbled out from my chest. They'd been slicing my flesh without any fear of retaliation for so long that they'd forgotten who I was. What I was capable of. It was time to remind them just who they'd been fucking with.

I ducked when the dagger-wielding vampire struck at my chest. A familiar heat spread through my muscles as I rotated until my back was against his chest. Grasping his hand, I pulled it back until his wrist snapped and he dropped the long dagger. I snatched it out of the air and slammed an elbow into his face. The vampire's head snapped back, blood pouring from his nose. My arm flew in a move based on nothing but muscle memory and sliced through his throat. He gurgled as his hands clenched at his neck, trying to hold back the blood gushing out between his fingers.

My fist slammed into his face once more, and he collapsed to the floor. With one downward motion, I shoved the blade through his mangled neck. I rose as his head rolled away from his body.

I tried to focus on where Magos was and the rest of the vampires, but it was so hard to think. The fog that was ever-present in my mind thanks to Sebastian's potion had lifted slightly during the fight, but now it was pressing back in. I gripped the blade harder and willed myself to stay here in this moment.

A loud crash from behind made me jump, and the lights

went out. My back was against the wall, but all I could hear was my frantically pounding heart.

Panic rose as I struggled to stay calm, breathing becoming difficult as my lungs refused to expand. The fog's pressure intensified, and my thoughts kept slipping away, replaced by doubts.

Maybe I'd been wrong. Maybe this was a trap. A new method of torture to break me.

I could still smell Magos, but too many other scents were present for me to pinpoint his precise location. My chest tightened further as I gripped the blade like it was the only thing keeping me anchored to this reality.

The sounds of bodies crashing into each other and snarls came from farther down the hall.

If this was real, I needed to get my shit together and help Magos, but I couldn't convince my feet to move from where I was rooted against the wall. Someone grabbed my arm, and my body moved on pure instinct.

I broke his hold and threw a punch but missed. I froze and listened, trying to pinpoint his location. *Got it.*

I spun and kicked out with my right leg. He danced out of reach, and I couldn't tell where he was. I shook my head, but whatever was in that potion made my head fuzzy. *Focus, damnit.*

Before I could throw another punch, my attacker grabbed me again but just as quickly released me.

My fist flew forward in his general direction only to be caught in someone else's much bigger hand. I hissed as I tried to pull free until moonlight filtered in through the nearby window, as if a cloud had hazed by, allowing a glimpse into the night sky. I relaxed when I saw Magos in front of me, holding a very dead vampire in his other hand.

"It's rude to assault the person rescuing you. I've taken care of the remaining vampires, but I'm sure more are on the way.

Also, you should watch your language." His face was turned away from me, but I was pretty sure he was grinning.

"You could have said something," I muttered.

Although, given the bodies on the ground, it looked like he'd been busy taking out several more vampires while I'd been having a minor panic attack. I looked down and saw another vampire at my feet. Well, his headless body anyway.

Magos disappeared around the corner, and I ran after him, down the stairs and out the front door. A break in the clouds allowed the full moon to light up the sky.

I slowed, breathing in the crisp night air. I was free. *Free.* But then the adrenaline coursing through my body faded and shock settled in. Before I could process much more, Magos pulled on my arm, and we took off at a sprint once more.

He glanced over his shoulder at me. "I have a car on the other side of the gate at the end of the driveway. We just have to make it there, and then you can rest."

I jerked my head in a quick nod and pushed my body to run a little faster as we fled into the night.

Chapter One

I woke with a start, gasping for air as my vision narrowed. Tears tracked down my face, and I frantically reached behind me, my fingers slipping under the pillow and curling around the handle of a dagger.

Breathing in, I focused on the feel of the cool, rough handle. My fingers traced the slight dip where a piece was missing.

My dagger. My bed. My room.

Slowly, the panic faded. I was free. No ties held me down. I let out a long breath, released the knife, and rolled onto my back. Sebastian may no longer have me, and he may have failed in binding me to him, but he had succeeded in breaking me.

I'd never been much of a crier, but now most mornings I woke up with puffy eyes and dried tears on my lashes.

Not that I'd been the picture of good mental health before I'd been captured. But that me, the one who ran purely on rage and the need for vengeance, felt like a distant memory. She was still there, lurking beneath the surface, usually making an appearance when something caused me to lose my temper.

But now there was this other layer between the new me and the old me. One filled with tears, panic, and numbness.

I hated it, but I didn't know how to fix it. And while I also hated the panic attacks, a small part of me enjoyed feeling numb after being so angry my entire life.

The magic inside me, however, felt… differently.

It despised the numbness.

Every time I had a panic attack, it would surge forward and try to break free. Sometimes I was able to shove it back down, while other times it succeeded, and we had to go into damage control mode to get it contained again. Clean up whatever mess was made. I'd destroyed more than one home since Magos had rescued me.

Outside the large windows that took up an entire wall of my bedroom, the sky was starting to lighten with the hint of sunrise.

I sighed. Whatever nightmare I'd been having must have been a doozy, but at least my magic remained safely contained. And *he* hadn't come to visit me in my dreams.

Any time I went to sleep and didn't have to see Sebastian's face was a gift.

I was still tired, but I knew there was no going back to sleep at this point. A quick glance at the digital clock next to my bed told me it was 5 a.m. I had been asleep for a whopping two hours. Ugh.

After rolling out of bed, I walked over to my dresser and pulled on a pair of stretchy black pants and a dark grey tank top. The large bedroom was sparsely furnished, containing only the bed and a modern dresser with two matching night-stands. The only personal effect I had rested on the dresser, a housewarming present from my best friend, Kaysea. A large electric blue flower rose from a thick stem that had smaller vines wrapped around it. A few long green leaves stretched outward.

Once the sun came up, they'd twist toward the window to soak up the rays. The flower picked up on my movement, turning its deep orange center towards me. The thick petals surrounding it trembled as it swayed back and forth slowly.

It must be hungry. I frowned. When was the last time I'd fed it? Two days ago? Maybe last week?

"I'll feed you soon," I promised.

The vines started to unwind, and I quickly left the room before they finished. It wasn't dangerous, but it was grumpy when hungry, and I didn't feel like getting slapped in the face. As soon as I stepped foot in the hallway, I heard the coffee grinder start up in the kitchen. Vampire or not, my roommate was simply the best.

A small part of me expected to wake up and find Magos gone one day. I had saved his life once, so he had saved mine. But the debt was repaid, and he didn't owe me anything else. Plus, he was a vampire, and I wasn't exactly on good terms with vampires these days.

But he had stayed by my side this whole time. Nursed me back to health and helped me as best he could when my magic raged out of control.

I'd tried to push him away in the beginning. I wasn't a safe person to be around. But nothing I did could make him leave, and finally I gave up trying. Now I didn't know what I would do without him. He was my anchor in the chaotic storm that was my life.

When I'd reached out to Kaysea and my other best friend, Pele, after getting free, they'd both been so relieved to hear from me. Kaysea had cried tears of joy, and Pele had cussed me out for being stupid enough to get caught in the first place. But once Pele was done throwing a bitch fit, she'd offered me a place to stay. I'd refused at first, both because I wasn't one to accept charity and because my control over my magic was too volatile after I'd first gotten free.

But Pele had eventually convinced me to come by promising to arrange gigs for me to take once I was feeling up for it in exchange for rent.

My magic had been tamed enough that I'd accepted under one condition: Magos came too.

She hadn't been thrilled about that part. Vampires weren't well-liked in the magical community, and after learning vampires had worked with Sebastian to capture me, my friend's dislike of vampires only increased. That she'd conceded to my request and allowed Magos to stay in the apartment and even gone so far as to adjust the wards for him spoke to just how worried she was about me.

I was glad I'd taken Pele up on her offer to move here. Before Sebastian had captured me, I'd been planning on visiting Pele in Emerald Bay. While she lived in the daemon realm, she ran the tavern of the daemon-run town on the Washington coast. I'd grown up in the human realm, and it was easier for me to travel around here. Whenever I was in the fae and daemon realms, I had to worry constantly about anyone looking too closely at my magic. But in the human realm, all I had to do was slap on a glamour and I was good to go.

It didn't hurt that I loved the old mill that Pele had renovated into three apartments. She claimed she'd done so with the intention of using it for visiting friends and family, but this one had been furnished to my tastes and overlooked the rocky coastline.

She'd even gotten me a motorcycle to ride and claimed that it "came with the apartment." I had no doubt she'd done all this when she'd learned I was alive and free. She'd wanted me to have a safe place to stay.

Pele was never one to talk about her feelings, particularly mushy feelings, but she always showed them with her actions.

I walked up to the bar in the kitchen and slumped onto one of the stools. My hand flopped out onto the countertop, and my fingers made a "gimme" motion.

Magos's eyebrows rose slightly, but he handed me a mug. I took a sip. Perfect.

"Did you work as a barista at some point in your life? Is that how you've been occupying yourself these last few centuries? Seems like that'd be difficult with the whole vampire thing. Or did you manage to find a coffee shop open only at night?" I tilted my head and arched an eyebrow at him.

Magos seldom smiled, but the corners of his mouth twitched as he strolled out of the kitchen.

I sighed and settled in to enjoy my coffee. Despite living together for almost a year, I barely knew anything about him. Figuring out his past had become a bit of a game between us, one I was sorely losing.

With his dark rich brown skin, short-cropped hair, and strange copper-colored eyes, Magos was jaw-droppingly gorgeous. At just over six feet with broad shoulders and a strong chest, he drew attention any time we left the house.

He pretended not to notice, but I was always entertained by all the stares he received from women and men. Granted, humans were pulled towards vampires regardless of their looks to a certain degree, and the older the vampire, the stronger the pull. Magos claimed they couldn't help it. I remained unconvinced.

Regardless of his ridiculously good looks, there had never been the inkling of anything romantic between us, despite what my brother and some of my friends believed.

Magos and I had met when I was a child. To be fair, that meeting had been fairly brief—less than a day, in fact. But when you save someone's life, you tend to remember it. I wasn't sure how to define our relationship now. I'd never had much in the way of family, only my parents and brother. But I supposed Magos would have fit well into the role of uncle.

I enjoyed my coffee and stared out the window, trying to ignore the unease that was always lurking in the back of my mind.

My friends and family had worked so hard to make me feel safe here, and I felt guilty about not being okay. Part of me wanted to run. Disappear somewhere in the human realm or one of the other realms for a while. It's what I usually did when things in my life went to hell.

But after centuries of running… I was tired. So instead, I shoved the feeling away and watched the waves crash into the rocky shoreline.

Pele truly had found and designed the perfect home for me. Similar to my bedroom, the rest of the apartment was sparsely furnished. The main living area was one big space that consisted of the kitchen, living room, and a workout area. The living room held a couch and a few chairs that faced a large TV. The rest of the space was dedicated to sparring and weapons storage.

"Up for some sparring?" I moved towards the large sparring mat without waiting for Magos's response.

No art hung on the bare brick walls. Only weapons. Lots and lots of weapons.

They had been the first thing I'd started to collect when we'd settled down here. My main swords hung next to the front door, but my collection of throwing knives and just-in-case-shit-really-hits-the-fan swords hung on the brick wall behind the sparring mat.

I walked past all the blades to grab my favorite fighting staff and twirled it in my right hand.

Besides being a clean roommate who served as my personal barista, Magos was also my sparring buddy. Shapeshifter healing is remarkable. It'd taken me only a few days to fully recover after escaping the vampires. Physically, at least. We'd started sparring shortly after that. I'd been training with my swords since I could hold them as a child. And after my parents' deaths, I threw myself into training even more. It was rare to encounter anyone with the skills to go up against me in a one-on-one fight.

Magos kicked my ass every time. It didn't matter what we chose—short swords, longswords, staffs, freaking nunchucks—the end result was always the same.

I usually grumbled a bunch of swear words in as many languages as I knew while Magos helped me back to my feet. I hadn't beaten him yet, but over the past couple of months, I'd made him work a lot harder to get me down.

Magos nodded, walked across the mat, and grabbed his favorite pair of bastons. The two-foot wooden sticks didn't look intimidating, but I was well aware of how much they hurt when he landed a hit with them.

He made no comment about me being up again so soon after going to bed. He had probably heard me screaming. Nor did he comment on me wanting to spar again after he'd given me quite the beating earlier in the night. He knew both the coffee and the sparring helped me settle.

Neither of us were good at talking about our past, but we *were* good at helping each other in other ways.

"Just going to stand there? Afraid I'll mar that beautiful face of yours?" I crooned.

As usual, he didn't move. Just stood there with a calm, easy expression in the middle of the mat as I circled around him.

"My apologies. I thought you wanted to exercise your body, not your mouth. You can assault me verbally just as well if I'm seated, can you not?" he said dryly.

Before my clever retort could come out, he spun around and slammed one of his bastons into my staff. I pushed back, only to receive a blow to my ribs with the other one. I bit back a cry and jumped out of his range.

We continued to circle each other, looking for openings.

"Plans for the day?" He closed the distance between us.

I blocked the blow to my right side and spun out of range of the follow-up coming to my left. Not quick enough. I felt the sting on my shoulder as I backed away.

"Going to check in with Kaysea this morning. She was planning on meditating to see if she could trigger a vision. If she's foreseen anything, I'd like to know. Might check in with Pele, as well. And I need to convince Andrei to spend my birthday here." My tone stayed steady even though the mention of my birthday quickened my pulse.

I moved to the left and stabbed with my staff, but he easily blocked it. I spun behind him and gave two more quick thrusts. Also blocked. I danced out of reach before Magos launched a counter offensive. He studied me calmly as I moved around him.

"There are no signs Sebastian knows where we are. It's unlikely anything will happen on your birthday."

"I know." I feinted towards Magos's left. He didn't fall for it. I made a face at him, and he just rolled his eyes. A habit he had definitely picked up from living with me. "I just don't want to be caught unprepared. He might not know where we are, but we also don't know why he worked with those vampires to kidnap me. He's been content for decades to torment me all by himself. Something must have changed.

"Since we don't know what, I want to err on the side of caution. Kaysea will be safe in the fae realm. Pele, likewise, will be safe if she remains in her bar. Andrei is the obvious target and the weak link. He'll be safer here with us."

"Very well."

Then he *moved*. One moment we were circling around each other and the next I was blocking his blows as fast as I could.

My staff shook each time it blocked a blow, and despite pushing myself as fast as I could, I had only a few more seconds before his blows made it past my defense.

Just *once*, I would like to get him on the mat. Winning was out of the question. Unless I used my magic, which I never did when we sparred. Magic wasn't something that could always be counted on. I'd learned my lesson on that.

Magos's technique was perfect. Every move was as graceful as it was deadly. He spent just enough energy for each strike and nothing more. Magos fought with perfect control, whereas I fought like a wildcat who had just escaped from its cage... which wasn't exactly far off.

I lunged towards him and jabbed with my staff. He knocked it aside, and I let it go as he swept me off my feet as I'd anticipated.

But I didn't land on my back like he expected. Instead, I arched my spine and reached out with my hands; as soon as they hit the ground, I pushed myself back and landed on my feet in a crouched position. Feline shapeshifter agility for the win! Launching myself forward, I pulled an absolutely stupid move that only worked in the movies. I crashed into Magos's knees, and we both ended up on the mat.

I reached for my staff, but before I could move, he switched our positions and was straddling me and pushing the wood baston against my throat. Game over.

Laughter erupted from his throat as he looked at me with amusement dancing in his eyes. He smiled so rarely, let alone laughed so freely. I might have lost the match, but I still considered this outcome a win of sorts.

"Satisfied? Can I return to my chair and coffee now?" he asked, still smiling.

"Sure. I'm going to lie here for another minute and enjoy my moment." I might not have beaten him, but I still got his ass on the ground.

Of course, I'd lost the match. Lost. Just like I'd lost the fight when the vampires had jumped me years ago.

My smile slowly faded.

I closed my eyes as the panic I'd fought back less than an hour ago rose again. My chest tightened, making breathing difficult, but I forced myself to maintain steady breaths. Something told me today was not going to be fun.

Chapter Two

Magos settled in a chair facing the window as he did most mornings, watching the sun peek over the horizon.

He'd been sitting waiting for the sun to rise when we'd met all those centuries ago, in fact. My family had just settled into our cottage on the coast of France, and I'd been out exploring the new terrain. I'd always been a terribly curious child, and finding a vampire sitting cross-legged next to a steep cliff had been quite the surprise.

I hadn't understood at the time why he was there. I knew a little about vampires, enough to know that the sun wouldn't kill them, but it was painful. He'd been sitting so close to the cliff that I was worried he would fall off and not be able to get out of the sun.

My father had been the one to tell me that while the sunlight didn't immediately kill vampires, it could kill them if they stayed out in it for days on end. Their magic would be forced to constantly heal the burns and would eventually run out. Without access to more blood to replenish itself, their magic would cannibalize their own body.

That was why when vampires had come to our door,

seeking shelter, my father had agreed. My mother had not been happy. But my father was always the kind-hearted one, and the vampires had left that night without causing any trouble.

Well, that might have been because my mother had watched them all night with her sword in hand and a promise of violence in her eyes.

I'd told Magos my concerns that day and he'd just given me a sad smile and told me he'd be fine and to run along. But I hadn't left him. Instead, I'd broken my promise to my parents and used my magic to get him out of there. I'd taken us somewhere the sun couldn't reach us and talked his ear off asking questions about where he was from and where he had been.

He'd answered all my questions and gradually started talking to me and asking questions about my life. I knew my parents would be horrified to know I was telling a stranger so many of our secrets. But even back then, I had just known I could trust him. When I'd brought him back to the cliffs after dark, he'd promised to tell no one of my magic and had thanked me for the gift of my company. He'd also promised to return the favor someday.

The memory of that day always came to me when I watched him wait for the sun to rise. I wondered how often he thought of it. We hadn't spoken of that day and what his intention had been since we'd been reunited. I didn't know Magos's age for sure. He was obviously older than me since I had met him when I was a child.

I suspected he was one of the original vampires, which would put him at over six hundred years old. He didn't volunteer any information, and I didn't push. It's not like there weren't plenty of things I didn't want to talk about, and he never pressed me on them.

I walked back to my bedroom, leaving him to watch the sunrise. I pulled off my clothes and tossed them haphazardly towards the laundry bin. My shirt missed and landed on my bed instead.

A furry grey head popped up to look at me from under my shirt, followed by a second furry black head.

Shit.

Luna just blinked at me with sleepy eyes, but Jinx glared grumpily. He was set in his sleep schedule and didn't like to be disturbed. Personally, I didn't think it was fair since he spent most of his time sleeping, so it was impossible not to interrupt him at some point.

Humans have this stupid superstition about black cats being the cause of bad luck. Go to any animal shelter, and black cats will be the dominant color. It was a bunch of bullshit, of course. The domestic cats of this realm had no bearing whatsoever on one's luck. Bad or good.

Unfortunately for me, that was not the case for grimalkins. Like the flowering plant on my dresser, Jinx and Luna were not of this realm. Their glamours made them look like a typical domestic shorthair cat, but their true forms were considerably bigger. Not quite as big as mine, but still big enough to be a physical danger. It was their magic that made them a true threat. Jinx, in particular, had a vindictive streak.

"Sorry. Sorry." I raised my hands in a placating gesture.

Luna moved slightly and settled herself against Jinx, her light silver fur contrasting sharply against his inky black coat. She started purring, and Jinx glanced down at her before shooting me one more dirty look. Saved by Luna again.

My instincts were screaming at me to stay inside today, but that wasn't an option. Technically, I could have met with Kaysea and Pele through the mirror in the living room, but given how my past birthdays had gone, I wanted to meet with them in person. Magos was probably right, and chances were slim anything bad would happen. But if something did, and if

I was taken again, I wanted to see my friends one last time in person and not through a mirror.

Gods, that's dark. I left Luna and Jinx to their nap and headed to the bathroom.

Standing under the shower head, I let the hot water wash over me. After scrubbing off all the dried sweat, I wrapped a fluffy towel around myself and headed back into my room. The two grimalkins stretched out across my bed were enjoying the sunlight beaming through the windows. Jinx was so adorable when he was sleeping and not terrorizing me.

I eased open one of the dresser drawers and pulled out a pair of loose-fitting black pants and a long-sleeve black shirt. Like most of my clothing, these came from the daemon realm and were geared towards fighters.

I pulled on the pants first and checked the various pockets out of habit, then slipped the shirt on. The fitted fabric clung to me before the sleeves widened below the elbow. Daemons never made anything that wasn't practical, whether clothes or weapons. The fashion and material were a little odd for the human realm, but not enough to stand out. And it wasn't like I interacted with humans all that often anyway.

Living in the human realm meant I could mostly avoid the politics of the fae and daemon realms, something I very much preferred. I'd lived in normal human cities and towns, but whenever possible, I tried to settle in daemon-run towns.

Places like Emerald Bay offered a thriving magical commu-nity, which made it easier for me to pick up jobs. And it usually meant not many humans were around, either. Daemons typi-cally chose remote locations humans didn't have any reason to visit, but they did have a presence in all the major cities as well. Emerald Bay had less than two thousand humans. Some knew about magic and all the things that went bump in the night. The rest had no idea and went about their daily lives, thinking they lived in a quaint coastal town.

Once dressed, I walked back across the hall to the mirror in the bathroom to set my glamour before going out. Emerald-green eyes with vertical slit pupils stared back at me. My mother's eyes. My father used to tell me that whenever he missed the infinite green fields of Ireland, all he had to do was look into our eyes and he felt like he was home.

As I stared into my irises in the mirror, I could almost hear him say it and hear my mother's lilted laugh. That brief moment of happiness dissolved as the laugh turned into her dying screams.

A flicker of anger flared to life before numbness surrounded me once more. I didn't fight it; instead, I sank into it further.

I touched the leather necklace around my neck. Really, it looked more like a collar, but the leather was soft and comfortable. I ran my fingers against a dark blue gem set into the leather. With a quick push of magic, a tingle spread across my skin, and the reflection staring back at me changed.

I studied my reflection in the mirror to make sure the glamour was working as it should. My eyes remained their vivid green, but my pupils were no longer catlike. Running my tongue around my normal-looking teeth, I could still feel my fangs even though I couldn't see them. The glamour also made my slightly tapered ears look more rounded and, most significantly, changed the appearance of my skin.

I wrinkled my nose in distaste. Human skin was so boring. My non-glamoured skin was a deep golden brown with lighter rosettes that matched my feline coat. With the glamour in place, my skin was just a boring flat brown. My ash-blonde hair remained the same color, and I pulled it back into a braid.

These days I could almost get away with not wearing a glamour. Humans would just assume I was wearing makeup and fancy contacts. If anything, it was my tattoos that would grab their attention more.

I stared loathingly at the brilliant blue flowers that wound their way down my arms. They were a similar shade of blue to the flowering plant on my desk. But these flowers were much more delicate and had smaller petals that tapered off to narrow points. Winding green vines connected all of them as they flowed over my shoulders and down my back.

Another flower would likely show up on my birthday, and I briefly wondered where it would appear this time.

Not for the first time, I wished the glamour was capable of hiding the tattoo. I'd still know it was there, but at least I wouldn't have to look at it every day. But the only one who could remove it was the warlock who'd cast the spell. And I didn't think Sebastian would be removing it anytime soon.

Slowly running my fingers over one of the blue flowers, I sighed and let my arm drop before leaving the bathroom.

I grabbed my bracers off a shelf by the front door and clasped them to my forearms, feeling the intricate glyphs carved into the silver on top. A silver dagger slid into the slim holster on the underside of each bracer, hidden by the wide sleeves of my shirt. I strapped the harness that held my two short swords on my back, shifting my shoulders slightly as I looked over the remaining knives and grabbed one to shove into the pocket in my boot. Helmet in hand, I left the apartment.

My bike was the only vehicle in the small parking lot. The Yamaha rumbled a bit but smoothed out. Heading toward the beach cove ten minutes away, I relished the chilly morning air.

Part of me wanted to keep going. But I needed to check in with Kaysea, so I reluctantly pulled into the beach parking lot.

I trudged up the beach, ignoring the humans getting their morning jog in. After a quarter mile, I came upon a small cove between large rocks where the water traveled in further. Any humans who bothered to walk this far would get a sudden urge to return the way they'd come. If they still moved forward, they would get a wicked case of vertigo for their troubles.

A tingle spread over my skin as I crossed the fae-created boundary. I stepped up the few stairs of a wooden gazebo and stopped by a small mirror with a cloudy surface. The symbol I traced across the mirror glowed a soft blue before fading away. Turning away from the mirror, I sat on the bottom step and watched the tide roll in and out. It shouldn't take Kaysea long to get here.

Most of the fae had returned to their realms during the Industrial Revolution. Despite common myths, they could handle iron and other metals just fine. But the fae found the pollution of the human realm to be distasteful. Some chose to stay behind, while others traveled back and forth. The merfolk in particular liked to play occasionally in the oceans in the human realm despite the growing amounts of pollution. The animals that swam in the oceans here were far less likely to eat them.

Everyone had an opinion on the fae. Humans told fairy tales and thought the fae were good beings who granted you fun little wishes and couldn't lie. The witches and warlocks thought the fae were manipulative and dangerous; I always chalked that up to jealousy, though. And others in the magical community thought they were patronizing snobs who didn't have nearly as much power as they claimed.

My opinion was that they were all of the above. Except for the power bit. They very much had all the magic they claimed and then some. Aside from Kaysea, I mostly avoided them. Any travel I made to one of the fae realms was quick and to the point. Not drawing the attention of the fae was on the top of my to-do list.

I glanced down the shore toward the portal to the Kaysea's fae realm. She had been my friend for a long time, over half my life. I'd met her while traveling in the fae realms after my parents had died. I'd been stubbornly staying in the fae realms, determined to discover the reason I always got the distinct impression I shouldn't be there, like what humans felt when they approached a boundary ward.

My brother, Cian, didn't get that feeling in the fae realms. No one I knew did. I'd come up with various reasons for why it was important, but really, I just desperately needed the distraction from the grief and rage I'd been feeling.

And then I'd quickly found myself in hot water.

Things were about to take a turn for the worse when Kaysea spoke up and said she'd brought me there, saving my skin in the process.

She got me out of the fae realm but stayed with me afterwards and we gradually became friends. The only person I'd been friends with longer was Pele. Although, Pele and I had been lovers first, our friendship coming later.

Movement in the waves caught my attention, but I didn't see Kaysea. I continued scanning until a familiar merfolk who was definitely not my friend came into sight. A disappointed sigh slipped from me as I walked towards the edge of the water and looked at the merman.

Kaysea's older brother Connor bobbed up and down in the waves, only his head and shoulders visible. His dark green hair was pulled back away from his face, making his already sharp features stand out more. Kaysea had light green eyes, but Connor's were several shades lighter and looked almost white. They freaked me out a little. Not that I'd ever admit it to him. It was hard to see any emotion in his eyes, but the flat expression on his face told me he was in his standard asshole mood.

He was a good twenty feet out, but I sure as hell wasn't getting in the water with a merman who held a massive grudge against me. I might be thick sometimes, but I wasn't stupid.

"Kaysea isn't feeling well at the moment. She asked me to

inform you that she'll reach out to you through the mirror later today," he said coldly. Pleasant as always.

Connor had barely hid his contempt for me ever since my lover, Kaysea's twin, had died a horrific death. I couldn't entirely fault him for that. Part of me understood I wasn't responsible for what Sebastian had done. But he had only targeted Myrna because of me. Kind, funny, and sweet Myrna had been the love of my life and more than I'd ever deserved. Kaysea understood how much Myrna's death had devastated me and grieved with me over the loss.

But Connor held me directly responsible; I held no doubt he would kill me the first chance he got. On land, he was no match for me, but the reverse was true in the water. My guilt over Myrna's death meant nothing to him. His anger and hatred hadn't softened over the decades.

"What do you mean, she's not feeling well?" I asked with the politest tone I could muster. *Must not murder bestie's brother.*

"I mean, she is feeling the opposite of well. Shall I procure you a dictionary?" he snapped.

"What, does she have a cold? Maybe she should get out of the cold water. I could run and get her some orange juice. Maybe some Airborne? There's a pharmacy right around the corner. I'll just go in and ask what they prescribe for a mermaid with a cold?" Annoying him always cheered me up a little.

"If you must know, one of the younglings was exploring some caves near our territory and encountered some not particularly pleased inhabitants. She was badly wounded and near death by the time she made it back. Healing her took most of Kaysea's magic, and my sister is exhausted. Both of them are resting, not that you care about the well-being of anyone besides yourself." Connor idly picked at some drifting seaweed.

"You could have told me that in the beginning instead of

acting like such a jackass," I retorted, annoyed that he'd ruined the fun I'd been having about teasing him and making me feel like a jerk.

"Perhaps one of these days you'll start acting your age and then you won't make such a fool of yourself every time you speak." He gave me a flat stare before diving under the surface. His tail rose out of the water, and he slapped it down, sending a wave of water crashing against me. I leaped back before I got soaked.

Asshole. *Pretentious* asshole.

Chapter Three

My mood continued to sour as I walked back to my bike. It was impossible not to think about Myrna after seeing Connor. Prior to being captured, her death was all I thought about every waking moment. I had let the grief consume me until I was a shadow of the person I used to be.

The grief was still there, but now thanks to the numbness I'd wrapped around myself, it was duller. But sometimes I'd still find a sharp edge and cut myself. Every time I did, a little of the former me peeked through. The one that felt nothing but rage and thirsted for violence.

I couldn't let myself lose it now. Not with my birthday coming up. I'd been hoping to spend a couple hours with Kaysea to try and trigger one of her visions. Normally, she only had visions related to the fae, but sometimes they involved me. It was a long shot, but I would have felt better if she didn't see any imminent deaths in my future. Plus, Kaysea always knew what to say and would call me on my bullshit. She had lived through what normally happened on my birthdays and understood things without me having to explain it.

Myrna and I had been together for forty-two years before Sebastian had killed her on my 352nd birthday. In the decades that followed, we'd been locked in a dangerous game of cat and mouse. But despite my skills at tracking people, he'd always stayed one step ahead. He used his dreamwalking abilities to slip in and out of my dreams.

To further taunt me, he'd leave flowers and other gifts throughout the year leading up to my birthday. The birthday gift was always the same.

A bloody heart. Usually still warm.

Occasionally, he would leave an item with the heart so I knew whose chest it had been torn from.

Sometimes I had no idea whose heart it was. I'd lived in constant fear that it would be the heart of someone I loved. Kaysea or Pele. Or maybe my brother, Cian. I walled myself off from everyone as best I could, but it's not like I could hide my history with them.

I still didn't know why Sebastian had changed the game and captured me. He'd been enjoying tormenting me all those decades. Based on the often one-sided conversations we'd had when I'd been his prisoner, something had changed between him and the other warlocks. I didn't know if they knew about me or not, but Sebastian had definitely wanted to keep me away from them. He was a selfish bastard who didn't like to share.

There was no way he was going to just let me go. Despite my friends constantly reassuring me that he didn't know where I was, I couldn't shake the feeling that this life I was building was going to fall apart. I needed to know what Sebastian was planning and where I fit into it.

My fingers rubbed the bright ruby gem that was embedded in the necklace around my neck. A little of the tension eased out of me as my fingers ran along its smooth surface.

This was my second birthday since Magos had rescued me.

The first one had been mere days after that rescue, and I didn't remember much of it.

As soon as I got my wits back after our escape, I went to one of the best daemon amulet crafters seeking a way to prevent Sebastian from using blood magic to track me. Gods only knew he had plenty of my blood leftover from my captivity.

The price would have been impossible for anyone else, and I agreed to it only because I was desperate and didn't see any other options. By that time, Jinx had found me, so the three of us had managed to get what the amulet crafter had requested in payment. In return, she had crafted me an amulet that blocked all tracking spells, including blood spells. Sebastian could still walk into my dreams, but he could no longer find me as easily as he once did. Magos and I hadn't seen any vampires since escaping, nor had I noticed any witches or warlocks in the area.

I chewed my bottom lip as I stood next to my bike, unsure of what to do next. If I went back to the apartment, Magos would be asleep, and I would just sit there and stress about my birthday. The more I stressed, the more the magic within me stirred and tried to break free. I needed a distraction, just for a little while, to give my mind a break.

It was still really early in the morning. Andrei was probably still sleeping and likely had only been asleep for a few hours. But waking up Pele this early could result in me being set on fire. Literally.

Andrei was the safer route. A grumpy werewolf was definitely the wiser choice over a grumpy daemon.

Plus, Pele could read me like a book and would instantly pick up on how stressed out I was and that I was hanging on by the barest of threads. Andrei didn't know anything about my past, so I could pretend to be someone else around him.

Someone that wasn't dragging centuries worth of pain and loss behind them.

Decision made, I hopped on my bike and made the short drive to the old boarding house that the werewolves were fixing up just outside of town. As usual, the front door was unlocked, so I let myself in. A glance into the large living room to the right revealed several bodies passed out on the couch and a few on the floor. Two lifted their hands in greeting but didn't bother to get up or look at me. I quirked a smile and headed up the stairs to the third floor.

The pack had gotten used to me coming and going these past few months; sometimes I'd even run with them under the moonlight in the woods nearby.

I went into the apartment, closing the door quietly behind me. A quick glance showed no one in the living room or small kitchen that took up this section of the apartment. The double sliding doors that led into the bedroom displayed the rumpled covers of the bed. Empty. The sound of falling water announced the shower had started.

I'd been hoping to catch him naked in bed, but naked in the shower would work just as well.

Grinning, I walked across the living room into the bedroom. I deliberately stepped on the creaky wooden boards to announce my presence.

"Hello?" a voice asked from the bathroom.

"You really should lock your doors, wolf. You're just asking for all kinds of trouble by leaving them open." I cocked one hip against the bathroom door frame.

A husky laugh sounded from the shower. The curtain pulled back slightly, and he poked his head out. "But I enjoy trouble so much. Especially the type of trouble you bring, kitty cat," Andrei replied with a sly smile.

If you really understood the type of trouble I'd bring to your life, you'd lock your door with me on the other side of it. Or maybe he wouldn't.

Andrei was a genuinely good guy. That worried the hell out of me. Good people didn't survive long in my world.

The guilt that I'd been purposely ignoring these past few months nipped at me. I shouldn't have let things progress as far as they had with Andrei. What had started as just a fun one-night stand to blow off some steam had turned into a second one-night stand. Then a third. Now it was common for us to see each other several times a week. Usually just for bedroom activities, but he'd started asking me to come over for dinner and stay for breakfast.

I knew what all that meant, that this was becoming something more than just a casual fling. But this was the only noncomplicated thing in my life, and I was determined to keep it that way. Once I was a little more confident in my mental health, I would break things off with him. Or tell him about my history and let him decide if he wanted to continue... whatever this was.

The water turned off and the shower curtain slid aside, revealing a lean, muscled body wrapped in tanned skin. His shaggy chestnut-brown hair was plastered against his face, darker while wet, which made his hazel eyes stand out even more than usual.

"Would you like me to do a little spin for you?" Andrei asked playfully.

"Mmm. Would you mind?" I practically purred.

He laughed and stepped out of the shower, offering me a satisfying turn. I squealed when he shook himself like a dog, sending water flying everywhere. I fled the bathroom and jumped onto the bed. Andrei laughed and followed me a moment later, a towel wrapped around his hips.

"You're up awfully early." I lay across the middle of his bed, head propped up on one hand. "I was hoping to find you still in bed. I had all sorts of plans." I bit my lower lip, and Andrei's gaze latched onto the movement.

He took a step towards the bed, and the towel started to fall. I grinned with anticipation. This was just the distraction I needed. I had several hours to kill before I could check in with the others, and I needed to get out of my head for a while. Andrei took another step and reached the bed. The towel fell completely away, revealing that he was *very* happy with this plan.

"Trouble, trouble, trouble," he growled, planting a knee on the bed and moving towards me.

I rose up to meet him but froze when I heard footsteps coming up the stairs.

"Shit." Andrei jumped off the bed and snatched the towel off the floor. He'd just gotten it wrapped around his hips when his front door flew open and Stela breezed into the apartment. She paused when she got far enough into the living room to see us, me still on the bed and Andrei holding the towel wrapped around himself.

Damn it. I sagged a little and put my libido on pause. Maybe this would be a quick conversation and then Andrei and I could get back to more important matters.

"Really? I literally called you fifteen minutes ago, saying I was coming up so we could plan how to handle the deliveries today before I head into town." She tapped her foot loudly, as if her exasperated tone wasn't enough to get her point across. But the move was ruined by the wide grin on her face. While Andrei was all lean muscle and rugged good looks, his sister was all soft curves and had a pretty face with bedroom eyes.

Very much aware of her appearance, she usually played up her curvy figure by dressing in retro pinup style. Today she was sporting tight red pants with a high waist and a low-cut white shirt with red polka dots.

"Sorry, sis," Andrei said as he walked to his dresser and pulled out clothes. "I was getting ready to come downstairs and meet you when I, uh . . . got distracted."

Given that I was still on the bed and Andrei had been frantically wrapping a towel around himself when she walked in, I supposed there wasn't really any better way to put it.

I wiggled my fingers at her. "Sorry, Stela. I didn't know you were on your way here; otherwise, I wouldn't have staged my little seduction."

Stela snorted. "Yeah, I'm sure it took a lot of effort to convince my brother to get in bed with you. Feel free to join our planning session, and then you can get back to it. Just maybe wait until I'm out of the house so I don't have to hear anything." She wrinkled her nose at the last part and turned back towards the door. "See you both downstairs in a few minutes."

I flopped down on the bed. Andrei pounced, his knees landing on either side of me and his hands on the bed frame above my head. I looked up at him, the corners of my mouth tugged downward, and he grinned.

"Don't look so glum, love. This won't take long, and I can't get started on anything until the rest of the pack wakes up anyway."

"Fine." I sighed and stuck out my lip in a pout.

He leaned down and nipped it. That led to us kissing and me wrapping a hand around the back of his head and kissing him harder. He parted his lips, and my tongue slipped in. Growling, he tangled his fingers in my hair. We broke apart a minute later and stared at each other. His eyes were wild, and the air around us was thick with lust.

A loud crash sounded downstairs.

Andrei sighed and leaned his forehead against mine. "Later," he said huskily.

"Later." A small smile played on my lips.

Andrei hopped off the bed and put his clothes on. I stayed put and enjoyed the show until he was done. We headed downstairs to the kitchen, where Stela waited for us.

"Coffee?" She held up the coffee pot.

"Yes, please." I plopped down on one of the stools at the counter and watched Stela pour the coffee while Andrei grabbed the cream and sugar. "I've trained you both well," I said proudly.

They made identical snorts and walked over to the table where Stela had a bunch of paperwork fanned out.

I sipped my coffee and watched them. It'd been a long time since I'd been around werewolves. The war between the vampires and werewolves had raged for centuries, and no one entirely remembered how or why it started. Attempts at peace never lasted. Events had turned decidedly in the vampires' favor towards the end, and they'd just about stamped the werewolves out of existence.

When I'd first reached out to Pele about moving to this city, she'd told me about the small pack living in the woods outside town. I'd sought them out mostly out of curiosity when I'd first moved here. They loved to run through the woods at night, so I had led them on several merry chases over the course of a week before finally introducing myself.

Andrei and I had hit it off right away. He and his sister were fairly new werewolves—so were a lot of the wolves in the pack. He hadn't told me everything yet, but I knew enough to understand a lot of pain and resentment existed between Andrei and the werewolves he'd met outside this pack.

It all stemmed from how he and his sister had been turned. Unlike vampire children who were born as vampires but didn't come fully into their powers until puberty, werewolf children were born human, and their werewolf side had to be activated. Normally, this process occurred when they were young adults, but it wasn't uncommon for some to choose to never activate their werewolf side and continue living as humans, especially as the war raged on and the vampires hunted down any werewolf they could find.

Despite my curious nature, I hadn't pried too much because he hadn't pushed to know more about me. If I started asking him questions, I knew he'd do the same, and I was enjoying having someone in my life who didn't know my whole history and all the baggage that came with it.

When I was with Andrei, I could almost pretend to be someone else for a few hours. It wasn't the healthiest way of dealing with all the problems in my life, but getting a break for a few hours was nice. I'd have to come clean with him, probably soon, but I could pretend a little longer.

Andrei stood up, and I tuned back into their conversation. "All right, I'll make sure all the lumber and supplies are stacked in the barn, and once everyone wakes up, we'll get started on the unfinished side of the basement. How long do you think you'll be in town?"

Stela stacked all the papers into a neat pile. "Probably a few hours. Jolie and I are going to grab breakfast and do a little shopping."

A creak announced the front door opening, followed by the sound of high heels down the hallway. Then a rosemary and lavender scent hit me, causing me to involuntarily stiffen.

"All done?" a soft feminine voice asked.

"All done." Stela walked over to the woman and gave her a quick kiss, letting her hand rest on the woman's shoulder.

"Hey, Jolie," Andrei said warmly. "You're here to help me unload all the supplies, right?"

"Not so much." The woman laughed lightly. She was a few inches shorter than Stela and had a more delicate build. Freckles stood out against her pale skin, and wisps of red hair fell out of a loose bun. If humans actually believed in the fae, they probably would have thought they all looked like Jolie. She could be a fairy princess in a movie.

Something about her bothered me, but I didn't know what exactly. I didn't interact with humans all that often, but that was primarily because most humans were clueless about magic and all the other realms. Jolie was one of the rare exceptions. She wasn't strong enough to use it, but she was sensitive and could see it. She probably had fae blood somewhere back in her family tree. My nose itched as her perfume soaked into the air. It always made me want to sneeze. Maybe that was why I didn't like her.

Stela held her hand out to Jolie. "Shall we? I could eat an entire stack of those lemon ricotta hotcakes."

"Mmm, that sounds delicious." Jolie clasped Stela's hand and nodded at me and Andrei. "It was nice seeing you both."

I offered a tight smile and tried to at least keep my expression neutral until they left. Letting out a sigh of relief, I turned and faced Andrei once they were out of the kitchen.

He raised a brow. "Still not a fan, huh?"

"Doesn't her perfume bother you? It's like she bathes in the stuff. I don't know how Stela stands it." I rubbed my nose, trying to make the scent go away faster.

"I don't notice it all that much. Maybe your little kitty nose is just too sensitive."

I stuck my tongue out at him, and he chuckled.

"Honestly, I wouldn't care if she smelled like garbage that had been baking in the sun all day. She makes my sister happy. And after everything that's happened, I'll put up with anything if it means I get to hear my sister laugh again." He kept his tone even, but I saw the darkness that crept into his eyes. Something really bad had happened to him and his sister.

Without thinking about it, I reached out and placed my hand on his cheek. He leaned into it and breathed in my scent. My guilty conscience flared to life once more, reminding me that I was getting too close to him for something that was supposed to be a casual fling. I squashed it down and we stood there for a few more moments.

"I'll be done here in just a few minutes, and then we can go upstairs so you can practice your seduction game some more." His lips quirked up into a playful grin.

"Psh. My game is perfect. It's yours that could use some work, wolf," I retorted before hesitating on the rest.

I'd always met Andrei at his place or sometimes at one of the bars in town. Jinx was grumpy, but Andrei could deal with that. I wasn't worried about the grimalkins. Magos being a vampire would definitely be a problem.

"Actually, before I forget… I have a question for you." I fidgeted with my shirt like I was a teenager asking out someone for the first time. Gods, what was wrong with me? "My birthday is in two days, and I was thinking you could spend the night at my place tomorrow night, and we could laze about all day for my birthday?" The words came out in a rush, and I tried not to wince at how awkward I'd sounded.

Andrei paused mid-step and stared at me, his eyes going wide in surprise and his lips slowly spreading into a smile. "Sure. But are you sure you don't want to go out for your birthday?"

"No," I blurted. "I prefer low-key, quiet birthdays."

"All right. That sounds great," he said eagerly. "I'm intrigued by what I'll find at your place. Your roommate has never hung out with us. And I've never been invited back to your place. You have a sex swing, don't you?"

"Yep. You nailed it." I huffed a laugh. "It's an apartment brimming with sex toys."

Andrei laughed as he walked around the bar and picked me up off the stool. I wrapped my legs around his waist and put my arms around his neck. Heat sparked in his eyes as he looked at me and kissed me deeply.

He pulled back slightly and said in a voice tinged with a growl, "I do believe you said I needed to work on my seduction game."

"Don't you need to finish up down here?" I quirked an eyebrow at him.

"It'll wait." His lips found mine again, and he walked us upstairs.

I'd tell him about the whole vampire situation later. Just a few hours of fun and then back to business. A little procrastination was fine once in a while. Totally fine.

Chapter Four

I WAS A COWARD. A nearly four-century-year-old coward. After Andrei quite convincingly proved that his seduction game was very much on point, I had chickened out on telling him about Magos. Maybe I could convince Magos to hide in one of the other apartments while Andrei was over? No, that wouldn't work. Damn werewolf's sense of smell was too good. Andrei would know there was a vampire present. Plus, Jinx would probably tell him just to spite me.

At least I'd remained strong when he'd tried to keep me in bed all day. I'd reminded him that he'd promised his sister that he would rouse the rest of the pack and get some work done. He'd begrudgingly agreed, and I'd slipped out to continue on with my day feeling slightly less stressed out.

A hot flash whipped across my skin as I crossed the boundary downtown that marked the beginning of daemon territory.

Technically, this entire town was daemon territory; the humans who lived in it simply didn't know that. But this area was similar to the fae section of the beach. Any humans who weren't capable of using magic or sensing it like Jolie wouldn't see what was truly inside the boundary. In this case, they thought this street was full of small office spaces, and built into the ward was a compulsion to make them uninterested in walking down the street and to make the existence of this part of town fade from their memory. The humans who lived in Emerald Bay didn't even bother entering this section of town anymore.

At lunchtime, only a few beings were ambling about, not nearly as many as closer to sunset. Most daemons were only just starting to wake up and wouldn't conduct any serious business until after sunset, so many businesses in town adapted to their schedule.

The windows of Pele's bar, The Inferno, appeared dark and cloudy. No sign stood over the door or in the windows identifying the business. Instead, carved in an arc on the door were seven words:

ABANDON HOPE ALL YE WHO ENTER HERE.

A smile tugged at the corners of my lips. No friendly poet would guide you to this place. I pushed the door open and stepped into hell.

All right, not exactly hell. But close enough.

Once through the door, you were expected to obey the rules as if in one of the daemon realms.

Of all the bars that catered to the nonhuman inhabitants of this town, this one was by far the most popular. And if you wanted to conduct business with daemons or needed a safe place to conduct other types of business, this was where you came.

Werewolves and vampires could make it past the wards into this part of town, although it did take some effort on their part, particularly the first few times. I'd never seen any wolves from Andrei's pack here, but I was pretty sure they knew about it and just avoided it.

Their decision was probably for the best. Werewolves and

vampires weren't exactly welcome in most of the establishments on this block and were definitely not welcome in The Inferno.

The gatekeeper at bars like this changed every century or so, with Pele holding the title for the past couple of years. She gave any vamp or werewolf ten seconds to walk their ass back out the door before setting them on fire. Of course, she never made that announcement officially, so it had to spread via word of mouth. There were a few well-done vamps and werewolves that the message passed around.

I walked over to the bar and rested my back against the dark wooden counter to survey the room.

Despite being early, the place was already crowded. Several groups of daemons were scattered around with a few fae in the mix. A group of lokis in one corner looked my way with some interest. Not what I needed today. I ignored them and finished my scan of the room before turning around to face the bar.

There was no sign of Pele, but Asmodeus and Zareen were working, and they'd know where she was. Like Pele, Asmodeus also had bright turquoise eyes, but their skin was more of a mahogany shade. They were currently dead in conversation with a somber appearing daemon, so I headed towards the other end of the bar and waved Zareen down.

She waved back and quickly made her way down the long bar to me. When humans typically thought of daemons, they thought of Zareen. Her skin was a deep red, and she kept her black hair cut short so it floated around her head in a wild nest of curls. Out of those curls rose two black horns which spiraled down like ram's horns. Bottomless obsidian black eyes gazed out at the world.

The fearsome daemon moved quickly down the long bar and crashed to a halt in front of me.

"Nemain! It is so lovely to see you! I made the most delicious pie this morning. I can grab you a slice in just a minute! I have some hidden in the back. I can also pack some to go so you can bring a slice to Magos!" She reached over the bar and hugged me before I could respond. "Are you going to be here for a while? Pele's busy with some important meeting upstairs, but she'll be free in a couple hours if you guys need to bang something out." She pulled back from her hug and waggled her eyebrows at me.

I laughed and shook my head. "Don't ever change, Zareen. Sadly, I don't have a couple hours. Can you go get her?"

"Negatory," she replied cheerfully. "Give me just a minute, and I'll pack up two slices of pie for you guys!" She practically skipped down the bar and disappeared through a door leading to the supply room. Truly the most terrifying daemon of all.

I snorted and turned around to face the rest of The Inferno's patrons, resting my back and elbows on the bar counter. Some movement to my right got my attention, and three fae rose from a table where they'd been talking to one of the locals and walked my way.

The local's name was Eddie. I'd spoken to him a few times when I'd been hanging out at the bar. He was fairly new to town but was already building a reputation for being able to find rare things quickly and quietly. I wasn't sure exactly what he was. He wasn't a daemon or fae. Obviously not a vampire or werewolf, since he was inside the bar and Pele hadn't fried him. Shifters like me weren't around much anymore, and he didn't smell like one.

He shot me an apologetic look and shrugged. Well, that didn't bode well.

I turned my attention back towards the fae heading my way. They were tall and slender, with elegantly pointed ears and long limbs. Sidhe. I couldn't tell if they were Seelie or Unseelie. Not that it really mattered. Not to me, anyway. The sidhe ruled the fae realms and were the most gifted magically of the fae, although a few other species in the fae realms gave them a run for their money. The two queens co-ruled, one in control of the Seelie realms and the other of the Unseelie realms.

Aside from Kaysea, I found the fae, sidhe in particular, to be arrogant and conniving. I had no interest in their games. Daemons could be tricky, but they were considerably more straightforward than the sidhe.

Remaining in my casual position, I offered them a bemused expression when they stopped in front of me. The Inferno was a neutral meeting place, and magic was forbidden. While nothing technically prevented one from using it, the penalty for doing so was severe. Pele was not known for her mercy. I doubted these three would risk her wrath. So that left weapons and good old fisticuffs.

Part of me was itching for a fight, but I should at least try to deescalate the situation. Not only because Pele would be annoyed if I trashed any of the bar furniture, but because the last thing I needed to do was attract the attention of the fae. Then again… a bar brawl was good for the soul.

A smirk spread across my lips as I watched them close the distance between us. Most of the sidhe leaned towards androgyny, with the males being slightly more masculine than the females. Regardless of their sex, they were all built the same way. Tall and slender, with angular, sharp features. And usually obnoxiously pretty. Still, I thought they were boring compared to the genderfluid daemons.

Two males stood slightly behind the female before me. They were clearly here to guard her, as both had swords strapped to their backs, but neither made a move to draw them.

I looked the female, who was apparently the leader of this little party. Her long chestnut hair pulled back in a high ponytail fell down her back to her waist. She wore a simple but elegant light blue tunic and pants. Typical fae clothes. No jewelry or weapons that I could see. She might be hiding knives somewhere, but she looked like the type of fae who relied solely on magic.

"Most of the time, I love me a good bar brawl. It gets me all hot and bothered," I said casually. "But I'm in a bit of a hurry today. How about we reschedule for some time next week? I promise to make it good for you." I winked at her.

The chestnut-haired fae clenched her jaw and spat out, "You stole from the family we serve, and you dare speak to me in such a manner?"

I blinked in surprise. Stealing from the fae was usually something I would remember because I took a perverse joy in it. But I'd only started doing jobs again in the past few months, and none of them had involved stealing. Pele arranged all the jobs for me, and all the recent ones had been tracking down some lost artifacts. And one had been finding some idiots who had wandered off in an uncharted realm.

My mind whirled as I thought over the last few jobs I'd done. Retrieved a sword that'd been lost in one of the devourer realms. Located a herd of pegasi that had strayed from their usual grazing territory in Alfheim. Recovered a necklace that had been lost in a shipwreck for some loki.

Oh. *Oh.* Well, shit.

"There's been a bit of a misunderstanding," I explained calmly. Pele would be pissed if I didn't at least try to avoid a fight in her bar. "I was hired to retrieve a necklace and some other items that had been lost in a shipwreck. I was under the impression that the individual who hired me was the owner of those items. It's possible I was mistaken."

And if I ever saw said individual again, I was going to punch them repeatedly in the face. This was why no good ever came from doing a job for a loki. Pele had warned me against taking the job, but I hadn't listened. I could already hear her saying, "I told you so."

"Who. Hired. You?" the fae female ground out.

Apparently, my attempts to exude calming thoughts weren't working. My hope of getting out of this encounter without a fight swiftly vanished. Oh well. I tried.

"I'm afraid I can't tell you that. I may not be particularly happy with the individual who hired me at the moment, but I did take the job and I never disclose information about a contract with outside parties." I pushed myself off the bar and shifted my weight into a good fighting stance.

The fae leader stood her ground and continued to give me what I'm sure she thought was a very intimidating stare.

"I don't have time for this," I muttered, what little amount of patience I had left dwindling down to nothing. "I have no quarrel with you. But I won't give you the information you seek, and picking a fight with me is a mistake."

"The mistake is yours in thinking you have a way out of this," she bristled. "We will take you with us and get that information from you one way or another. You might even have a mind left by the time we're done."

"As threats go, that wasn't bad. But I'm guessing you're relatively new to this thug business. Trying to work your way up the ladder, eh?" I grinned wide enough to display my fangs. "I get it. We've all gotta start somewhere. But I'm a little more experienced than you, so your attempts at intimating me only reveal how ignorant you are of this situation."

"Just who do you think you are, bitch?" Her face flushed red. "You look like mongrel trash to me."

"Ah yes, that fae arrogance," I said, still smiling because it was irritating the crap out of her. "Always assuming those of us who live in the human realm are trash or powerless. If you were more important, you'd know who I am, what I can do. And we'd probably be having this conversation upstairs on a comfy couch over some drinks. I may be a mongrel, but I'm very good at what I do, and I've worked for several of the Tuatha Dé Danann."

Granted, that work was through Pele, so I didn't have to interact with them. The Tuatha Dé Danann were the elite of the sidhe, many of them generals or advisors to the queens, and I had no interest in meeting them face to face. But they still knew my name. My reputation was solid.

"So you either don't work for anyone important," I continued, "or you're about to make a serious mistake in picking a fight with me, and whoever you're working for is going to be pissed when they find out. They might even send you back to me to apologize. Wouldn't that be delightful?"

The two sidhe behind her glanced at each other, but their leader wasn't deterred. "I think you're full of shit."

At her words, the other two moved away from her to better flank me. Her hand shot out shockingly fast, trying to punch me in my solar plexus. With the fae males on each side of me, I had no room to dodge, so I dropped to a crouch and dove between her and the sidhe on her right. I sprang upward, slamming the sidhe male's jaw with an uppercut. He flew backwards and crashed into the bar, collapsing to the floor. One down.

The female threw a vicious punch. I blocked with my left arm and hammered a blow to her face. Bones crunched and blood poured.

She screamed as she stumbled a step back, clutching her nose. The other fae male moved to her side but didn't attack.

In a matter of seconds, I'd completely knocked out one of them and scored a brutal hit on their leader. He'd done the math and decided he probably wasn't going to fare much better. The fae were crazy powerful when it came to magic, but many of them relied on it too much. That was clearly the case with this lot.

"Wow, that was really embarrassing for you guys." I

laughed, though truth be told I was a little disappointed they hadn't put up more of a fight. That didn't even count as a warmup. "Had I known you'd go down that quickly, I wouldn't have bothered trying to talk you out of the fight."

The female glared at me through her tear-stained eyes. Blood still streamed from her nose.

The rest of the bar had been quiet while they watched the interaction, but they went back to their conversations as if nothing had happened. Violence was common in our world, and this was a relatively minor interaction.

I caught the gaze of one of the lokis that'd been hanging out at the bar, and they winked at me.

I raised my hand in an obscene gesture in return, and they laughed. *Argh.* Freaking lokis. When I saw the one that had hired me for this job, I was going to punch them right in their shapeshifting face.

Since Pele wasn't available, it was time for me to head out. I'd have to catch up with her later. "Thanks for not breaking any furniture!" Zareen called out happily from the bar. "I'll keep the pie safe for you!" I waved my hand in the air as a goodbye and walked out to get on with my day.

Chapter Five

I HEADED STRAIGHT for my bike after leaving the bar. Instead of making me feel better, that pathetic fight had only succeeded in wiping away what little calm I'd had since leaving Andrei's. I thought briefly about going back inside to see if they wanted to go for round two, or maybe pick a fight with some other people. But it wasn't worth the lecture I'd receive from Pele.

The tension I'd managed to temporarily silence came back with every step. Couple that with the guilt of my friends' lives possibly being in danger and it was too much.

My magic was straining against the chains I kept wrapped around it. I was one panic attack away from losing control and announcing to everyone exactly what I was. The warlocks and vampires would be the least of my problems then.

If the fae and daemons knew what I was truly capable of, they'd hunt me down and kill me. Keeping my magic locked down and under control had been drilled into me since I was a child. I was good at it. Or, at least I used to be. My time being held captive and tortured by Sebastian and his vampire cronies had shattered that control.

The first few months after my escape, Magos and I had

stayed in a remote cabin in the Sierra Nevada Mountains because I couldn't stop my magic from erupting. I'd been in a near constant panic all the time. It had taken months, but ever so slowly, I got the chains once again wrapped around that part of me. Sinking into the numbness I felt most of the time helped keep it at bay, along with daily sparring sessions with Magos.

Sometimes the jobs I took through Pele sent me to remote places where I could let it out for a little while. But it'd been almost two months since I'd been able to do that, and now every time my magic pushed, I felt the chains get weaker.

I started to pull on my helmet but paused. Something tugged my attention to the alley that stretched between the buildings next to me. Shadows filled the space, but I could scarcely make out a slight figure standing at the end.

I opened my mouth and inhaled deeply. Even with the distance between us, I knew that scent.

Vampire.

"Not possible," I whispered. The air in my lungs felt like it froze, and a sharp pain echoed in my chest.

My magic rumbled beneath my skin, straining to get free. To annihilate the threat. I couldn't lose it here. Mere steps away from a bar full of fae and daemons.

Not now, dammit! I pleaded with my magic.

Whoever was at the end of the alley cocked their head to the side. They knew. They sensed my fear and panic.

My heart pounded. I tried to push my body to do something. Start the bike. Drive away. Get off the bike and run back to the bar. Anything. But my body wasn't taking requests at the moment.

I waited for the vampire to seize this opportunity to grab me, but they just stood there, staring at me. Slowly, they raised their hands to the side with palms facing out and took a few deliberate steps back. Away from me.

It was enough for me to seize some control of my body back from the panic. As much as I didn't want to take my eyes off the vampire, I closed them. I forced my lungs to take even breaths in and out. The tightness in my chest eased, and the sharp pain dulled.

I waited a few more seconds before opening my eyes. The vampire was gone.

I carefully looked over the alley and up and down the sidewalk. There was no sign of whoever had been at the end of the alley. I must have imagined it. It was the fear and stress wreaking havoc with my mind.

Vampires couldn't handle being in the sun. Unless Sebastian had worked out an amulet or something for them. Creating amulets and charms wasn't really his thing, but maybe he'd gotten better at it over the years…

"Nemain?"

I snapped my head to the left and let out a sigh of relief when my eyes landed on Pele. "Thought you were busy?"

Pele shrugged, her deep fiery red skin looking exceptionally bright in daylight. "My meeting wrapped up early, and I have a few minutes before my next one starts. Zareen filled me in. I told you that loki job would be trouble."

I rolled my eyes. "Never said it wouldn't be. But given a choice between working with the loki or working with the fae, you know which one I'll always choose."

It was Pele's turn to roll her eyes.

Silence stretched between us before Pele spoke. "Everything okay? Zareen said you wanted to speak with me?" Her eyes ran over me over carefully. A worried look flashed across her face, but she hid it behind a calm mask.

It was hard to hide anything from Pele. She was incredibly observant when it came to body language. I had no doubt she was perfectly aware I'd almost lost my shit a few minutes ago.

We'd been lovers that had gradually become friends,

although we still frequently ended up in each other's beds. Our friendship was odd, but it worked for us.

I had specifically avoided sleeping with Pele since I'd moved to Emerald Bay. As much as I wanted to, it was hard enough to keep secrets from her when she wasn't doing extremely clever things with her tongue. Andrei was different than being with Pele, but he was just as fun, and I didn't have to worry about him grilling me immediately after I orgasmed.

I had no doubts that Pele was very much aware of why I hadn't sought her bed, and it only made her more worried about me.

My eyes drifted back to the alley where I'd sensed the vampire. "Just getting a little anxious. My birthday is in two days, and there's still so much we don't know. I'm planning on holing up in the apartment starting tomorrow night. Magos will stay with me. So will Andrei."

"A dog and a bloodsucker. Lovely," Pele said in distaste. "I've heard nothing on my end. But truth be told, there is not a lot of gossip regarding warlocks and vampires. They're not important enough for anyone to care about."

I let out a frustrated breath. Daemons and fae were considerably more powerful than the vampires and warlocks. Even if all the vampires and warlocks united, they could still be wiped out in a day if a handful of fae put their minds to it. All of which made figuring out motivations behind recent events more challenging.

"Think those fae from the bar will cause trouble?"

Pele shrugged and studied her long nails, which were currently filed into claws and painted a bright turquoise to match her eyes. "The job checked out and was fair. It's not our problem that they failed to retrieve their shit after they lost it. Finders keepers."

I snorted. Definitely no love lost between the daemon and fae.

"Not that I don't like seeing you, but this is all stuff we could have chatted about through mirrors," Pele said slowly.

"I know." I chewed on my bottom lip and stared at the handlebars of my bike. "I've been so tense these last few days. I just wanted to see everyone in person one last time before my birthday."

A flash of movement and Pele grabbed my chin and snapped it up, so I had to look at her. Her eyes were a sea of turquoise with just a narrow black slit in the center. "We didn't know about Sebastian having help before. Now we do. So if they ever succeed in taking you again, I will personally burn through every vampire and warlock in this realm until I find you. Do you understand me, Nemain?"

I saw the promise in her eyes, leaving no doubt that she meant every word. "Yes," I breathed.

"Good." Pele gave me a savage smile and stepped back. "I've got to head back inside. My next meeting will be starting soon."

Weariness flashed across her face. Most wouldn't have noticed, but I'd known Pele for centuries.

"Everything okay?" I asked.

Pele looked back at her bar and up to the second floor as though she could see through the walls at whoever was waiting for her in one of the meeting rooms. "Everything's fine. Just typical fae bullshit. It's nothing to worry about. Just tiresome to deal with."

"Have fun with that," I muttered.

She flashed her teeth at me in a quick smile. "See you later, Nemain."

I put my helmet on and started up my bike, still feeling a little unsettled. I'd feel better after a couple of hours of running. Tomorrow night, Andrei would come over, and we'd stay at my apartment behind the wards Pele had put in place.

With that plan firmly in mind, I pulled away from the curb and headed back out of town to the woods.

Olympic National Park was farther down the coast, but forest reserves were scattered all along the Washington coast. The one I was heading to was a mix of public and private land. Despite the daemon-run town, the private land was mostly owned by the fae, although they rarely bothered to come to this area anymore.

Driving past the road that led to Andrei's, I headed deeper into the forest and pulled off at a small dirt turnout. This section was private land with no trails or markers anywhere. But I'd been here often enough to know my way around. I walked a quarter mile at a leisurely pace before coming upon a dry creek bed. There, I stripped off my weapons and clothes and folded them into a neat little stack that I tucked into a hole between some colossal boulders. I had taken my throwing daggers out of the bracers, but the bracers themselves I kept on, along with my necklace.

I quickly shifted and felt the weight of the world come off my shoulders. All the stress and fear was still there in the back of my mind, but the sounds of the woods helped drown it out. My senses were so much sharper in my feline form. I sucked in a deep breath of air and filtered through the scents. Pine. Old leaves. Rabbit. Deer. Even miles from the shore, I could faintly smell the saltiness of the ocean.

A quick shake moved the necklace into a more comfortable position. The bracers turned into a tattoo in this form. The tattoo wasn't visible because of my fur, but it created a slight pattern on my front legs where the fur was darker. It was elegant and beautiful, like most things the fae made. The necklace was a daemon creation and lacked some of that elegance but was still every bit as functional. It changed size when I shifted, so it fit comfortably around my neck.

The glamour spell that hid my nonhuman features didn't

work on my feline body. From a distance and with poor lighting, I could almost pass for a mountain lion. Maybe.

At over five hundred pounds, I was almost triple the size of most mountain lions. And there was the minor detail of my coat being a vibrant gold that shimmered brilliantly in the sun. But I wasn't worried about humans spotting me. I would sense any humans in the area long before they had a chance to see me. And even if they did, so what? I'd be just another tall tale or internet sensation.

I took a few steps to become accustomed to being on four legs again before breaking out into a run. Pushing myself hard, I flew over the ground, leaping over fallen branches and brush.

The smell of the ocean and the woods was exhilarating, and I pushed myself harder and faster. Soon, I caught the fresh scent of a rabbit and gave chase. After enjoying my snack and cleaning myself, I trotted off in the direction of my favorite spot in the forest.

Miles later, I reached a group of boulders surrounded by redwoods. In a perfect indent in the trees, the sun warmed up the stone.

I channeled my inner Jinx and spun around three times, curling up with my tail covering my eyes. My fur coat soaked up the sun, and I enjoyed the feeling of being completely content and happy, drifting off to sleep.

THE SMELL of saltwater hit my nostrils, and I smiled. The warm sand felt good against my cheek. I twisted my head and looked over at Myrna. Her light green hair fell across her face as she dug through the leather satchel she kept her paint supplies in.

"You should stop whatever you're doing and come lie next to me instead." I winked at her.

She laughed in that husky tone of hers that drove me crazy. "What, this morning wasn't enough for you?"

"I'll never have enough of you," I replied honestly. "Besides, when you told me to strip off my shirt and lie down, I was sort of expecting something else."

"Of course you were," she said wryly and dug further into the satchel before pulling out two small containers. "Aha, found them!" She held the containers up in the air triumphantly and moved to kneel next to me.

I settled back down as she made broad strokes between my shoulder blades while whispering something to herself. My skin tingled pleasantly where the brush fell, and I closed my eyes to enjoy the feeling. I was just about to drift off to sleep when Myrna sat back and admired her work.

"It's not fair you always do this where I can't see it," I complained.

Myrna laughed. "But *I* can see it, and I like to admire my own work."

"Such a vain artist you are."

"I have to be good at something. I'm not a seer like Kaysea or a strong fighter like Connor. Wouldn't want to let the family name down." Her voice was light, but I knew this bothered her. I twisted until I was on my side and grasped her hand, kissing the back of her knuckles.

"You're perfect." I kissed her hand once more. "Now tell me what you painted."

"Remember those blue flowers that grow around my parents' house?"

I thought back a few years to the last time we'd visited her family. "The ones that grow on the trees? Bright blue with the orange center?"

"Those are the ones." She traced her thumb over my fingers. "When I was a little girl, my mother told me that if you hold one on your birthday and make a wish, it'll come true. I was her wish. Well, me and Kaysea. She wanted a little girl and was blessed with two. Since we don't have access to the flowers at the moment, I thought I'd paint one on your back."

"I don't think magic works that way." Skepticism coated my voice.

"Hush, you." Myrna flicked my nose. I did as I was told and relaxed into the sand while she packed up her supplies. "You are forbidden from coming to the house for the next two hours. I have to prepare for the party tonight and don't want you distracting me."

"In what ways would I distract you?" I turned my head and arched an eyebrow at her.

"You're impossible." She laughed and rose to her feet. "Two hours, Nemain. Take a nap and relax for a bit. I want you in a good mood for tonight."

I stretched out on the sand and waved her off. A nap did sound nice. I hadn't planned on doing anything special, but Myrna had insisted on having a small celebration. Kaysea would be coming, along with their brother Connor.

Cian would also be attending. I was hoping my brother wouldn't be bringing his annoying lover with him, but that seemed unlikely.

Sometime later, I woke and groggily glanced up the beach towards our cottage. How long had I been sleeping? I climbed to my feet and pulled on the loose shirt I'd tossed aside earlier. Jogging up the beach to the cottage, I stopped at the front door. It was open.

I inhaled deeply. Death. Death waited for me inside.

I took a trembling step forward.

"Not a good idea," a smooth, lightly accented voice said. "We both know what you'll find in there."

I turned and faced the man who'd spoken those words. He hadn't been there that day. I'd only found his scent and the note he'd left behind.

You will always be mine. And I do not share.

But he was here now. I stared at the face I had once found so attractive but now found repulsive.

Sebastian could make himself appear however he wanted in dreams, but he always chose to appear to me as he had looked during our time together. His golden-blond hair was pulled into a ponytail at the base of his neck, a few strands breaking free to frame his face. Large brown eyes full of humor and warmth looked at me.

"Of all the dreams you could have made me dream. Why this one?" I asked as an old ache fluttered in my soul.

"Actually, this dream"—he wove his hands around—"was of your doing. I wanted to stop by for a chat and see what you were dreaming. I thought I'd let it play out a bit. I was curious. But if I let you walk inside that cottage, we both know what you'll find. And there will be no talking to you after that." He said it so casually. As if he weren't the one responsible for tearing out Myrna's heart.

"I loved her." My voice caught at the words.

"You loved me once." The elegant, handsome mask he wore cracked, and I saw the real Sebastian. The warmth vanished from his eyes, and they became cold and calculating. "And you will be mine again. But time is running out."

"You're insane if you think I could ever love you again," I growled.

Sebastian's eyes went distant, and I knew he was talking to someone outside of this dream. I took a step towards him. I couldn't actually hurt him here, but that wouldn't stop me from trying.

His eyes snapped back towards me. "I'll be seeing you soon."

He vanished a second later, and I stared at the spot where he'd stood and at the front door. He was right. I did know what waited for me inside.

I stood there trembling for a few seconds before turning away and walking back onto the beach. I sat down and watched the waves roll in and out. Trying not to think about what he'd done. About what he'd just said.

Be seeing you soon.

A short amount of time passed before I felt a tapping on my shoulder. I sighed and looked to my right at the red door I knew would be there. At least my brother was a polite dreamwalker. I brushed the sand off my clothes and walked through the red door, leaving the cottage and what it held behind.

Chapter Six

As soon as I was through the door, my brother pulled me in for a hug.

"I've been worried to death about you!" he exclaimed.

I wondered if he knew who had just been in my dreams. Given that my brother rarely liked to enter my mind like that, I assumed he didn't. That's why he always made a door appear as an *invitation* to join him in the death realm. Cian was a polite dreamwalker. I returned the hug and started detangling myself from him.

My brother and I looked nothing alike. All we had in common was our height and our mother's emerald-green eyes. He'd taken after our father, black skin with faint silver rosettes. He kept his silver hair in a long braid trailing down his back. I was pretty, but my brother was beautiful. I'd always been slightly jealous I hadn't taken after our father as well. Not just for the striking looks, but for the black coat that blended into the darkness far better than my bright gold coloring.

Cian had also taken after our father in other ways. He was quieter and far less prone to violence than me. If necessary, he was perfectly capable of defending himself, but he never had the vicious streak my mother and I possessed. He also held our father's groan-worthy sense of humor.

"Worried to death?" I quirked an eyebrow at him. "Really, Cian?"

My brother's smirk told me he was very proud of his little joke. I just shook my head while I rubbed my arms. Death realms freaked me out a little. My physical body was still slumbering away in the forest. But souls were corporeal in death realms.

While Cian took after our father in looks, he inherited our mother's magic. Necromancy. Which was why despite being very much alive, he preferred to spend his times in death realms where his magic was most powerful.

Necromancy could be used in any of the realms, but in the death realms was where its abilities really shone. Reality and magic were warped here. Things like distance and time worked differently. And nothing was truly real. Death magic swirled around to create vast illusions, and necromancers could harness that magic to make whatever they wanted. My brother argued that if your mind perceived it as real, then that was really all that mattered.

I was of the opinion that if I grabbed a rock from this realm and took it to a different realm, and that rock disappeared from my hand, then that was some freaky shit, and I didn't want anything to do with it.

As far as death realms went, Mag Mell was pretty nice, but it still weirded me out. I had no death magic, and the power in these realms felt odd to me. Magical talents among the feline shifters varied quite a bit. Really, all we had in common was the ability to shift into our feline forms. Feline shifter children commonly inherited magic from their parents, but sometimes their magic would be completely different. Cian had inherited our mother's talent for necromancy, but his dreamwalking magic had come out of nowhere.

He'd also inherited our father's ability at guilt-tripping. In fact, he'd improved on it. Cian was a master of guilt trips, so I visited him more often than I would like.

My definition of "often" was apparently different from his.

"I've been saving that one for you. But really, where have you been?" A crease formed between his brows as he looked me up and down.

Not for the first time, I was glad that he hadn't inherited our mother's other magic: the ability to read souls. That fun one had gone to me, although I was a weak candle compared to my mother's bonfire. If Cian had that magic, he would have been able to see just how fucked up I was inside.

I chewed on the inside of my cheek and wrapped my hands around my stomach. It'd been months since we'd spoken. He'd reached out twice through the mirror, but I'd ignored it.

Our relationship had always been strained, and that was mostly my fault. I was not an easy person to love.

"I'm sorry. I meant to come here sooner or at least chat through the mirror, but I've been busy with some gigs Pele arranged," I said, and that was mostly true. "In what little free time I've had, I've been reaching out to some contacts trying to gather information about whatever the hell Sebastian is planning. Or even better, where the hell he is. It's not going well." I offered a close-lipped smile.

"Not surprising." Cian shrugged. "No one pays attention to the warlocks."

"I know." I tapped one of the gems on my collar. "Assuming this thing is still working, and it better be for the price I paid for it, Sebastian can't use blood magic anymore to track me, so he should have no idea where I am. I'm still not taking any chances for my birthday. I'll be holed up in the apartment, which has been warded heavily against warlocks, witches, and vampires. Even if all the warlocks combined their power, they wouldn't get through Pele's wards."

"True enough."

"Kaysea promised to stay in the fae realm on my birthday. I know you rarely visit the human realm, but if you get the sudden urge to do so on my birthday . . . don't." I grinned at him. "Or hit me up on the mirror, and I'll come and get you. You can join in on my birthday party."

"I take it the vampire will be there?" Cian asked. His tone was casual, but I didn't miss how his eyes hardened.

"You damn well know his name," I snapped, dropping my hands to my sides as I clenched them into fists. I was so sick of having this argument. "And he was the one who found me and saved me when everyone else failed."

My brother narrowed his eyes. He was no doubt about to say something that would enrage me further. Less than five minutes here, and I was already on the verge of getting in a brawl with my brother. Typical.

"Tsk. Tsk. Still so quick to anger, Nemain," a smooth, deep voice cut in.

My body went on high alert at the same moment my magic stirred at the threat. Things worked differently in the death realms. Unless your magic was some flavor of death magic, you were significantly less powerful in this realm. I could still shift if I needed to, but I wasn't as fast or strong.

My ability to open gateways didn't seem to be affected at all, but the rest of my forbidden magic was sluggish while in the death realms. On the one hand, it was nice to not feel the constant push of it, but it didn't make up for the fact that I was considerably less powerful here. And that was not a feeling I liked.

My brother was a strong necromancer, but his lover was on another level. And he hated me. I hated him back and did not like being around him when he was at his strongest and I was at my weakest.

I walked towards the white leather couches in front of the fireplace and sat on the ottoman so I could glare at Dante. If he weren't so arrogant and if his eyes weren't so cold, he would be handsome. He was a little over six feet tall and had perfect olive skin with short black hair and a neatly trimmed beard.

Everything about him screamed Greek god, but I knew that couldn't be the case since most of them were dead and kicking it in Elysium.

No, despite being a cold bastard, Dante was very much alive. I knew who the few survivors of the Greek gods were, and Dante wasn't one of them. Cian must know more about him, given that they'd been together for almost a century. But my dear brother was keeping his lips sealed in that department.

"So glad to see you're still here," I grumbled as I tried not to give him a once-over.

It took me about five seconds to give in and check him out. Black leather pants. Check. Tight black shirt. Check. Full pouty lips. Check. Eyes so dark it was easy to lose yourself in them. Triple check. Whatever Dante's faults, and there were many, I had to give it to my brother. He sure had picked a pretty one.

"At some point, you're going to have to accept that I'm not going anywhere."

"A girl can dream, can't she?" I turned to face my brother, who was sitting on the couch to my left. "I'm fine, Cian. As is Magos. There really hasn't been anything exciting happening. I just got caught up with An—with someone. Nothing special." I cursed myself for the slip.

Cian raised an eyebrow but said nothing. Dante, however, leapt at the opportunity to dig at me.

"It's not like you to refer to a lover by name. Not since the mermaid." My heart clenched, but I forced myself to remain still. He was trying to bait me, and I wouldn't fall for it. "You haven't had many since her, and you've never once mentioned their names. Honestly, I figured you never bothered to learn their names or anything about them. Why bother given the short life expectancy of your lovers? Did this one get more than into your pants?" he purred as he gave me a sly grin.

The leash I had around my temper snapped at the truth in his words. Dante knew exactly where to push for maximum pain, but two could play that game.

"Still pissed off I wouldn't fuck you all those years ago? You may be eye candy, but your personality is so repugnant I'm not even sure you have a soul. Maybe you died and your necromancy just animated your body afterwards," I said snidely. "I don't know how my brother stomachs being with you. Frankly, I don't know how anyone could sleep with you, let alone love you. You may be hot, but not many people want to fuck a corpse."

I didn't see so much as feel him move. I dove off the couch and rolled so my butt was on the floor and I was scooting backwards. Dante landed where I had been sitting and whirled, lunging after me. I caught him by the throat as he landed on me and flipped so I was sitting on top of him.

He grabbed my wrist and ripped it off his throat, throwing me off him. I jumped to my feet but wasn't quick enough.

A large hand wrapped around my throat and lifted me off the ground. One hand gripped his wrist while the other struck at him, but he blocked my hits easily, and I had no leverage in this position.

"Get over yourself, Nemain. I'm glad you turned me down all those years ago because it led me to your brother, who is worth far more than you," he sneered.

I gasped quietly as I tried to pry his fingers off my throat.

"Congrats. You charmed a werewolf. Little more than a dog in heat. Does fucking him make you feel more alive? Make you forget everything you've done in the name of revenge? Who could possibly love *you* given what you've done?" His dark eyes bore into mine, and I bared my teeth at him.

Magic leached into me, and a coldness spread through my blood. My magic raged, and I started to rip the chains off, but I was already feeling so weak. I should have released it sooner. My vision went black, and Dante threw me across the room into the wall. The wood cracked, and all I could do was sit there as the coldness slowly left my body. Dante stalked out of the room without another word.

Cian, who had made no move to stop our fight, sighed. "What is it with you two? Can't you at least be civil to each other for my sake?" My brother, the king of guilt trips.

"He started it."

And finished it. But I didn't say that part out loud. This wasn't the first time Dante had kicked my ass, and it likely wouldn't be the last. We both had short tempers, and we both loved Cian and wanted to protect him.

The problem was that we also viewed each other as the greatest threat to my brother's well-being.

"Let's just forget it, okay? What's going on with you?" I stood up slowly and made my way back to the couch, determined to ignore the fact that I'd just got my ass handed to me. I had to stop letting Dante goad me into a fight while we were in a death realm where he held such a high advantage.

I snatched the blanket that had been thrown across the back and wrapped myself in it. Cian glanced at the wall I'd crashed into and casually waved his hand. The damage disappeared. Nothing in this realm was truly real. Not the wall. Not the couch I was sitting on. It seriously weirded me out. Cian propped his feet up on the coffee table and stared at them a moment before giving me a hard look.

"I love him, Nemain. And he loves me. I would appreciate it if you would treat him with respect while you are in our house." He wasn't yelling, but his fury was burning behind each of those words. A wise person would have nodded and apologized.

Wisdom wasn't really my thing.

"You mean like the way you treated Magos when you visited me after he rescued me?" I asked lightly and continued to meet my brother's gaze.

He rose in one motion, kicking the coffee table away. "I looked for you! Damn it, you know I did! He's a fucking vampire! You know what they are and what they're capable of! He wants you for himself. He wants you to trust him, so he doesn't have to lock you up to make you stay around. He wants you to love him, so you won't object when he feeds from you. When he uses you!"

"I do trust him. And I do love him. There is nothing he could do to make you like him. You despise him for what he is." I crossed my arms and glared, annoyed that he'd brought me here just so Dante and him could take turns fighting with me.

Cian turned away from me and rubbed his temples with his hands and muttered, "I never thought you would be such a fool."

"There is a fool here, but it certainly isn't me," I said tiredly.

We'd had this fight so many times over the past year. Part of me knew it wasn't fair that I kept throwing the fact he hadn't been able to rescue me back in his face. He had looked. They'd all looked. They would have kept looking until they knew for sure I was dead. And even then, I had no doubt my brother would have kept searching for me in the death realms.

I knew what I said wasn't fair. But I was so sick of having this argument over Magos that I always lashed out in whatever way would hurt my brother the most. And he did the same. It felt like we were at an impasse that neither of us was willing to budge on.

Cian moved to sit by me. "I'm just trying to look out for you, sis," he murmured. "It's not like you to trust so easily, and you barely know him."

"I know him well enough," I said coldly. "I don't have many friends, but the ones I do have, I'll fight for. Even if that means fighting you."

I rose from the couch and stalked towards the red door that was my ticket out of this hell. Cian grabbed my arm and yanked me back around. I hissed in his face.

"You need to leave him, Nemain!" He shook me hard, and I shoved him away. "He's hiding something!"

My brother's eyes were wide with fear and panic. I hated seeing that, but my anger was burning too hot to back down.

"And Dante isn't?" I asked incredulously. "Your lover is just as mysterious, but you don't hear me telling you to sever all ties with him. I may hate the prick, but you're far too old for me to lecture you about who you should be hanging out with. Perhaps you should do the same. The only reason you dislike Magos is because he's a vampire." I closed the distance between us until I was in his face. "Get. Over. It."

"Just like you've gotten over your hatred of witches and warlocks?" he retorted sharply. "Perhaps I should make some new friends in the magical community."

"Go fuck yourself!" I snarled.

"What's wrong, sis?" Cian taunted. "You hate them every bit as much as I hate vampires, but I don't throw it back in your face by hanging out with them."

"It's different." I gritted my teeth and tried to stop myself from shaking. Damn him for always knowing where to push.

"How? How the fuck is it different? You have condemned all witches and warlocks because of what one warlock did to our parents! Although you did make an exception once, and that didn't turn out so well, so—"

My fist caught him in the jaw before he could finish. He stumbled away from me, his hand flying up to hold his face in shock. He didn't stop me this time as I strode through the door and slammed it behind me. Granted, the door led into my own head, so I was essentially giving myself one hell of a headache.

But I didn't care. I was beyond pissed and just wanted out. So much for my peaceful nap.

Chapter Seven

Despite how worked up I was after seeing my brother, I fell into a deep sleep as soon as I returned to my body. Something about my feline form kept the nightmares at bay when I slept. When I first escaped from Sebastian and the vampires, I slept as a cat every night until I decided I couldn't run away from my fear anymore. The nightmares seemed to be getting better, and I hadn't destroyed the apartment yet, so I considered that a step in the right direction.

A screeching magpie roused me from my slumber. I seriously considered going after the stupid thing so I could return to my sleep when I noticed the sun was setting.

It was official. Nap time was over.

I wasn't all that eager to return, so I jogged back to my clothes at a leisurely pace. Stretching my legs felt good after napping for so long. By the time I reached the dry creek bed, darkness had fallen. The new moon meant no moonlight. I'd forgotten how dark the woods could be at night.

I stopped in front of my clothes pile and took a deep breath. My skin tingled as the fur slid back into it. Bones crunched and muscles rearranged themselves as my massive feline form shifted back to a body a third of its size. No pain, just a tingling sensation and a slight feeling of pressure, and seconds later, poof. I was human again. Well, human-ish.

Pulling on my underwear and bra quickly, I tried not to dwell on the blackness of the forest. The forest I had so loved running through mere hours ago now seemed ominous. I tried to shake the feeling off when I realized something else. It was quiet. Most of the birds would have settled down for the night, but a few would still be up. Plus, the other night critters and insects should be singing their evening songs. But only silence reigned.

Their scent hit mere seconds before I recognized their presence. Vampires. My blood ran cold as fear seized me, but I kept the panic in check. I wasn't helpless. My weapons were close, and if it came down to it, I could use my magic. It wasn't ideal, but if I left no survivors, there'd be no one to tell on me.

"Fancy meeting all of you out here," I said lightly, edging closer to my swords.

None of them had appeared yet, but they were there, lurking in the shadows. Branches snapped and rustled on both sides of me. I was pretty sure there were at least three of them, but I needed to know exactly how many and where they were before I did anything rash.

"Come out and play, you shitheads." Did antagonizing count as rash?

My bravado abandoned me completely when a vampire walked into the clearing from my left. Echoes of pain trailed across my skin as my body went absolutely still. Of course it had to be him.

The vampire strolling across the clearing looked no older than twenty, but he was far older than that. With his boyish good looks and brilliant blue eyes, he appeared harmless. Dark blond hair fell in soft curls around his face, adding to his whole charming boy next door image.

Everything about his appearance was a carefully crafted lie. I knew those eyes; they had sparkled as they caused me pain.

"You gave a good chase, but the old warrior can't save you now," he drawled with a faint southern accent.

He'd been turned in Louisiana in the late 18th century. One of his favorite pastimes while cutting into my flesh had been to tell me about his younger days in New Orleans and the havoc he had wreaked. He'd always been a monster in a pretty package.

"Nice to see you again, Ryder," I said evenly as I tracked movement behind me and in front. Three vampires, *in addition* to Ryder.

"Forgive me for doubting the sincerity of that statement," he replied with a smile. "Sebastian will be so happy to see you again. He apologizes for not being able to be here in person, but he's wrapping up a few things on his end."

My jaw clenched. *He knew.* Sebastian knew I was here. He was coming. "How? How did you track me?" I ground out.

Ryder just smiled wider. I would have given a century off my life to wipe that look off his face.

The vampire behind me stilled, waiting for something. The two in front had come close enough that I could now see their faces. The twins. I had so hoped they wouldn't be here. They were creepy, even for vampires. Ryder to my left, one behind, and the twins in front. I could take four vampires. Especially if I could reach my swords.

Additional vampires moved behind the twins. At least another half dozen. Fuck. My weapons were close, but the vampires would be on me before I grabbed them. And I was standing in nothing but my underwear and bra against almost a dozen vampires. I was so fucked.

If I hit them hard and fast, I could shift and maybe beat them back to the parking lot. They were fast, but my motorcycle was faster. That plan involved a lot of "ifs." I could use magic, but I kept it chained down so tightly it would take me a minute to set it free. And unlike my magic that allowed me to open gateways, I wasn't good at wielding this side of my power. In my panicked state, I had no doubt I would lose control.

The daemons and fae rarely came to this section of the woods, but I would still leave behind one hell of a magical echo. It would take weeks to fade. Unleashing that part of myself meant I might survive the vampires only to be killed by the fae or daemons. Not ideal. Fight and run it was then.

I shouldn't have slept for so long. And I should have been more aware of my surroundings. Magos was going to lay into me once he found out.

But first, I needed to survive and escape.

Take the twins out first. Losing track of where they were was not a good idea. A split second before I dove forward, movement to my right drew my attention.

I took a swift step back with my right foot and threw a quick jab. My fist connected with solid flesh, and I stilled at the sight of the vampire who held my fist in his palm. His eyes were a dark blue with flecks of purple that reminded me of twilight. As they locked onto mine, my heart skipped a beat. He was the vampire who had looked at me from the alley earlier. I don't know how I knew that. He'd stayed in the shadows then, and I hadn't been able to see his face. But this *was* the same vampire. I was sure of it.

"This doesn't have to end in violence. You're outnumbered, and you have no weapons. Come with us and live to fight another day," he said quietly. His accent was faint but sounded so familiar.

He released my hand, and I took a step back. "Who are you?" I breathed.

"Mikhail."

Recognition flashed through me. Even those who didn't give a shit about vampires had heard of Mikhail, the famed assassin of the Vampire Council. He had one hell of a body count attached to his name.

I watched as he casually put his hands in his pockets. He probably meant for the move to make him appear non-threatening, but it didn't fool me. He was more dangerous than all the other vampires combined.

Time to shift and get the hell out of here. I reached for my magic, but pain made me fall to my knees gasping. I tasted blood in the back of my throat. My eyes darted around the trees, finding small pouches hanging from them in a circle around us. *Fuck.*

"I can't believe you fell for this again." Ryder laughed and slapped a hand against his thigh. "We actually had a bet going about whether you'd be able to sense the pouches and avoid this little trap. The twins were quite sure it would work. Apparently, I put too much faith in you because I thought you'd sense them and take off running. Happy to be wrong in this case."

"In my defense, it's not like they give off a scent, and there's no moonlight tonight. Hardly my fault for missing them." Shit. I was so fucked.

My heart pounded against my chest like a sledgehammer. I was surprised I couldn't hear it. As long as I was in this circle surrounded by those damn pouches, my magic was out of reach.

No shifting, no opening gateways to other realms. Nothing. They had me right where they wanted me.

I was so *fucked.*

But maybe...

I reached for my chained magic and was slightly surprised to find it still there. Whatever magic was in those pouches, it wasn't quite as powerful as what they'd used before. That remained the nuclear option, though.

Now that it was dark, Magos would be wondering about me. I needed to stall for a few minutes. Maybe I would get lucky, and he would come looking for me. Or maybe I had pissed off Jinx and was stuck in a bad luck rut. That would certainly explain my current situation.

Mikhail remained silent, watching me with those unusual twilight eyes.

"Sebastian will be delighted at this turn of events. He was hoping he could get you back in time for your birthday. I do believe we'll get a bonus for this." Ryder stalked towards me.

My fingers clawed into the earth as I desperately thought of options to get myself out of this.

Ryder paused a few feet from me and looked at Mikhail. He shifted his weight back and forth uneasily. "You're not supposed to be here. She's my responsibility. I do believe the Council gave you other orders. Shouldn't you be elsewhere dealing with *that* little problem?"

A small smile played across Mikhail's lips as he looked at Ryder. "I am quite good at dealing with things I find problematic."

Ryder snarled. "This isn't your business. She's mine."

A growl rippled up my throat. "I'm not yours. Nor am I *his*," I spat and prepared to jump to my feet and make a run for it. If they spread out while chasing me, I'd have a better chance of crippling or killing some of them.

Ryder flashed his fangs at me in a grin. "Bind her."

Before I could react, the twins moved in unison and snapped their whips at me. The sting of leather wrapped around my wrists just below the bracers. The twins spread apart and jerked my arms out to the sides painfully. I was still kneeling on the ground, so I couldn't even kick out with my legs.

Bound. Helpless. *No, no, no, no,* the word repeated frantically in my mind. I couldn't let them take me again.

There was nothing I could do as Ryder stepped in front of me and sank a punch into my gut. Bile rose in my throat, and I struggled to compose myself, but then he hit me with a right hook and my head snapped to the side. Left hook. *Snap*. Another gut punch. I coughed up blood, and the world went fuzzy.

I tried to fling myself back, but the twins' grips on my arms were too strong. I rallied my strength to make one last stand. If I could get to my feet, I could try to unbalance one of the twins with a solid pull to one side. I'd probably dislocate my shoulder, but it'd be worth it to get free.

Despite Mikhail's advice, I wouldn't go down without a fight. If this didn't work, I'd go with the nuclear option and release my magic. I'd just have to hope my luck changed and the daemons and fae never found out.

I would not let them take me again.

The vampires behind the twins moved towards me but came to a sudden stop. The twins looked behind me and swore as the smug grin slid off Ryder's face. I tried to twist my head to look behind me, but I couldn't see anything. Something was crashing through the trees. A lot of somethings.

"Grab her!" cried Ryder as he lunged for me.

A dark form leapt over me and snapped at him with a snarl. He managed to yank his hand back before he lost any fingers. Pity. They would have grown back, but it would have hurt like hell.

I looked to my left, and Mikhail gave me a small smile and stepped back into the dark, vanishing from sight. Before he was gone, I heard him whisper, "I'll be seeing you."

Alarm shot through me at his words, but that was a problem for later. Right now, I needed to get the hell out of here.

I turned my attention towards the chaos in front of me and almost blacked out from the movement. Ryder hadn't held back in his punches, and I was lucky to still be conscious. My head swam, but I was able to make out the snarling shapes in front of me.

Werewolves. Right. Forgot about that.

I finally lost the battle to stay awake. The last thing I remembered was a large dark grey wolf stopping in front of me before I blacked out.

Chapter Eight

THE SCENT of lavender seeped its way into my consciousness. I kept my eyes tightly closed as panic caused all my muscles to tense. My mind had jumped straight into panic mode, and it was hard to think. The leviathan that was my magic started to rumble and push against its cage. It remembered the sweet floral smell as well and how the room the vampires had kept me in always reeked of it thanks to Sebastian liking to use it in his spells.

Another scent hit me, a musky earthy smell. Werewolf.

"You're safe," someone said in a kind, reassuring voice.

I knew that voice. *Andrei.*

My panic slowly eased, and rational thinking returned. Right. The werewolves had shown up. They rarely ran in that part of the woods, but they must have picked up the scent of vampires and headed that way.

Andrei and the rest of his newbie werewolves might want nothing to do with starting up a war again, but that didn't mean they liked vampires. Their natural instinct would always be to hunt them down. They would never tolerate vampires in their territory.

My body relaxed, and my magic settled within me. Opening my eyes at last, I took in my surroundings. I was on a bed in a small room with warm wooden walls. On the dresser, across from the foot of the bed, was a vase full of lavender and flowers. This was probably one of the guest bedrooms on the first floor of the lodging house. Pack members took all the rooms on the second floor.

Finally, I looked to my right at the werewolf sitting next to my bed. Andrei leaned back in the chair with his legs stretched out lazily in front of him. A smirk stretched across his face as he watched me gain my bearings.

"Even though you smell like a wet dog, I still find you delicious," I purred. "Although I had everything under control and did not need to be rescued, for the record."

Lie. I was damn lucky the werewolves had shown up. Not that I would ever admit that to anyone, especially not my brother and his annoying lover. Rescued by a pack of dogs. I'd never live that down.

Andrei's smirk grew into a full-fledged grin. "Wet dog? Moist dog at most."

"Nope. There are no degrees of wet dog smell. There is only dry dog smell and wet dog smell. Doesn't matter if the dog is only slightly wet." I pointed a finger at him.

Andrei laughed, standing up and moving the chair back against the wall.

"Care to tell me what you were doing in the woods tonight?" he asked with a casualness I didn't buy for one second.

"I went for a run this afternoon and took a nap. Lost track of time and ended up staying out later than I intended." I shrugged.

"If you wanted to go for a run, you could have said something this morning. I would have made time to go with you."

"I know." I smiled at him. "I've got a lot on my mind right now, and I needed some alone time to blow off some steam."

Andrei nodded in understanding.

I swung my legs over the side of the bed to stand up and regretted it immediately. Sharp pain shot across my ribs, and I winced. Any broken ribs had healed, but it still hurt. I sat back on the bed and looked down at my arms. A few abrasions and cuts were still healing where the whips had wrapped around my wrists just below the bracers. If I'd been a little faster, I could have positioned my arms so the whips would have hit the bracers instead of my flesh.

I'd have to hide that from Magos. I could just hear him now. "What's the point in wearing those things if you're not going to use them? Or are they just a fashion accessory?" Ugh. I'd never hear the end of it.

Shit. Magos. I needed to let him know I was okay before he tore the town apart looking for me.

"Do you have a mirror I can use?" I asked hopefully. "I need to let my . . . uhh . . . roommate know I'm okay." I really would have to tell Andrei about Magos soon, considering they would be meeting very soon. But I didn't think telling my were-wolf lover that my roommate was a vampire was a good idea at this moment, considering I'd just been attacked by vampires. I didn't see any scenario where that conversation would go well. I'd explain after I spoke to Magos and assured him I was okay.

"There are a lot of mirrors in the house... Not sure what that has to do with contacting your roommate," Andrei said as he pulled a cell phone out of his pocket and waved it back and forth in the air. "I have this crazy little contraption that lets people communicate over vast distances. It's called a cell phone. They're quite popular, I hear."

I frowned, even though I knew that would be his answer. "It's fine. I just need to get home quickly to let him know I'm okay." I realized I was only wearing a t-shirt over my underwear and looked around the room. "Don't suppose you guys grabbed my clothes?"

"Sorry, must have slipped our minds, what with all the vampires and damsels in distress that needed rescuing."

I arched an eyebrow at him. "You're really terrible at this whole rescuing thing."

"Thought you said you didn't need to be rescued?" He mirrored my move and raised an eyebrow.

"Well, my clothes did." I tugged at the t-shirt.

Andrei let out a wolfish laugh that made my toes curl and left the room. There wasn't a clock in the room, but a glance out the window told me it was still dark out. Bantering with Andrei had distracted me, and while I enjoyed it, I needed to go.

Sebastian knew where I was, and he was coming for me. My blood chilled as all amusement from bantering with Andrei fled. The vampires were already here.

Magos and I needed to talk and come up with a new plan. The only options I could think of was to stay and fight or run and hide. Before we could do the latter, we needed to know how they'd found us. My amulet protected me from all tracking spells, including ones using blood magic. Either the amulet had failed, which was unlikely but possible, or someone had sold me out.

I heard light footsteps coming from the hall and looked at the doorway just as Stela walked into the room. "Good, you're awake. How do you feel?" she asked with a sympathetic smile.

"Lovely." I gestured towards my various cuts and bruises that were almost healed at this point. It was mostly just dried blood. "I mean, don't I look fabulous?"

She snickered and walked towards the window. "Please, I know you well enough to know you're perfectly aware of your looks. A few cuts and bruises are hardly going to detract from your beauty."

"Oh, I don't know about that," Andrei said as he walked back into the room and tossed some clothes on the bed. "I frankly think you're hideous now."

"Really?" I pulled the t-shirt off. "Is that so?"

Andrei stared. His eyes focused on me with an intensity that made my breath quicken. I reached for the clothes on the bed.

"Hideous? Isn't that right, Andrei?" I teased.

Stela laughed under her breath while Andrei just followed my movements as I pulled the clothes on. Before I could poke at him a little more, footsteps sounded from the hall.

"Are you coming to bed, Stela?" Jolie swept into the room and walked around Andrei to Stela, who wrapped an arm around her and kissed her on the forehead. The scent of lavender and rosemary followed her. My nose twitched. That was why she always bothered me. I'd subconsciously reacted to that stinky perfume she always wore.

Stela opened her mouth to say something but was cut off by a scream coming from further inside the house. Several growls followed, along with the sound of large bodies crashing into walls and furniture.

"What the hell?!" Andrei darted out of the room and down the hallway towards the chaos.

I ran out of the room after him before skidding to a halt where he'd paused at the end of the hallway. Peering around him, I looked into the living room and took the scene in.

All the furniture was in pieces strewn about the floor, some of them embedded into the walls. Over a dozen werewolves were spread out across the room in both wolf and human forms. Some were picking themselves up off the ground, shaking their heads and holding onto broken limbs or trying to stanch the bleeding from various wounds. A few seemed relatively unharmed, just a little freaked out. A couple remained on the floor, moaning or whining.

And there he stood in the center of the room. Mist curled off his impeccable black suit as he casually brushed off some wooden splinters that had landed on his jacket. I flinched slightly. I should have introduced Andrei to Magos before now. Because this wasn't going to go well. Stupid procrastination.

"This is exactly what I'm talking about, Magos!" I waved my hands towards the broken werewolves and furniture. "You always have to be so dramatic and such a show-off about everything!"

Andrei shifted, so he was no longer blocking me, and I moved to stand beside him. "Magos? As in your roommate?" He looked back and forth between me and the vampire.

I could practically see the gears turning in his head as Andrei tried to figure out why someone who was being hunted by vampires would also be on friendly terms with one. Whatever conclusion he was drawing, I was guessing he didn't like it based on the impressive scowl he had going on.

As I stepped towards Magos, two werewolves decided I'd provided enough of a distraction and moved in on the vampire.

I had to give it to them; it was a beautiful attack. Clearly, these two worked together often, as they were able to coordinate and implement this attack with no words, merely relying on each other's body language. Both were in their wolf forms, possibly siblings because they had matching light silver coats with darker silver and black fur mixed in. The slightly larger one moved behind Magos while the other one remained in front of him.

"Nathaniel! Clint! Stop!" Andrei snarled.

The wolves ignored him. Both beasts lunged for Magos at the same time, one going for his legs and the other for this throat.

Magos disappeared in a cloud of mist, and the wolves collided into each other. The mist solidified once more, and

Magos snapped into existence. He grabbed the larger of the wolves by the back of the neck and flung him across the room, where he crashed through the wall and into the next room.

The remaining wolf tried to dodge to the side, but Magos was faster and grabbed him by the throat, lifting him up off the floor. He turned to face me and Andrei.

Showing absolutely no strain at holding what was probably a four-hundred-pound werewolf that was frantically fighting to get free, Magos simply looked at me expectantly.

"Yes, I know I should have called. I was literally about to head back to the apartment to check in with you. But come on, you have to admit this little show was a bit flashy." I gestured at the demolished living room and werewolves strewn about the place.

Magos spun, building up momentum, and chucked the werewolf he'd been holding. I winced as it slammed into a couple of wolves who thought they'd been sneakily coming up behind the vampire.

Magos brushed his hands together and shrugged. "Personally, I thought I was very restrained about the whole affair."

I choked back a laugh and turned to face Andrei. He hadn't moved and gave me a hard stare. Apparently, he didn't find this nearly as amusing as I did. I chewed on my lower lip and glanced around the room. Several wolves were still lying on the ground, alive but unconscious. The others were keeping their distance but were clearly on the edge of violence.

"Umm . . . so I may have forgotten to mention that my roommate is a vampire?" I hadn't intended to make that a question, but it just came out that way. I lifted my hands out, palms facing up. "Surprise?"

Chapter Nine

MAGOS SNORTED SOFTLY, and I glared at him. A light danced in his eyes and the corners of his mouth twitched, fighting a smile. Clearly, this was very amusing for him.

"I'll wait for you outside," he said smoothly and vanished, leaving only a curling mist where he had been standing.

Andrei glanced around at the other werewolves in the room. "Give us some space," he said quietly but firmly.

They clearly weren't happy about this turn of events, but they filtered out of the room, taking various exits, some heading upstairs, others to the kitchen.

"I would suggest you leave the vampire alone. He's not with the others, and he will cause you no harm if you leave him be. We'll be going soon." I kept my tone light and made sure my words were more a suggestion than an order.

Werewolves could be touchy about receiving orders from those outside the pack power structure. This pack was more of an odd assortment than the highly organized and militant packs I'd run into in the past, but dominance games were part of their nature. I had no interest in getting into a pissing contest with them.

A few growls floated my way, but a snarl from Andrei cut them off, and they left without argument. Hopefully, they'd leave Magos alone. His patience would go only so far if they tried to attack him again.

I looked back at Andrei, and he met my stare with yellow eyes. My eyebrows crept up. Andrei was still struggling with his wolf nature and usually kept the wolf side contained when he was in human form. I'd never seen the wolf this close to the surface when he wasn't rocking fur. Power and dominance radiated off him, with the other wolves naturally falling in line behind him.

Had the werewolves not been so decimated and scattered by the end of the war, he would have been snatched up and trained by some of the older wolves and placed somewhere important. It was interesting to see this part of him, so different from his normal carefree and charming side.

"Explain," he growled.

I tilted my head in a very feline gesture. His words held power. His wolf was trying to assert dominance and make it clear who was in charge.

Cute.

"Dominance games don't work on cats." I smirked. I owed him answers, and I had every intention of telling him the truth, most of it anyway, but I wouldn't allow his wolfiness to push me around.

Some of the hardness faded from his eyes, and his stance eased a bit. He took a deep breath, then another. His eyes slowly faded back to hazel. "Please."

"I know I haven't told you much about my past." I swallowed. "You haven't pushed me on it, and I appreciate that. Spending time with you these last few months has been amazing. It allowed me to take a break from everything else and just pretend my past didn't exist for small amounts of time. I know you didn't realize it, but it was truly a gift you were giving me." I paused as I thought about how to continue. "Over a century ago, I met a warlock named Sebastian. He was smart, funny, and passionate. And he hated other warlocks. Particularly the leadership of the warlocks known as the Circle. I fell for him. Hard."

"I'm going to take a wild guess and say it didn't end well?"

"No." I gave him a tight, close-lipped smile. "It did not. The first couple of decades were amazing. But things shifted. It happened so slowly I didn't really notice. He became obsessed with gaining more power and started playing all these political games within the warlock power structure. I didn't want any part of that, and I started to realize that whatever love there had been between us was gone. He was using me, and I just hadn't wanted to see it. I left and told him not to follow me."

"He just let you go?" His brows furrowed together as a look of puzzlement settled over his features.

"He tried to win me back at first. But I made it very clear to him that we were done. I didn't see him for a couple of decades and fell in love with someone else." My throat constricted, and heat built behind my eyes. "We were happy. Before Myrna, I thought I'd known love with Sebastian. And maybe I had in the beginning. But not nearly on the same level as what I felt for Myrna. If such a thing as soulmates is real, I think she was mine."

I blinked rapidly to clear the tears threatening to fall.

"Sebastian killed her. He ripped out her heart on my birthday." Pain edged my voice. "He said he wanted me back. And he would share me with no one else. In addition to being a very talented warlock, Sebastian has a natural skill for dreamwalking. He would enter my dreams and manipulate them. Or he would make me relive things I'd rather not. Outside of dreams, he'd leave me gifts throughout the year, always ending with the same gift on my birthday. A bloody heart."

Andrei's eyes shone with sympathy, and I had to look away.

I'd hoped to never tell him about this. I liked having someone look at me without knowing my past.

"I haven't known you long, but I know you well enough to know you're not the kind of person to let that go unanswered. Why haven't you stopped him?" Andrei asked.

"I've tried," I said bitterly. "Sebastian was never particularly talented with combat magic, but he's very good at crafting tracking spells and illusions. He had some of my blood from when we were together. I had nothing of his. Nothing I could give to my friends to help find him. I tried other means of locating him but never could. So, we continued this fucked-up game of me trying to find him and him leaving me gifts as I failed over and over again."

I stared at the flower tattoos that ran down my arms. Each one a reminder of my failures.

"Two years ago, something changed. He worked with a small group of vampires to capture me. They held me captive and tortured me for almost a year. Sebastian oversaw everything and kept pushing for me to accept a binding between us."

I felt the wolf rise in Andrei and wasn't surprised his eyes had turned yellow again. "What would a binding do?" he asked in a rough voice.

"There are different types of binding. The one he wanted would have enslaved my will to his. It's rarely done because it requires both participants to agree and accept the binding."

I managed to keep my voice even as I stared at the worn hardwood flooring, beating back the memories playing in my head. Bound to that table while the vampires came up with new ways to break bones. While they sliced into my skin and fed from me. Sebastian's smile as he asked if I was ready to accept my fate. Magic rippled under my skin as my breathing quickened.

You are free. You are safe. I repeated the words in my mind to combat the rising panic.

Andrei rested his hand on my shoulder almost tentatively, like he wasn't sure whether he should touch me. I appreciated that he hadn't tried to hug me, as any confinement when I was in this state would only push me over the edge. I focused on his hand and the strength radiating from him. It was enough for me to push the panic back.

I reached my hand up and laced it on top of his, where it still rested on my shoulder. "Thank you," I whispered.

"Anytime," he said softly, stepping back to give me space.

I turned around to face him again. "It was Magos who saved me. We have a history, and I saved him once. He returned the favor and stayed with me afterwards. We traveled for a while before settling in this area. The vampires shouldn't have been able to track me here. Either the magic I've been using to protect myself has been compromised or someone has sold me out." And if it was the latter, I would find that person and cut them into tiny little pieces.

"You live together," Andrei said flatly. Of all the things I'd told him, that was what he latched onto.

I rolled my eyes. "We're not sleeping together. Why does everyone always assume that? It is possible for two people to live together and not have sex." I threw my hands up in the air.

Andrei gave me a look that said he clearly didn't believe that but was willing to let it go for the moment.

"Look," I said calmly as I raised a hand in his direction, "I need to take care of some stuff tonight before returning home. Why don't you come with me while I check on a few things, and when we get back to my place, I'll answer more of your questions?"

What I didn't say was I couldn't leave him alone now. There was too big of a chance of him being snatched by Sebastian or the vampires. He'd be staying with me for the next forty-eight hours, whether he wanted to or not. It would just be easier if he came willingly.

"All right." Andrei nodded and moved towards the door that led to the kitchen. "But I have more questions, and you will answer them. I'll meet you out front. I'm going to tell everyone to stay inside for the night and keep alert."

I made a face at his back, then headed out the front door. I'd forgotten how pushy werewolves could be.

Magos stood on the front porch with his hands clasped behind his back, gazing out into the darkness. "I brought your clothes and weapons. Found them in the woods before tracking you here."

I glanced down and saw them piled neatly by the porch railing. "Sweet." I yanked off the clothes Stela had given me and pulled mine on, fastening the weapons.

Magos kept his attention on the tree line. "Plan?" he asked.

"Andrei will give me a ride to pick up my bike. Then we'll head into town." I rubbed the blood ruby gem embedded in my necklace with a frown. "I need to know if this is still working."

"Very well. I'll follow." Magos vanished.

Andrei came back out just in time to see Magos disappear. He stared at the spot where Magos had been. "Care to explain how he does that? I didn't know vampires could do that."

"I have some theories, but I'm not entirely sure," I said honestly. "I've never encountered another vampire that can do that either."

Andrei looked at me sharply. "And you never asked him?"

"No. It's his business. If he wants to tell me someday, he can. Otherwise, I don't pry." I shrugged.

"I thought cats were curious?" he said with a trace of humor.

I gave him a sly look. "I didn't say that I wasn't curious. Or that I wasn't looking for answers elsewhere. I merely said I wasn't asking *him* for answers."

Andrei laughed, and I smiled. Despite the events of the evening and what I'd told him, that laugh was still so joyful. I'd never get tired of hearing it.

"You know the small turnout right before the main parking lot for the forest reserve?" I asked as we walked towards his beat-up Bronco.

"Yep. I take it that's where you left your bike?" He hopped into the driver's seat.

I opened the passenger door and climbed in. "You assume correctly, my dear Watson."

"That's not the expression." Andrei frowned. "Also, why do you get to be Sherlock?" he asked as we pulled out of the long driveway and onto the main road.

I sniffed and looked out the window. "Truth be told, I always considered myself more of a Ms. Adler."

Andrei chucked softly, and we rode in a comfortable silence for the rest of the trip, which was less than five minutes. I paused before hopping out. "Follow me back, and we'll regroup when we get there." He nodded.

I headed back to town on my bike with Andrei following in his Bronco. Magos was around, despite not being seen. Given the late hour, the streets were mostly empty on the human side of town. I pulled over just before the boundary that led to the nonhuman blocks.

Andrei parked behind my bike and sauntered over to me. He glanced around. "So what are we doing here, exactly? This place is just a bunch of office buildings. Not much to see around here."

Before I could answer, Magos materialized right next to us. I was used to my friend's dramatic comings and goings. Andrei was not.

"Fuck!" Andrei jumped back a few feet. His startlement

gave way to anger, and he took a step towards Magos with a growl bubbling up in his throat.

Magos merely stood there with a disinterested look on his face, but I knew him well enough to know he found this entertaining. Damn vampire.

I stepped between them and calmly said, "Can we not, please?" I looked at Magos. "You know what you did. Knock it off. And you, wolfie, calm the fuck down."

"My apologies. I didn't mean to frighten the poor boy," Magos said in a tone that sounded sincere, but I knew it wasn't.

He didn't hate werewolves like most vampires, but that didn't mean he liked them either. He basically tolerated their presence and took a weird joy out of needling them. Under normal circumstances, I found it amusing, but not so much when it was being directed at my sort-of boyfriend. It would be a long night if they kept this up.

Andrei hadn't taken another step towards Magos, but the look on his face said he wanted to punch the vampire in the face very much. But his eyes held no trace of yellow, so his wolf hadn't pushed itself to the surface. Good enough.

"This section of town isn't just a bunch of offices. It's under the daemons' control. They have wards up around it to keep the humans out. You'll be able to cross the boundary created by the ward, but you won't be able to enter the bar where I need to go. Neither can Magos. So the two of you need to wait here."

I held up my hand, halting the objections that came from both Andrei and Magos.

"Neither of you are allowed into the bar. You might be my friends, but Pele has a very strict 'no vampires or werewolves' policy, and I don't want to smell burnt fur or skin. It's highly unlikely the vampires or warlocks will attack here."

Magos mulled it over. "All right."

Andrei looked like he was about to argue, but something

about the expression on my face must have changed his mind. "Fine," he bit out. "My first question still stands. What are we doing here?"

"I have an amulet that is supposed to stop the bad guys from tracking me via magic. A friend of mine can tell me if it's still working or not. I'll be back in ten minutes."

"If you're *not* back in ten minutes, I'm coming after you, and the vampire won't stop me," he growled.

The vampire could totally stop him, but I wasn't going to tell him that. Besides, if I wasn't back in ten minutes, I had no doubt Magos would come looking for me. He might have agreed to this rather easily, but I knew he wasn't happy about it.

I gave Andrei a quick kiss. "Thank you. See you in ten minutes."

I jogged up the street heading towards The Inferno, anxiety building with every step. It was unlikely that the vampires would attack me here. The human side of town might be empty, but this part was busy. I nodded my greetings at various groups, recognizing many of them as locals who lived here full-time.

Hopefully Pele was here and available. She spent most of her time at the tavern and even had a suite built on the top floor that she stayed in most days instead of returning to her home in the daemon realm. But sometimes her duties required her presence elsewhere. Asmodeus could probably help me in a pinch, but I'd have to give them some sort of explanation. Pele trusted them, but I still didn't like telling others my secrets.

A few minutes later, I pushed open the heavy wooden door to The Inferno and looked around. The tavern was full tonight. I let out a sigh of relief when I spotted Pele standing behind the bar chatting up Eddie.

As I walked up to stand beside them, he lifted his shot glass towards me in greeting.

"Hey, Eddie. Mind if I borrow Pele for a few minutes? Something urgent came up that I need to get her opinion on. Won't take long." Without waiting for Eddie's reply, I glanced at Pele. "Can we step away from the bar for a few minutes?" I asked calmly and ran my fingers across my necklace.

"Sure," she replied without missing a beat. "I'll be back in a moment, Eddie."

Pele headed down the bar, and I followed. She moved aside the heavy curtain that separated her office from the rest of The Inferno, and we walked through the doorway. All the chatter and noise fell away.

I glanced around the sparsely decorated room. The main piece of furniture was a simple but beautifully crafted dark wooden desk with two chairs made of the same material sitting in front. A larger, more ornate chair sat behind the desk. One wall was full of shelves with various books, trinkets, and other objects filling its space. The wall opposite the entry had a wooden arch that spread across most of the wall. Words were carved into the wood, and the space inside the arch rippled a dark purple color. My magic told me the gateway was currently closed.

Pele brushed past me and leaned against the desk. Her tailored suit fit her curves perfectly. I'd gotten Magos some suits from the same daemon tailor for his birthday. I didn't actually know when his birthday was, so I had just picked a day and declared it his birthday. He thought it was ridiculous, but I knew for a fact he loved the suits.

"What's going on?" Pele crossed her arms.

"The vampires working for Sebastian are in town and tried to grab me tonight." Pele's nostrils flared, and her eyes flashed in anger. "Sebastian isn't here yet, but he's coming. I need you to tell me if this is still working." I tapped the ruby gem embedded in the necklace around my neck.

Pele pushed off the desk and stood in front of me. I was

tall, but she had a couple of inches on me, so I had to tilt my head back a bit to give her better access. She laid her fingers against the gem, and the turquoise in her eyes swirled, changing to a dark red. Pele hadn't made this particular amulet, but she understood the magic behind it. Her magic brushed over me as she prodded the gem some more.

Pele pulled her magic back, and her eyes slowly returned to turquoise. "Kali's work is perfection. The amulet is still working as it should. No one can track you with magic. They must have found you some other way."

"Someone in this town sold me out," I growled.

"That is definitely the likeliest explanation," Pele agreed. "What's your plan now?"

"We're heading back to the apartment for the night. Nobody is getting past your wards. We'll game plan what to do from there. If we run, at least I know they can't track us," I said tiredly. I didn't want to run; I liked this town. I liked my apartment. We hadn't been there long, but it already felt like home.

"We could just kill them all," Pele offered.

"The problem is, I don't know who *all* is," I replied, letting out a frustrated breath. "Something has driven Sebastian to these measures. There's a desperation that wasn't there previously. I would love nothing more than to kill Sebastian and all the vampires working for him—and will probably do so before this is over. But what if Sebastian has told other warlocks about me? When he had me, he made it sound like others were after me, too. What if the Circle knows?" I swallowed as an icy dread sank into my chest. "I know the warlocks aren't as powerful as the fae or daemons, but the members of the Circle aren't lightweights, and they command all warlocks. I can't fight all of them."

Not without using the magic I kept hidden anyway. And

doing that would draw the attention of the fae and daemons. Neither Pele nor Kaysea would be able to protect me then.

"Go home for the night and stay there," Pele commanded. She had a tendency to get extra bossy when she was worried. "Let me do some more digging and push some of my contacts more. If an opportunity arises, try to catch one of the vampires alive."

"I'm fairly certain Magos is already plotting that," I said wryly. "Thanks, Pele."

"Always." She waved me away.

I left her office and walked outside—almost straight into Magos, who'd clearly been hovering outside the bar. "What are you doing here? I thought we were going to meet down the block?" I looked around. "And where's Andrei?"

His mouth twisted in distaste. "Vampires are here."

Chapter Ten

"Shit." Adrenaline pulsed through me as I pulled both my swords free. "Where?"

"Close. I didn't want to chance you running into them before reaching our meeting place." He walked down the street towards our vehicles.

I fell into step beside him and stayed on alert. "And Andrei?" I prompted.

Magos spared a glance at me. "I didn't think you'd want him involved in a fight, so I had him wait in the vehicle. Not ideal, but you and I are their targets. They have no reason to look for him, so he should be safe there for a short time."

"And he just voluntarily stayed behind?" I narrowed my eyes at Magos.

He didn't look at me and kept scanning the path ahead. The small suspicion I had at his words erupted.

"You did your vampire mind whammy on him!" I said incredulously. "Seriously?! He already doesn't like you. Now he's going to be pissed."

Magos shrugged. "That's your problem. I wasn't going to waste time arguing with him."

I sighed. It was probably the right call. If we ran into vampires, Magos and I fought well together. Andrei would be a wild card. I'd just have to deal with the fallout later.

"Did you recognize the scent of the vampires?" I asked.

"No," Magos said slowly. "Something is different about their scent. I'm not sure what."

"Hmm. Well, we have another block to go, and that section is quieter than the rest. So if they're going to spring a trap, that's where they'll do it."

Magos made a sound of agreement and slowed down. "Their scent is getting stronger. They're near."

"There's an alley up ahead. You scout, I follow?"

Magos didn't bother to answer; he just vanished into mist. I quietly stalked towards the alley.

We were still in the daemon section of town, but this block was mostly restaurants and a few shops that closed earlier in the night. Most had apartments above them, but all the lights were off. Either the residents were asleep, or they were out. Some of the apartments were also used for those visiting from other realms, so they might not even be inhabited.

A high-pitched shriek erupted from the alley. What the hell? That almost sounded like . . . a kid?

I sprinted towards the alley entrance and skidded to a stop to take in the sight. My head cocked to the side, and I slowly lowered my swords. Well, that wasn't what I expected.

Three kids cowered next to a dumpster, and Magos held what appeared to be a teenage girl against the wall by her throat. I inhaled. Yep. Vampires. Great.

I put my swords away as I entered the alley. I very much doubted these kids were going to attack us, and even if they did, I could handle some vamp kids just fine.

"I've had a long day and an even longer night." I rubbed my forehead. "What little patience I had ran out about ten minutes ago. So can someone explain to me why there are a bunch of vampire kids hanging out in a dark alley in *my* town?"

The girl that Magos held by the throat calmly tapped his arm. He let go and took a step back. He seemed shaken. I doubted anyone but me would be able to tell. But his calm façade wasn't as convincing as it usually was.

Something about this girl deeply disturbed him.

I pursed my lips together as I studied her. Tall, only a couple of inches shorter than me. Thin, willowy build with pale milky white skin and black hair. She was striking. I put her age at around eighteen. She probably hadn't settled yet. Unlike other beings, vampires had a choice about what age they settled at. They had to perform some ritual. Most chose their early to mid-twenties because no one wanted to be stuck as a teenager forever.

The girl rubbed her throat and calmly said, "We mean you no harm. We're actually hoping you can help us."

I sighed and closed my eyes. *Why me?* Opening them again, I turned my attention to Magos. "Did you put out an ad or something? Post on some vampire-only board about our availability to help wayward teens?"

Magos didn't acknowledge my words. He just continued to study the vampire girl. Alrighty then.

I glowered at the vampire kids. "Help you with what, exactly?"

"Hide from the Council," she said. I rubbed my forehead as she plowed on. "Something big is happening. We don't know the specifics, but the Council is working with the warlocks. A few months ago, we were moved from our various houses to Seattle. They didn't tell us why, but they kept us under lock and key. And warlocks started coming regularly to study us."

"Why?" I turned to look at the others who were still huddled by the dumpster. Suspicion formed as I thought of all the reasons vampire leadership would be so interested in some vampire kids. "Why were they interested in you four specifically?"

The girl chewed her lip and glanced back at the others. After a few moments, she turned and looked back at me, holding my gaze. I felt a pulse of magic from her. One moment, she was a teenage girl. And then she was a large black wolf.

Because we're all from Apex bloodlines, a voice calmly said in my head.

"Holy shit," I whispered, mostly to myself. "All of you?"

The wolf vanished, and the girl reappeared. "Yes."

I processed that information. Most of the first vampires were human before they were changed into vampires. But some hadn't been human, or at least not completely human. Whatever magic they had possessed came along for the ride and mutated in odd ways when they were changed into vampires. Those beings had unique abilities and were referred to as the Apex bloodlines.

Some of the original Apex vampires were still kicking around. I was pretty sure Magos was one, and I suspected Mikhail as well. Over the generations, the Apex bloodlines got watered down and their descendants usually didn't possess the same magic as the original Apex. Or it was so weak it didn't matter.

But this girl didn't seem weak. And if all four of them were like this . . . Holy shit.

"And you're here . . . you escaped, I take it? Why?"

"We want no part of what they're planning. We've spent our entire lives locked away and just want a chance to be free." She gestured towards the others. "There is no life for us among the vampires. They're obsessed with war and power. They defeated the werewolves and immediately began negotiations with the warlocks. It never ends.

"That's no way to live," she continued. "We planned our

escape and waited for an opportunity and then came here. To ask you for help."

I heard the desperation in her voice, and it pulled on something inside me, but I kept my expression neutral. It was a hell of a coincidence for these kids to show up in town at the same time the vampires working for Sebastian had finally tracked me down.

My eyes narrowed. "How did you find me? And why *me?*"

The girl gestured towards one of the kids crouching by the dumpster. "Damon can read minds. The guardians and teachers we've had over the years knew he could do it, but we've all been downplaying our magic for years. They thought their mental shields were enough to keep him out, but he's been able to pull information out of them for some time. We knew about you months ago. The shifter on the run with the old warrior."

Her eyes flickered warily to Magos. "You've escaped them before. And you've stayed ahead of them all this time. They only found out about you recently. We figured you would disappear again and thought maybe . . . you'd take us with you? We don't know anyone. You're literally the first being I've ever spoken to that isn't a vampire or a warlock." Her eyes filled with hope. "You can help us."

Her words replayed in my mind: *They only found out about you recently.* "Do you know exactly when they found out about me? Or how?" I asked.

This was so not good. I had assumed the Vampire Council knew something about me. The group of vampires working for Sebastian was small, but the Council knew everything when it came to vampires. They would know if a small contingent of theirs was working for a warlock, even if they weren't directly involved. But it sounded like they were *very* much involved. Which meant this definitely went beyond Sebastian and the vampires working for him.

I'd already suspected as much, but this just added more credence to my suspicions. As I thought about how to proceed, I looked at Magos and found him staring at the girl with an intensity I'd never seen before.

"Magos? What's wrong?" I looked back and forth between him and the girl. "Do you know her?"

"No," the girl said softly. "He knows my ancestor."

She took a step forward. Then another. Until she was standing in front of him. Magos continued to stare at her and say nothing.

"I'm sorry. I wish I were descended from someone else. But I can't help what I am." Her voice was gentle but firm.

"I know," Magos replied. His expression softened, and his voice held an echo of pain. "His sins are not yours to bear." A mixture of concern and curiosity stirred in me. Whoever this girl was, she had some connection to Magos's past.

He lifted his gaze from the girl and looked at me. "We must help them."

"I know. But how?" I raised my hands in the air. "We can't even help ourselves, and we're not exactly safe to be around at the moment." I turned to the girl. "Does anyone know you're here?"

She shook her head. "We only got to town last night. I'm sure they'll send someone after us, but I don't know why they would come here. We covered our tracks well."

I snorted. "Kid, you said yourself that you've rarely interacted with the outside world. We should assume you've been followed. A group of vampires is already here after us. They wouldn't divide their attention between capturing us and tracking you."

I remembered what Ryder had said. *I do believe the Council gave you other orders. Shouldn't you be elsewhere dealing with that little problem?*

Shit. The Council sent Mikhail after them. Seemed like a

little overkill to send the vampire assassin after a bunch of runaway vampire kids, even if they *were* Apex vampires. My brows furrowed as I thought about our options.

We would help them. I didn't have it in me to turn away kids. Even vampire kids. Besides, they could provide us with more insight into what the Council was up to and maybe shed some more light on our situation. But we couldn't just take them back to our place. It was only a matter of time before the vampires figured out where I lived, and I didn't want them to know the vampire kids were there, too.

Our place was ideal, though. No one would be able to get to them, and the two apartments below ours were empty. Pele wouldn't be happy about it, but I'd explain it to her tomorrow. I needed to get the kids inside the building with no one seeing or creating a scent trail.

"We can't just take them there," Magos said, echoing my thoughts. We looked at each other. I knew what he wasn't saying. "Can you do it?" he asked simply.

"Yes. Not directly. We'd have to stop somewhere else and go home from there." I tapped my fingers against my thigh.

This was such an insane idea. I'd pulled crazier stunts when I was younger and considerably more reckless, but still. As much as I tried, I couldn't come up with another plan that didn't also come with a long list of issues.

Magos held my gaze as I said softly, "There's no hiding my magic from them if I do this."

"I know." He clasped a hand onto my shoulder. "I won't let anything happen to you," he vowed.

A sniffle came from the kids by the dumpster. I hadn't looked at them closely before. Two teenage boys crouched protectively around a young girl. She looked to be around five or six years old.

I closed my eyes. This was such a bad idea. "What's your name?"

"Elisa," the older girl replied and pointed to the others. "That's Misha and Damon with Isabeau."

I took a deep breath. "All right. Here's the deal. We're going to get you to our place. There's an empty furnished apartment below ours you can stay in for now. The entire building is heavily warded, particularly well against vampires. I'm going to get you to the apartment, and you're going to stay there and not move, understand? We'll be home shortly after you. I have a lot more questions for you."

She nodded.

"Magos, cover the front?" I moved farther into the alley.

Both the daemons and the fae made amulets that could detect gateways, but they weren't all that common, and most of them had a pretty limited radius. So unless someone had a specific reason to investigate this area, I should be safe. Any leftover magic residue would fade within a few days.

I reached the end of the alley and faced the brick wall. Even someone standing at the front of the alley wouldn't be able to see anything between the dumpsters and the dark. I glanced up at the roof; Magos was crouched on the corner where he had a view of the top of the buildings and the street. I took his silence to mean the coast was clear.

I stretched my hand out to the brick wall, fingers spread wide, and concentrated. The air directly in front of the wall rippled. With another small push, a gateway snapped into existence, providing a doorway to another realm. Where the air had been rippling, there was now a dimly lit cave that appeared beyond it.

This wasn't the magic that I kept chained and locked away. But it was just as likely to get me killed if the fae or daemons ever found out I could waltz in and out of their realms despite their fancy wards. On the off chance they didn't kill me outright, they would definitely scrutinize me further. And if they discovered what else I was hiding . . . the Circle would be the least of my worries.

A small gasp sounded from behind me, but the vampire kids kept their mouths shut as they stared at the cave in wonder. I stepped through the gateway and looked back at them.

"Come on." I gestured for them to join me. "This is just a pit stop."

Elisa stepped through with only the slightest hesitation, and the others followed her. I kept that gateway open and reached my hand out again. A ripple formed in the air. I pushed a little harder.

Pele had some intense wards around our building, and opening a gateway into it was a little bit more difficult. She probably thought such a thing was impossible and would be none too pleased to find out no wards I'd ever encountered could keep me out.

Sweat broke out on my forehead as I fed the gateway more magic. Finally, a tear appeared where the air rippled and the apartment on the first floor became visible in front of us. I'd only been in it a couple of times. While our apartment had a large living room and kitchen, this one had a smaller living room with three bedrooms. Unfortunately, it also had floor-to-ceiling windows.

"Go. Remember the rules. Don't try to leave. Also, don't break anything. I haven't exactly cleared your stay with the owner of the building."

Elisa herded the rest of the kids through the door between realms I had opened and faced me. "We won't. I promise. See you soon?" I nodded. "Thank you," she said.

"Thank me by not breaking anything. Don't worry about the windows. They're spelled so no one can see in them from the outside. Really, though . . . don't break anything." I grimaced.

Once the gateway to the apartment closed, I returned to the alley and closed the one there as well. Magos appeared beside me as I stepped out of the alley.

"It's been a long night. Let's get home before we run into more trouble."

As we walked around the corner, I spotted Andrei's Bronco and a man leaning casually against the passenger door. Every part of me froze. Mikhail was waiting for us. He must have seen Andrei in the car. My heart raced as I thought about how to get to Andrei and make sure he was still okay.

Mikhail smiled. "Hello, Uncle. Quite the situation you've gotten yourself into."

Chapter Eleven

"Uncle?" I shot Magos a disbelieving look. "Tell me that the vampire assassin of the Council isn't your nephew? Please tell me you haven't been keeping that from me?"

I knew Magos had to have some sort of history with the Council. He was a vampire after all, and they all seemed to know of him since they kept referring to him as the "old warrior". But I never would have guessed he was related to their goddamn lapdog.

"It's complicated." His expression remained stoic.

I waited for him to say more, but he didn't elaborate. "That's it? That's all you have to say?"

"Yes," he said in an irritatingly calm voice.

"Fine." I clapped him on the back before crossing my arms. "I've already gotten into two fights tonight. I do believe this one is all you. Plus, it seems there's some family drama here to sort out."

Magos rubbed his forehead. "You're going to ask me a ton of questions about this later, aren't you?"

"Obviously." I waved a hand towards Mikhail. "Go on, then."

Leaving Magos to frown at Mikhail, I walked across the street, angling my direction slightly towards the front of the vehicle. I stopped about ten feet from the bumper and could scarcely make out Andrei's form in the passenger seat. He sat there unblinking, completely oblivious to what was going on around him. But his breathing was even, and he looked unharmed, likely still under Magos's compulsion. He was going to be so pissed later, but at least for now he was safe.

Some of the tension eased out of me, and I turned my attention back to the vampire assassin . . . who was apparently Magos's nephew? That was a hell of a thing for him to never mention to me.

"Now isn't the best time, Mikhail," Magos said, moving until he stood a few feet in front of the other vampire. He didn't draw his sword like I expected but instead clasped his hands behind his back. "I can explain things later."

Mikhail ignored him and turned slightly to scrutinize me. "So . . . this is the reason you've come out of your centuries-long isolation? I suppose she's pretty enough, but plenty of pretty ones are out there. What *exactly* does she do for you that's worth incurring the wrath of the Council after all this time?"

My lips curled in disgust. "First, real subtle on the innuendo there. Second, gross. Magos and I have never, and will never, have that type of relationship. We're friends. A concept, I'm guessing, is foreign to you."

"Not so much a foreign concept as a memory slowly slipping away," Mikhail murmured as he stared at me with an intensity that made me want to run in the opposite direction.

Mikhail pushed off the Bronco and walked towards me. Magos stiffened but made no move to stop him.

"Not lovers then." Mikhail snapped his fingers and glanced over his shoulder at Magos. "Ah. She's the child, isn't she?" Mikhail returned his attention to me and started circling. "Tell me, what did you tell him that day? I'd been trying to get through to him for weeks with no luck. But one conversation with you had him pulling out of that downward spiral."

I took a step towards him, and he stopped circling me. We stood, almost touching. I couldn't help but take in his appearance.

Strong jawline, sharp cheekbones, full lips. He was more pretty than handsome with his mix of masculine and feminine features. If I'd had to guess what he was based on appearances alone, I would have sworn he was sidhe. Most sidhe had the same sort of androgynous beauty.

Some part of me stilled when I looked into his bottomless eyes and saw pain, violence, and insanity. It should have scared the shit out of me, but I found myself drawn in instead.

I breathed deeply, finding he smelled a bit like Magos. The scent of rainfall. But there was something else there, too. I'd never come across anything like it. My magic stirred, but for once, it didn't feel like it was trying to break free. Instead, it felt like it was intrigued by Mikhail.

Mayday, mayday! What the fuck was wrong with me? I fought the urge to step back and create space between us.

"Well?" Mikhail said softly as he continued to stare at me with an intensity I suspected he couldn't shut off. "What did you tell him?"

A tremor ran through me at being the sole object of his attention. Despite the weird ride my emotions were going through, I kept all that off my face as I gave him a lazy smile. He was crowding my space, trying to intimidate me, and I didn't like it. Well, the *sane* part of me didn't like it.

I held his unflinching gaze and slid a knife into my palm. "That's for me to know, and you not to." I jammed the knife into his side, between the ribs and a mere inch away from his heart. He grunted, but the bastard didn't even take a step back.

Magos appeared between us in an instant and thrust us

apart. I kept my grip firm on the blade, and Mikhail hissed as it tore from his flesh.

"Enough," Magos said firmly. "We don't have time for this. Put the knife away, Nemain."

I took a step back but kept the knife out.

"A bit of an extreme reaction to my question, don't you think?" Mikhail snapped. "A simple 'none of your business' would have been sufficient."

The wound I'd dealt him hadn't been fatal, and I hadn't intended it to be. But it should have hurt like hell and slowed him down. Yet nothing in the way he was standing indicated he was in any kind of pain. Bastard had likely already healed. Picking a fight with him had probably been a mistake, and it was good Magos had broken it up. But I wouldn't be admitting that anytime soon. I'd just have to be aware for future reference that I'd have to deal him a lot more damage to put him down.

"Exactly what was going through your head?" Mikhail continued. "Here's the infamous vampire assassin who clearly has a history with my lethal companion. How about I stab him in the ribs?"

"I stabbed you because you're annoying! And you were there when the vampires tried to grab me earlier and did nothing, even though you clearly knew Magos and I were friends!" I wanted to throw my dagger at him, but Magos shot me a "don't you dare" look, so I clenched my fingers around the handle instead.

"I could have slaughtered all those werewolves before they ever got to you. So actually, I did help!" Mikhail's fingers twitched like he was imagining wrapping them around my throat.

"You moth—"

"Enough from both of you." Magos held up a hand to silence me and asked Mikhail pointedly, "What are you doing here?"

"I'm here to save you from yourself. I stayed with the Council all these centuries to keep them away from you. I worked for them; they left you alone. That was the deal. A deal that was working just fine until you teamed up with the stabbity shifter over there who the Council and the warlocks want to capture at any cost. I can't protect you from that." He glared at me as if it was my fault that the Council was after me.

Prick.

"You stayed with the Council because you wanted to kill werewolves. Don't act like I was your first thought in that decision. I never wanted that life for you," Magos said calmly.

"Wait," I cut in, "is the Council working directly with Sebastian? Or is there another player in this besides Sebastian? Until recently, we assumed he had hired or coerced a small group of vampires to work directly with him and the Council wasn't directly involved in any of this."

Mikhail looked at me like I was an idiot. "Of course they're involved. The Council and Emir have agreed to an alliance."

Emir. That name sounded so familiar, but I couldn't place it. "Emir is the warlock currently leading the Circle?" I guessed, my brows furrowing as I tried to process this.

"Yes," Mikhail replied in a somewhat bored tone. "Sebastian was told to bring you in no matter what. Whatever was going on between you and him before is irrelevant. They all want you now."

A chill ran through me. "If that's true, then why didn't he hand me over to the leader of the warlocks when he captured me last year?"

Mikhail shrugged. "Don't know. I do know he hadn't told them he'd captured you. And they were none too pleased to learn about it after you'd escaped. I'm surprised Sebastian's still breathing, to be honest."

It had bothered me that they'd sent the vampire assassin of the Council after the runaway teenagers. I'd assumed something more was going on there. Had that just been a cover so he could work behind the scenes to find me? Magos didn't exactly look happy about Mikhail's presence here, but he also didn't seem super worried. Once we were alone, I'd have to get more information from him about their family history.

"Why exactly are you telling us all of this?" I arched an eyebrow. "Don't you work for the Council? Kind of telling on your own side right now, aren't you?"

"I work for myself," he replied flatly. "In the past, my work and that of the Council coincided. That may no longer be the case. That said, if I deliver you to the Council, it *would* ensure my uncle's safety." The look Mikhail gave me was that of a pure predator. He was definitely thinking about making a grab for me.

"That won't be happening," Magos said, voice stern. He held his blade out against Mikhail's throat. I hadn't even seen him move. Mist was still rolling off the broadsword he'd summoned.

"I see you still have the blade," Mikhail said, eyes narrowing. "What will you do now, Uncle?" He leaned into the sword until it bit into his skin and blood dripped down his neck.

I watched both of them carefully but said nothing, trusting Magos to handle this for now. I'd get more information out of him later.

Magos pulled the sword away and moved between me and Mikhail. "If you turn her over to the Council, nothing will stop me from getting her back. You won't be able to stop me. You'd have to kill me. What will you do then, Nephew?"

Mikhail glared at his uncle in frustration.

"Thought so," Magos said. "We need to go. But you and I will speak about this more."

Without another word, Magos and I walked over to the SUV. I opened the passenger door and looked at Andrei. He was sitting upright in the seat, staring straight ahead without focusing on anything in particular. I cringed. Gods, he was going to be so pissed when Magos snapped him out of it. I closed the door and glanced to where we'd left Mikhail standing. I wasn't surprised to see he was gone.

"Well," I drawled, "for a long overdue family reunion, I guess that went well."

Magos laughed softly and winced. "Think you can hold off on assaulting me with questions about all this until we're back at the apartment?"

"Fine." I pointed to the passenger seat. "Should probably leave him like this until we're safe in the apartment. He's not going to be happy when you wake him, and I don't want to deal with it here."

"All right. I'll drive this hideous vehicle back, and you can follow on your bike." Magos slid into the driver's seat of the Bronco. I got the impression he was trying to touch as little of it as possible.

I snickered and walked to my bike, started it up, and followed them back to the apartment.

We parked in the side lot next to the building, and Magos swung Andrei over his shoulders in a fireman's carry position. Once we got through the front door, I pointed to the stairs. "Take Andrei up to our place. I'm going to let the kids know we're back."

Magos nodded and headed up the stairs, showing absolutely no strain at carrying the two-hundred-pound man with him.

I walked up to the bright red door and knocked. "It's me." I heard sounds of movement from the other side. A few seconds later, Elisa opened the door. "Just wanted to let you know we're back. We live in the apartment on the third floor; the apartment on the second floor is empty. I have some things I need to take care of right now. Do you guys need anything?"

Elisa chewed on her lower lip. "Umm . . . we're kind of

hungry." I looked at her, and she rushed on. "We haven't eaten in almost a week. There wasn't time before we left, and we've tried to keep a low profile while on the run."

I looked up and stared at the ceiling. "Right. You can't mesmerize anyone yet, and leaving bodies with two holes in their neck would be a bit of a giveaway. All right, I'll send Magos out and have him bring back something for you."

Elisa smiled. "Thanks."

"No problem." I turned and headed up the stairs to let Magos know he was on food duty. Just as I reached the top of the landing, I heard a crash come from inside our apartment, followed by a growl that very much sounded like a werewolf.

I sprinted the last few steps to the door and threw it open. Magos stood on one side of the living room, just in front of our sparring mat. And a very pissed off Andrei in wolf form stood on the wreckage of our coffee table.

I stepped inside the apartment and closed the door, exasperated. "I told you he'd be pissed."

Chapter Twelve

"How about you help me keep the werewolf from breaking anymore furniture and crack jokes later?" Magos replied as he studied the werewolf where it crouched across the living room.

"What, you can't handle one little wolf on your own?" I grinned at him and leaned back against the door with my arms crossed.

"Sure." Magos casually shrugged. "But I assumed you wanted the boy in one piece. My way of dealing with him involves ripping his head off. Especially if he damages my favorite chair."

I snorted and cautiously entered the apartment, heading towards the kitchen. Andrei remained crouched, muscles tense, waiting to attack. His eyes tracked my movement, and his growl rumbled louder.

I looked around the living room and saw no signs of Jinx or Luna. Probably sleeping in my room. I could use Jinx's help, but convincing the fae cat to do anything he didn't want to was pointless. There was no way he didn't hear what was going on, which meant he'd decided not to get involved. He was such a jerk sometimes.

"Easy, wolf." I passed the kitchen counter and paused a healthy distance away from Andrei.

Calling a werewolf a wolf was a bit of a misnomer. It was more that they were wolf-like in appearance. Andrei's lupine body was covered in dark grey fur with some black and white mixed in here and there, which was a common coloring among werewolves. His head was canine in shape, but the jaw was wide enough to make room for two rows of teeth. I estimated his weight to be around 800 pounds, which made him one of the bigger werewolves I'd seen. Definitely bigger than me in my feline form.

"What are the chances of you shifting back so we can talk this out?" I asked hopefully. "I've got steak in the fridge. And beer."

The werewolf pivoted slightly until he was facing me, and his jaws opened wider as he snarled, allowing me a nice view of his teeth. The front row contained sharp teeth and two massive canines perfect for slicing into flesh. The back row was equally sharp but curved back slightly.

Getting bit by a werewolf sucked. If they latched on, it was hard to pull away, and if you managed, the cost would be a pound of flesh. Literally.

"Right, I'm guessing Andrei's not home right now."

"Of all the beings in this town to date, you had to pick the werewolf who has zero control over his wolf?" Magos said dryly.

"We're not dating," I retorted automatically. I didn't look at Magos, but I knew he was giving me that skeptical look with one eyebrow raised. "We're just enjoying each other's company in a casual and non-committed sort of way."

"If that's the case, then why are we going through all this trouble to keep him safe?" Magos replied. I knew his stupid eyebrow was still raised.

"Because I might in six months to a year consider dating

him, and I need him to be alive for that to be a possibility," I snapped back. "Are you going to help me or not?"

"Fine," Magos grumbled. He took off his jacket and carefully folded it over a nearby chair. I rolled my eyes. "You distract and I'll get him in a chokehold. I can hold him for a few minutes, but you'll have to find something to bind his legs and keep his muzzle shut."

I nodded and prepared to jump forward. I'd need to be fast. Jump towards him to get his attention and jump back. And keep that up while Magos got in position. This would be easier in my feline form, but that would require time to strip and shift. Chances were pretty good the werewolf would attack me then. The muscles in my thighs tensed as I prepared to lunge forward.

Seconds before I made my move, a flash of movement to the left got my attention. Luna sleepily walked out of the hallway and into the living room. She stopped and took in the sight of the werewolf less than twenty feet from her and sat down. Then she yowled loudly. The werewolf swung his massive head towards her and licked his lips.

Before any of us had a chance to move, magic flooded the room, and Magos and I got pushed to our knees and locked in place. Andrei did a not so graceful belly flop.

A long hiss sounded from the hallway, and Jinx stalked out. His glamour was gone, and I watched his hundred-pound sleek form walk menacingly towards the wolf. The fae cat was dwarfed by the werewolf, even though Andrei was flat on the ground. It wasn't a fair fight. It wasn't even a fight at all.

"Don't kill him, Jinx!" I said frantically before he decided to do something drastic like rip out Andrei's throat. "It's okay. Good kitty." Jinx swung his head towards me, and glittering gold eyes glared at me a few breaths before returning to stare down the werewolf. "Please," I ground out, still trying to rise from the floor where I'd landed.

Jinx's tail twitched as he continued to stare at the werewolf. A soft meow sounded from the hallway as Luna slowly crept back in. Jinx glanced back over his shoulder at her and looked at the werewolf one more time before turning and walking back to the hallway where Luna greeted him by rubbing her face against his and caressing her body against his legs as she weaved in and out.

Fine. But keep that dog away from my chair. I don't want his stench on it. Jinx's voice rumbled through my head.

He released me and Magos but kept the werewolf pinned to the floor. I sagged in relief. Jinx was normally the less volatile one between the two of us, at least when it came to killing, but all bets were off if he felt Luna was in danger.

"Think you can convince the werewolf to shift back?" Magos asked after climbing back to his feet.

"I think so," I replied. "But it will be easier if you're not here. The wolf side of him is probably still pissed at you." I looked over at Jinx, who had decided to stay in the living room and had settled on his favorite chair, with Luna curled up behind him. "Jinx, would you mind blocking sound from Andrei for a few minutes? I need to have a chat with Magos."

I was pretty confident that Andrei wouldn't remember any of this given that his wolf side was fully in control. But I didn't think Magos would want the werewolf knowing his business, so I didn't want to take any chances.

Jinx grumbled something that I took as a yes. Andrei jerked his head, and his eyes darted around the room wildly. He was pinned to the floor and no longer able to hear anything around him. He was definitely not a happy werewolf. I could practically feel the rage radiating off him.

Magos had moved to the kitchen, and I slid onto one of the stools at the counter. "Do you trust Mikhail's information?" I asked.

The coffee machine beeped, and Magos poured the delicious black sludge into the two mugs. He poured some cream and a ridiculous amount of sugar into mine and handed it to me. He stared at the steam rising from his mug for a few seconds. "Yes. We can trust him."

"I think it's time you filled me in on your history a bit more," I said slowly. "I won't push you on this if you don't want to talk about it. But I get the impression Mikhail isn't going away. And if what he said was true, our problem just got a lot bigger than worrying about what Sebastian had planned for my birthday."

"You're right." Magos sipped his coffee. "I'm guessing you know I wasn't human before I was turned into a vampire?"

"I've suspected you were an Apex vampire. I take it Mikhail is too?"

"Yes. Our realm fell to devourers over six centuries ago." Magos's wide shoulders bowed slightly as he wrapped both hands around the coffee mug. "We were lucky our city had an active daemon gateway they were able to keep open for us to evacuate everyone. Most of the other cities weren't so lucky. And those who lived in small towns or out in the country . . . they had no chance."

The way he spoke, with that forced clinical detachment, was achingly familiar. My parents' realm had fallen to devourers. Their village was one of the few that made it out of the realm. It was why so few of us feline shifters were walking around. They rarely spoke about what their realm was like. I'd met others with similar tales. The human realm was full of survivors from realms fallen to devourers.

"My people's magic was elemental. We weren't particularly powerful, but we could do small things. Most of what we did was weather-related. Manipulating weather patterns to make it rain. Harnessing the power of the sun to help our crops grow faster."

"Were you always a warrior? Or were you something else

before your realm fell?" I asked, tilting my head to the side. The thought of Magos as anything other than a warrior felt weird.

"I was always as I am now. Our existence was mostly peaceful, but another race in our realm was not particularly peaceful. They liked to raid our cities and villages. So some of us trained to be warriors and learned how to use our magic for things other than crop growing." Magos gave me a wry smile.

"Mikhail, too?"

"No." Magos's expression softened. "He was too young. My sister didn't want that life for him. His father had died in a raid on their village when Mikhail was young. Mikhail wanted to be a warrior to protect others from losing their loved ones. Whenever I visited, he would plead with me to convince his mother to let him train. He was starting to wear me down when our realm fell and we all fled to the human realm."

Magos paused, and I sipped my coffee, waiting for him to collect his thoughts enough to continue.

"Our city had been a large one, and over twenty thousand of us made it to the human realm. We ended up splitting into two cities off the coast of the Black Sea, Nouă Zori and Speranţa Nouă. At first, I lived with my sister and Mikhail in Speranţa Nouă, but eventually I relocated to the other city. I . . . had someone. Hasina. Her family had business in the other city, so I went there."

He placed both hands flat on the counter on either side of his coffee mug and watched the steam rise with a vacant, hollow look. It was the same look he had when we'd met the first time.

My heart clenched, and I swallowed hard.

He had someone. A wife? A lover? He'd never spoken of her before, but after all these centuries I could still see the pain in his eyes at remembering her. I reached across the counter and squeezed his hand gently before wrapping it around my mug once more.

Magos blinked and cleared his throat. "My sister had her own community in Speranța Nouă, and she didn't want to leave. I did convince her to allow Mikhail to start training. Our people were resilient, and both cities prospered. Everything went well for years, and Mikhail excelled in his training. I often traveled with some of our top merchants when they were establishing new trade routes. One of the merchants wanted to stop at a particular town that was becoming an important trading post, Dragodana."

I recognized the name immediately. "The town that gave birth to the first werewolves and vampires. That's some shitty luck."

"Yes," he agreed, a hint of anger breaking through the flat detached tone he'd been using up until now. "Had we just gone a different way or left earlier or later, everything would have been different."

He blamed himself, I realized. Not for the devourers attacking his realm, but for leading the group to Dragodana and being unable to prevent what'd happened there. He had survived his realm falling to the devourers only to have the unfortunate luck of being in the wrong place at the wrong time later on.

Kaysea would spin some seer bullshit about everything happening for a reason. I accepted that life just sucked sometimes.

"Mikhail and I were the only ones from our group who survived the transformation," he continued, his voice once again flat and distant. "All the merchants died. It took us a while to get out of that town. Prior to being turned into vampires and werewolves, the people in that town had some form of deep feud going on. After the turning, it broke into an all-out war."

Magos shook his head, exhaling. "It was madness. We wanted nothing to do with their war and just wanted to go back to our people. Once we were confident we could control our bloodlust and had learned all we could about our new . . . condition . . . we left. It took some time since we could only travel at night, but we made it back to Nouă Zori. Mikhail returned to his mother in Speranța Nouă a few days later.

"Of those turned into vampires, we were among the most powerful, and those who would eventually become the Council wanted us back. In my arrogance, I dismissed their threats," Magos said bitterly.

"They went after your people," I murmured as the truth dawned on me.

Magos raised his gaze to meet mine, copper eyes burning with fury. "My people survived the devourers. They learned to thrive in a new realm. And they were annihilated because of a war they had nothing to do with. *Wanted* nothing to do with."

His voice held so much anguish I wanted to scream on his behalf and kill everyone who'd caused him such pain. I knew life wasn't fair. I didn't think I'd ever been naive enough to think it was. But gods, I was still so angry hearing Magos recount the ending of his people after all they went through.

"My city. My *wife*." His voice shook. "The entire life I had built was destroyed by vampires. The Council claimed those responsible were led by a rebel and had not been given the authority to do so. A vampire named Marius who had the ability to shift into a wolf."

Shit. "Elisa is a descendant of the vampire that slaughtered your family." I squeezed my eyes shut.

"It's not her fault." He took a deep, shuddering breath. "I know this. It's hard, but I'll manage."

"What happened to your sister? And Mikhail?" I asked, already dreading the answer I knew was coming.

"Werewolves," Magos said, and we both looked at Andrei,

who was still pinned to the floor growling softly. "The werewolves attacked his city. It was a few days after Noua Zori fell. Mikhail argued for the city officials to send a scouting party to look for survivors. They denied him and said they needed everyone there in case something happened. Mikhail was halfway to Noua Zori when the wolves attacked his city. I'd survived the attack on Noua Zori and had been traveling to Speranța Nouă. We met on the road and raced back to his home. We found nothing but death."

"Your sister?" My voice caught on the words. As much as Cian and I fought, I couldn't imagine what I'd do if something happened to him.

"We found nothing but death," he repeated, his eyes hollow. "The werewolves slaughtered everyone."

"And Mikhail signed up to help the Council kill all the werewolves."

Given my history with hunting down witches and warlocks after the death of my parents, I couldn't really criticize Mikhail's decision. I shifted uncomfortably. I didn't like having something in common with the vampire assassin.

"Yes." Magos cleared his throat, slipping back into his typical reserved expression. "There's more, but we can discuss that later. Mikhail is loyal to me. Despite our disagreement over the years, he would never act out against me. The Council has always known this. They want him because he's quite possibly the most powerful vampire in existence. But they know they can't fully trust or control him."

"Which means there's probably a lot he doesn't know," I finished. "All right, I'll deal with Andrei and get him calmed down. Can you get some food for the vampire kids? They haven't eaten in a week, and they're hungry."

"I'll take care of it," Magos replied.

"Are you sure you're okay with Elisa being here?" I asked gently.

"Seeing her was a shock," he admitted. "I don't know how I knew exactly; she looks a lot like Marius. Her scent is similar as well. I saw her . . . and I just knew in my soul who she was."

"I can find some other place for them to stay." I didn't know Elisa and the others well, but I didn't think there was any chance of splitting up their group. It would be hard to relocate them, but I'd figure it out.

"No." Magos shook his head firmly. "I meant what I said. It's not her fault whose blood runs through her veins, and they've been through enough." He swallowed. "I think it will be good for me to help them. Hasina would have wanted me to."

He walked across the living room and grabbed his jacket from the back of one of the chairs.

"I'll be back in a couple hours. I want to talk with Elisa some more and see if she can give us any useful information about the Council. Don't leave the apartment."

"All right. Are you sure you'll be fine on your own?" I tried to keep the anxiety from my voice.

"I'll be fine." He shot me a reassuring grin. "Unlike you, I have yet to be captured."

I made a face at him. "Haha. Go play babysitter for a bit, and I'll play wolf whisperer."

Magos gave one last look at Andrei. "Good luck," he said skeptically and left.

"All right, Jinx, you can let him hear again, but keep him pinned." Jinx flicked his tail in answer, and I walked over to Andrei with my coffee. His low growl kicked up a notch. "Oh, enough already," I snapped.

The growling stopped.

"The magic is going to hold you until you shift back into a human," I said calmly. "I know the human side of you isn't really driving things right now. But the wolf side is perfectly capable of logic. Right now, you're in a compromising position, and you can't defend yourself."

I pulled one of my throwing knives out and held it against his throat. His growl rumbled through the living room, and I felt it in my bones.

I raised a brow. "Impressive. But that won't stop me from slitting your throat. You're defenseless in this form. Shifting back to human is your only option. Decide."

Yellow wolf eyes stared at me, and I could see the calculation running through his mind. Werewolves were violent and aggressive, but they were smart predators. Even when the wolf was in control, they could still be reasoned with. The growling died off.

"Good." I pulled the knife away.

The werewolf jerked, and I heard bones crunch and the telltale sounds of a change coming on.

I walked to my bedroom and pulled out a pair of sweatpants. They were stretchy enough that I figured they'd fit him. I didn't bother grabbing a shirt since nothing I had would fit, and Magos would be really annoyed if I gave the werewolf one of his shirts.

By the time I walked back into the living room, the shift was complete, and a panting, naked Andrei greeted me. He was still lying on the floor but had propped himself up on one elbow. I paused in the hallway and looked at him. Okay, it might have been more like gawking.

"I know. I know. I'm ridiculously hot." He smirked and stood up in one smooth motion. His eyes were hazel once more; the wolf had retreated, and the human was running things again.

Andrei casually walked over to me, and I slowly looked him up and down. He stopped in front of me, and I swept my eyes back up to meet his, holding out the sweatpants.

I smirked. "I've seen hotter."

He took the clothes and leaned forward to whisper in my ear, "Liar."

Hot breath brushed my skin, and I swallowed. Andrei pulled on the sweatpants while I worked on getting my brain back online after that one word had derailed all thought. He sniffed and looked at the kitchen.

"Where am I? And do I smell coffee?" he asked hopefully.

"My apartment. And yes." I walked into the kitchen and poured him a cup. He sat on one of the barstools, and I handed him the mug and leaned on the counter across from him to sip my own coffee. "So, what do you remember?"

I kept my tone casual. He wasn't going to like it when I told him that a vampire had put him under this thrall. Hopefully he didn't wolf out again.

Andrei sipped his coffee and put it down, his eyebrows bunching together. "We went to that weird part of town that I didn't know existed," he said slowly. "You left to go check out a bar, and the vampire and I waited by the car. He sensed something, and I asked him what was going on, and he turned to face me . . ." Andrei's face looked puzzled. He glanced at me. "I don't remember anything after that."

"Yeah." I winced. "Magos sort of mesmerized you into being under his thrall. It's a vampire thing. It doesn't always work on werewolves—in fact, it rarely works on werewolves— but you don't have the best relationship with your wolf side, so it makes you vulnerable to that type of magic."

Andrei glared at me angrily. "So, the vampire—"

"Magos. His name is Magos."

"Fine," Andrei spat. "So *Magos* did his vampire thing on me. Why? And how did we end up here?"

I thought about it. Andrei was new to this world and clearly missing a lot of information. But he already had the 'werewolves hate vampires' part down. He wouldn't be happy about there being a bunch of vampires two levels below him, even if they were kids.

"There was a complication," I said simply. "We dealt with it but decided it would be best to get you back to the apartment before snapping you out of it. I assumed your wolf side wouldn't be happy about the whole vampire whammy thing. I was right. Minor fight ensued. You pissed off my cat. I negotiated with your wolf side to shift back. And here we are." I raised my mug to him.

He stared at me for another moment and snorted lightly, clinking his mug against mine. "Well, at least the coffee is good."

"The vampire made it," I said cheerily, and Andrei frowned.

I laughed and walked over to the refrigerator to pull out a container with pieces of leftover rotisserie chicken. After I'd got a couple bites down, I looked at Andrei, who had taken a seat at the counter and was eyeing the chicken. I nudged the container towards him.

"You gonna explain what the hell is going on?" Andrei grabbed a piece of chicken and bit into it.

I popped another piece into my mouth and chewed. "Yeah, I probably need to bring you up to speed on a few things. And maybe elaborate on some things that I may have glossed over in our previous conversations."

"You mean your sketchy ass past that you've barely told me about because you were too busy seducing me with your wicked ways?" He tilted his head with an amused scoff.

I grinned. "That about sums it up."

Chapter Thirteen

"WHILE YOU WERE . . . napping, we received some new information." Andrei didn't say anything, but his eyes narrowed at the "napping" comment. "Good news," I said with a false cheer. "Stressing over what Sebastian has planned for my birthday is no longer our biggest problem."

"Meaning we now have much bigger problems than your psycho stalker who had you kidnapped and tortured? And has been leaving you bloody hearts for your birthday for the last few decades?" Andrei said casually, somehow managing to maintain a completely straight expression.

I snapped my fingers and pointed at him. "Yup. Sebastian is still a problem. Actually, the vampires he's working with are in the area, and he'll be here soon. But my birthday is somewhat irrelevant at this point." I glanced at the clock and saw it was past midnight. "Technically, my birthday is tomorrow, but Sebastian might make a move today or after my birthday. Also, he's not the only one after me. Apparently, all the warlocks are. The warlock leadership, known as the Circle, has entered into an alliance with the Vampire Council. Sebastian is trying to get me before they do, which is why my birthday doesn't matter anymore. He'll take whatever opportunity he can to capture me. But the Circle is the bigger threat."

"Why?" Andrei studied me. "I get your history with Sebastian. But why is the Circle after you too?"

I gnawed my bottom lip as I thought about how to answer. Andrei and I had been seeing each other for several months now. We rarely discussed magic, other non-humans, and the realms beyond the human one. Andrei knew some of it but not much.

I liked Andrei. I liked him a lot. And one of the things I liked the most about him was he *wasn't* part of my world. But I also felt guilty about not giving him this information sooner. I could have enlightened him at any point over the past few months. Could have eased him into this. That was no longer an option.

"You spent some time with older werewolves before you moved here, right?" I asked, and Andrei nodded. "I'm assuming they mostly told you about the history between werewolves and vampires. Did they tell you about the rest of the magical community? The other realms?"

"I know there are other realms besides this one. The fae and daemons are the supposed heavy hitters in our fun little magical world," he said sarcastically and wiggled his fingers in the air for emphasis. "They mostly stay in their realms, but some of them linger in the human realm. Lots of others who don't have a realm of their own live here as well."

"Did they talk about the Cataclysms? Devourers?" I asked.

Andrei frowned. "They mentioned Cataclysms once. I asked about it more, but by that time they were starting to clam up on information. Stela and I were making it clear we wanted nothing to do with restarting the war with the vampires, so they began withholding information. They said they'd only tell us more if we joined their cause. We left shortly after that and moved to this town. I didn't really care about learning any more to be honest." He shrugged. "Things had been going pretty well for us here, and I didn't really see how the rest of it mattered."

The guilt I'd been feeling nipped at me harder. I should have left him alone. He might not have always been able to remain so innocent and removed from my world, but he probably could have made it at least a few more decades.

"What does this have to do with why the warlocks and vampires are hunting you?" Hazel eyes brimming with curiosity and a small amount of wariness met mine.

My magic shifted under my skin, and I pushed it back. I was feeling antsy and wished Magos were here so we could spar; that would have at least taken the edge off. I cracked my neck from side to side and walked over to the fridge. I moved some containers around until I found the one that still had some raw ground beef. I grabbed a spoon from the nearby drawer.

"I need to explain a few things for you to understand why they're after me."

"Okay," Andrei said slowly and sniffed the air, looking in confusion at the container I was holding. "I'm curious about how ground beef fits into your explanation."

I huffed a laugh "This"—I shook the container a little bit —"is for my plant. It actually prefers chicken, but this is all I have at the moment, so it'll just have to deal."

Without bothering to explain further, I headed towards my room. Andrei followed close behind.

"You were told about the fae and daemons being heavy hitters. It's no joke. They're seriously powerful," I said over my shoulder as I walked over to the flowering plant on my dresser. Its large blue flower sat on top of a stem thicker than my arm with smaller vines growing out of it. It had been facing the window, but it shifted towards me at my approach and swayed slightly, sending a tremor out through the petals.

Andrei stumbled slightly and came to a slow stop next to me, staring wide-eyed at the plant. Slowly, the flower turned to face him and waved its petals again. Andrei reached out towards the edge of the petals, and I smacked his hand away.

"This plant is from one of the fae realms. I'd advise you to never touch anything from the fae realms until you know a bit more."

I popped the lid off the container and scooped out a chunk of meat. The flower forgot about Andrei and zeroed in on the meat. The thin green vines snapped the meat off the spoon and pulled it toward the flower. The bright orange center split open, revealing a mouth full of small teeth, and the vines quickly shoved the meat in. The meaty bulge made its way down the stem, but it stopped. A high-pitched hissing sound came from the flower, and one of its vines swiped at my face.

I barely leaned back in time to avoid the vine. It was hard to see, but each vine was covered in tiny thorns. In addition to being sharp, the thorns were also slightly sticky, which helped the plant capture small rodents and other prey in the wild.

"Enough of that!" I snapped at the plant. "This is all I have. I'll get you chicken next time." I scooped out another chunk of beef and held it out. "So, what's it going to be?"

The flower shook angrily at me one more time and swiped the spoon and the container out of my hands. The green vines covered the container. Ugh. I'd get it back later.

"Another important thing to know." I turned to walk out of the room. "You can pretty much assume anything fae is an asshole."

"Okay, but—what the fuck?!" Andrei swore, and I whirled back around. The werewolf rubbed the back of his head as he gaped at the plant with an expression of annoyance and disbelief.

I glanced at the spoon lying on the ground. "It was probably aiming for me. But it doesn't have eyes, so you can't really blame it for having shitty aim." I shrugged and walked back out to the living room to stand in front of the windows, watching the waves crash into the rocky shoreline.

"So, the fae are powerful assholes?" Andrei asked when he joined me and leaned against the window frame.

"Pretty much. Power ranges among them as well as their general assholerly. One of my best friends is fae, and she's actually super nice. But yeah, when it comes to power, the fae are at the top of the food chain. Or at least they were until a few thousand years ago."

I looked at Andrei. "I'm sure you've heard the expression 'there's always a bigger fish?'" Andrei nodded. "The devourers *are* that bigger fish. No one knows exactly where they came from. They started appearing a few thousand years ago, but there is no record of them before that. The main theory is that in some realms, species evolved to prey on those with magic. Their own magic warped in a way that allowed them to feed on the magic of others and make themselves stronger. And they themselves are immune to magic. There are all sorts of devourers. I've encountered at least a dozen different kinds."

If it wasn't for my impressive healing abilities, I'd have the scars to prove it too. Several of those encounters I'd barely walked away from. I rubbed my side as the phantom pains of one of the more brutal fights echoed through my body.

"Really?" Andrei looked at me with interest. "Where? What do they look like?"

"Here and there," I said dismissively, not wanting to get into more of my history that wasn't relevant to this conversation. "They're always a predator species. I've encountered some that looked almost like the bears of the human realm. Some that looked like small flying dragons. Lupine and feline ones." I thought back to one of the gigs I'd taken through Pele before getting captured by Sebastian. "One time I encountered some that were basically giant worms. The ground would literally rumble as they traveled underneath it, and they'd shoot up and try to swallow you in one gulp."

Andrei gave me a skeptical look. "So, the monsters from *Tremors*, then?"

I pondered this for a moment before nodding. "Actually, they were exactly like that." I huffed a laugh.

Andrei shook his head in disbelief.

"I've never met any that could talk, but maybe they exist somewhere. Anyway, the fae and daemons rely pretty heavily on their magic in a fight. Some of them don't even know how to battle with weapons, so they're at a severe disadvantage when it comes to the devourers. Fortunately for all magical beings, the devourers are contained to their own realms."

"This is where the Cataclysms come in, right?" Andrei furrowed his brows together. "I vaguely remember this before the older werewolves stopped giving us information. Realms are accessed through gateways. Sometimes those gateways occur naturally . . . When that happens on a large scale, it's referred to as a Cataclysm."

"Right." I nodded. "Cataclysms can last for hours. Sometimes days. One of the largest ones was several thousand years ago, and it was the first time the devourers were encountered. After that one, most of the survivors relocated in the human realm. It took a while for things to settle down. All that early human mythology about gods wreaking havoc and doing fucked-up shit? Those were some of the new inhabitants getting comfy into their new world."

"You're talking about the gods?" Andrei's eyes widened. "Zeus, Odin, Hades, Shiva, Osiris?

"Way to only name the dudes," I scoffed. "But yeah. Pretty much all of human mythology is about those who came here after Cataclysms. Although, some were here before that."

"What happened to all of them?" Andrei frowned. "I mean, clearly, they're not still doing what they were thousands of years ago. Pretty sure people would notice half-naked people riding around in chariots throwing lightning. Are they still in this realm?"

My eyebrows raised. "First you only name the male gods, and now you're referencing Greek mythology. They were always the lamest of the gods."

He shrugged. "What can I say? I was a big *Xena* fan, and that was mostly Greek mythology."

I laughed. "Fair enough. We're getting a bit off track here. To keep it short, all those gods were getting a little out of hand, and the fae and daemons stepped in. Some of them were moved to other realms. Some were killed. Others fell in line. Some like the seraphim actually still had their own realm. They were just flat out banned from the human realm."

"Angels?" Andrei looked at me with a puzzled expression. "Why were they banned?"

"Oh gee, I don't know. Maybe because they had a habit of getting into drunken fights that lasted until dawn or fire-bombing cities," I said dryly.

I'd encountered seraphim a few times while traveling around the realms and would be thrilled to never encounter one again.

I added, "They were given multiple warnings and didn't listen, so they got themselves kicked out."

"Oh." Andrei frowned.

I eyed him. "You're taking all of this pretty well so far."

He shrugged and gave me a lopsided grin. "I know I'm somewhat new to all of this, but I'm still a werewolf. It's not too hard to accept the existence and history of other supernatural species when you have a wolf crawling under your skin all the time."

"Is that what it feels like?" I asked curiously. "That the wolf and you are two separate beings?"

"Sometimes." His forehead creased. "Is that not how it feels for you?"

I shook my head. "My nature is the same whether I'm in this form or my feline one. There is no difference." Although the magic that I kept hidden deep within me sometimes felt like its own entity. But I wasn't ready to talk about that.

"Must be nice," he muttered. "So, what does this history lesson have to do with why these warlock assholes want you so bad?"

"A thousand years ago, the fae figured out a way to protect entire realms from gateways opening naturally. Any realm with this protection in place would be protected from a Cataclysm. It's an incredibly complex spell and requires a constant stream of magic to keep it powered. The human realm is unique among the realms because humans and other native species generate a large amount of power. But very few of them use it, so the human realm is bursting at the seams with magic."

I glanced at Andrei to see if he figured out where I was going with this, but he just stared at me expectantly, waiting for me to continue.

"The daemons figured out how to feed the magic from the human realm into the spell created by the fae. Their realms and the human realm have been protected from Cataclysms since then. Sometimes they make deals with other realms, but only if they get something significant in exchange."

"You're telling me the human realm is basically one big magical *battery*?"

"Yup." I smirked as his mouth gaped before he snapped it shut. My fingers twitched at my sides as my amusement bled away. "As far as why I'm such a popular shifter?"

I stretched my hand out and let my magic pour out of me. A dark ripple formed in the air to the left of the couch and split open. Just through the portal, I could make out the edge of a cliff, and far below was a sprawling city with a large castle in its center. Andrei froze and stared wide-eyed at the gateway and city beyond it.

"I can open gateways. To *any* realm. That fancy magic spell the fae created to protect their realms?" I stared at the city stretched out before us with a flat expression. "Doesn't stop me or even cause me to break a sweat. I could open a gateway straight from a devourer realm into a fae queen's bedchamber."

Andrei slowly moved closer to the gateway. "Holy shit," he breathed. "I never thought I would see another realm."

"This is the capital city of one of the fae realms." I let him stare at it for a few more moments before closing the gateway.

Andrei gaped at the space where the gateway had been before turning his attention back to me. I shifted uncomfortably at his expression. He was looking at me like I was a wonder and not a freak with magic that would get me killed. And likely anyone close to me.

"I don't advertise this particular skill of mine," I said seriously. I needed to make him understand the gravity of this situation. "I've gained a reputation as someone who can easily find objects and people in other realms, but no specifics are provided for how I do that. A friend of mine arranges the gigs. If the fae or daemons learned what I could do, they would imprison or kill me. And they'd likely do the same to anyone who knew about me, just to ensure their silence."

Andrei's eyes darkened in understanding. Good, he was finally getting it.

"Very few know I have this skill," I continued. "Sebastian is one of them. He must have told the other warlocks, or they found out from him somehow. This is why they want me."

Truth. But not all of it. The rest of my magic pushed

against the chains I kept around it as if it were sentient and didn't like being left out.

Tough shit, I thought at it.

My ability to open gateways would definitely bring the attention of the fae and daemons my way. But my other magic would get me killed. I'd have to tell Andrei about that part of me, but I wasn't ready yet. I needed to be sure he understood everything at stake before I told him the rest.

Andrei stared at me. "Well . . . shit."

"Yeah." I laughed humorlessly.

My magic strained harder, and I reinforced the chains I kept wrapped around it.

I looked at the clock on the coffee maker. Magos hadn't even been gone an hour yet. I should reach out to Pele to fill her in on the situation, but my magic was being so twitchy, it was hard for me to focus.

Andrei shifted slightly, and I glanced at him. He watched the waves below with a tight look on his face.

For someone who had been content in not knowing about my world, he was taking all of this pretty well. He had a resiliency I hadn't appreciated before. Maybe I hadn't been giving him enough credit.

"Spar with me?" I headed over to the large sparring mat without waiting for a response.

"What?" Andrei asked, startled from whatever thoughts he'd been having.

"I need to blow off some steam. It helps me focus." My magic was pushing too hard, and I needed a distraction. Magos wasn't here, so the werewolf would have to do.

I walked over to the back wall of the mat and pulled my boots off, along with all my weapons. I took my throwing knives out of the bracers but left the bracers on. Walking back to the center of the mat, I made the universal "bring it" motion with my hand.

Andrei sighed and walked over. He paused at the edge of the mat and stretched. Muscles rippled across his broad chest and abs. I gave him an appreciative once over. One never saw an out-of-shape werewolf.

He walked onto the mat with easy confidence and took up a fighting stance across from me. "You sure you want to do this? I've dabbled in MMA fighting, and I'm pretty good."

I gave him a bored expression before knocking his feet out from under him with a lightning-fast sweep kick. A slap echoed across the living room as his back made contact with the mat.

"Yeah," I drawled, "I can see you're *real* good."

Andrei leaped to his feet, and yellow flashed across his eyes. Good. It'd be fun to play with the wolf. We moved around each other slowly, with Andrei studying my movements more carefully.

"Have any other information bombs you want to drop on me?" His left fist shot forward in a jab. Fast for a human but nowhere near as fast as a werewolf could be.

I stepped to the side and grabbed his wrist, wrenching his arm forward. His body followed awkwardly, and he crashed to the ground.

"You can be faster than that." I stepped back to let him recover. He snapped back up and growled at me. I smiled. "Do you know how werewolves and vampires were created?"

I took a quick step towards him, and he darted back. Getting faster.

"What do you mean *created*?" He danced around me, looking for an opening.

"During the early fifteenth century, two sorcerers came from their realm and set up shop in a small town in what is now called Romania."

Andrei took two steps forward and threw out a strong left hook which I easily blocked. He darted back before I could land a blow. Heat spread through my muscles, and my body loosened with every step. Even my magic settled down a bit.

"Are sorcerers different from warlocks?" he asked.

"I would pay good money to see you ask that to a sorcerer's face." I chuckled. "Warlocks are just humans who can do magic. Sorcerers are a different species and have their own realm. They don't spend much time in the human realm but do come over here occasionally. And yes, before you ask, Merlin was a sorcerer."

Andrei smirked at me. "I mean, I feel like that's a given." He tilted his head slightly. "So, these two sorcerers set up shop in town and created werewolves and vampires? Why?"

I snapped a kick to his ribs. Andrei dropped his elbow and brought his knee up so it connected with his elbow and blocked the kick. A growl rumbled from his throat. I flashed my teeth at him and took a couple of steps back.

"Nobody knows exactly why they did it. Sorcerers are a weird, antisocial bunch. There seemed to be some sort of competition between the two. Possibly a bet."

"A bet?" Andrei asked incredulously. "I'm the result of a bet?"

"Probably. All we know for sure is they imprisoned the village along with any other poor souls who happened to be passing through and split the population between them for their experiments. They used whatever weird magic they had to combine the humans with other magical creatures."

"What creatures?"

"Devourers." I closed the distance between us and shot a swift punch to Andrei's throat.

He blocked and followed up with his own jab, which I evaded. We danced away from each other. His eyes turned yellow, and he bared his teeth at me. I grinned savagely back at him. This was more like it.

"Tell me you're joking," he growled and feinted forward before diving back. The wolf was definitely out to play.

"Nope. Vampires and werewolves are fucked-up devourer/human hybrids." My lip curled in distaste. "The only reason the fae or daemons haven't hunted all of you down is you guys are determined to wipe each other out and you're not really much of a threat to them."

I took a quick step forward and snapped a kick up. Andrei caught my leg, and I pushed off the ground and spun my other leg. My foot caught him across the jaw. His head snapped to the side, and he dropped my leg. I twisted, landing on my feet, and quickly followed up with an uppercut. Andrei barely managed to move his head to the side to avoid the blow. He grabbed the back of my head and thrust his knee into my ribs. I had no way to dodge, and pain flared through me as the hit landed.

He was holding back, but it still hurt like hell. My elbow shot up and connected with his jaw. He stumbled back a few feet and wiped the blood from his mouth. We grinned at each other.

"Plus, you're not exactly devourers," I continued. "There are different kinds of devourers, but most can absorb or nullify magic from a distance. That's what makes them so dangerous. Neither vampires nor werewolves are immune to magic. And they can only absorb it by, well, by consuming it. Vampires drink blood. Werewolves eat flesh. If the blood or flesh of a particular magical creature is consumed, that makes you at least partially immune to that creature's magic, but only for a short time."

"Not a fan of this origin story," he grunted.

"Sorry." I laughed. Footsteps came up the stairs, and my head snapped to the front door. I hadn't expected Magos to be back so soon.

Andrei's retort was interrupted as a vampire crashed

through the door and flew across the living room, slamming onto his back. I moved to stand between Andrei and the newcomer, already on high alert.

Magos strolled in and shut the door. He casually took off his jacket and laid it neatly over the back of the chair in the living room, waving his hand towards the vampire. "I brought you an early birthday present. Apologies for not wrapping it."

I stared at the vampire who was struggling to get up from the floor. Blood poured from a wound on his head.

When his light blue eyes met mine, I smiled.

Chapter Fourteen

"Hello Ryder," I purred and punched him hard. Bone crunched, and blood poured down his face.

"Bitch!" he snapped as he tried to wipe some of the blood off. His eyes darted around the room, and he seemed to realize he was outnumbered three to one. He grimaced and remained on his back, propped up by his elbows. "My guys will follow me here. As I recall, you're not so brave when you're faced with all of us."

My vision turned red as my muscles tensed, remembering the many beatings I'd suffered at Ryder's hands. I felt Magos's gaze on me, and the rage lifted enough for me to think. We needed answers before I could enact my revenge.

My magic pushed, feeling my eagerness. I didn't try to shove it down. Instead, I let it out a little so it could lurk just beneath the surface.

Wait. Just wait a few minutes, I promised it.

"As I recall," I started, "you led me into an ambush, poisoned me, and jumped me with two dozen vampires. So, it's not like you were all that brave either."

Ryder glared at me but said nothing.

"Tell you what. Answer a few questions for me, and you'll leave this apartment alive," I offered.

Magos started to speak, but I raised my hand. His mouth clamped shut, and he went back to staring coldly at Ryder. I could practically see the gears turning in his head as he tried to figure out what I was up to.

"Bullshit," Ryder scoffed. "You've probably been dreaming of this moment. No way are you letting me leave here alive."

I walked over to the kitchen and grabbed a knife from the cutting block. I swiped it across the back of my hand, creating a gash. "I swear on my blood that if you answer my questions truthfully you will leave this apartment alive. And no one in this room will raise a sword or dagger against you for twenty-four hours." Magic sizzled in the air as the blood oath snapped into place. "That's enough time for you to get out of town before I hunt you down."

Ryder stared at me with those pretty blue eyes, calculating his odds. He knew I couldn't break the blood oath and would have to let him leave the apartment alive. He probably assumed I'd take him outside the apartment to fulfill the blood oath and then attack.

I could kill him with my bare hands, true, but it wouldn't be quick. And if the other vampires had indeed followed him here, they would join the fray, and the odds would be in their favor. I let him think through all his options.

"Fine. I'll play," he said warily and sliced the back of his hand open on one of his fangs. "I accept your blood oath and will answer your questions truthfully. What do you want to know, kitten?"

The magic in the room sizzled once more as it accepted Ryder's agreement. My skin crawled, and I couldn't stop my fingers from flexing. I wanted nothing more than to grab one of my daggers and slice him to ribbons.

Ryder smiled. "Missed me, haven't you?"

Rage and magic spiraled in me, and the cold fire strained against my skin, wanting to be set loose. Ryder was still grinning at me when Magos slammed his foot down on him. The vampire grunted and curled around his stomach.

Magos loomed over him. "Nemain promised you would leave here alive. She didn't say when or in what condition. I'd be happy to keep you here for a few weeks and break every bone in your body repeatedly before throwing your broken body outside," Magos said in a deadly calm voice. "Keep that in mind when you speak."

Magos hammered one more kick to Ryder's gut and took a few steps back, resuming his stance with his hands behind his back as if nothing had happened. I blinked at him, momentarily surprised by his burst of violence. Ryder shot him a death glare but kept his mouth shut.

"We know your Council and the Warlock Circle have entered an alliance," I said. Ryder's eyes narrowed slightly. "Three simple questions for you. What did each side promise the other in exchange for entering into this alliance? Why is Sebastian trying to get me on his own rather than work with the warlock leadership? And how did you find us? Answer those questions truthfully, and you'll be free to go."

Ryder mulled it over. "Ain't nothing you won't figure out on your own eventually anyhow. The Council doesn't exactly fill us foot soldiers in on every detail. We've been told an alliance with the warlocks will benefit us in 'meaningful ways.'" He raised his hands and made air quotes. "Warlocks are going to make it so we can move around in daylight again. And they've promised to make the powers of Apex vampires available to all vampires. Don't know the specifics of how they're going to do that."

Shit. No wonder the vampires had agreed to the alliance. If they created an army of Mikhails, they'd become a force to be reckoned with very quickly. Even the daemons and fae would take notice. "What are the warlocks getting in return?" I asked.

"Don't know." Ryder shrugged, disinterested. "Like I said, the Council doesn't fill us in on all the details."

As much as I wanted to assume Ryder was lying so I could beat the truth out of him, I believed him. The Council ruled the rest of the vampires with an iron fist. It made sense they would keep the specifics of the alliance to themselves. If I had to guess, the Council had promised the warlocks a vampire army in exchange for giving them more power. The warlocks were powerful, but their numbers had always been few. Witches and warlocks didn't always pass on their magical abilities to children; more often than not, their children were just ordinary humans.

Plus, not all warlocks were good at combat magic. An alliance with the vampires made sense. Especially if they were plotting something major. We'd have to capture someone higher ranking than Ryder to get more information on that.

"What about Sebastian? When you kidnapped me, that wasn't for the Council, and it wasn't for the warlocks. It was for him specifically. Why?"

When Sebastian and I had been together, he'd been on the outs with the rest of the warlocks. It took me a while to piece things together, but I was pretty sure he had made a play for power and lost. I wasn't sure if he was still working on his own or if he'd made amends with the rest of the warlock leadership.

"I ain't exactly well-liked by most of the Council."

"I'm shocked," I said flatly.

"My charm isn't for everyone." He gave me a lopsided grin. "The Council will pick their favorites to get the benefits from the warlock deal. Me and mine would be on the bottom of their list. Sebastian will ensure we're at the top."

"Where does he fit in with the warlock leadership?"

"We got a good working relationship, but we ain't buddies who confide our hopes and dreams in each other," Ryder said lightly. "Best I can tell, him and the guy in charge of the warlocks, think his name's Emir, have some sort of beef with each other. Don't know where he falls in terms of their leadership hierarchy. Don't even know how their hierarchy works."

"Fine," I ground out. "Last question. How'd you find us?"

Ryder gave me a charming smile, making his dimples stand out.

I wanted to punch the shit out of him. If Magos got to hurt him, it was only fair I did too. But I wouldn't be able to stop myself. And if I killed him, the blood oath would take its toll on me.

I'd survive . . . probably. But it would hurt like hell and knock a good chunk of my power offline for gods only knew how long. Given my current situation, that was basically a death sentence.

So instead, I tapped my fingers against my side and gave Ryder a hard stare.

He offered me a pouty look. "You're no fun anymore."

Andrei and Magos growled at the same time and glared at each other. I rolled my eyes. "Just answer the fucking question, Ryder."

"A birdie whispered about you in Sebastian's car." Ryder laughed.

"What. Birdie?" I demanded.

"A witchy one." He smiled knowingly. "Haven't had the pleasure of meeting her myself. But she's some relative of Sebastian's, and she's trying to get in good with the warlocks. After you escaped, Sebastian told her to come to this town and keep an eye out for you. He sent others to other places he thought there was a chance of you showing up at. He's a clever bastard."

I kept my face carefully blank. I wasn't aware of any

witches in town. Yet another problem I'd have to deal with sooner rather than later.

Magos glanced at me, and I nodded. He strode over to Ryder, who tried to scramble away from him, and kicked him in the face, placing his boot on Ryder's throat. Ryder tore at Magos's leg as he gasped for breath.

"You swore!" he choked out.

"Don't worry. I won't break my word. You will leave this apartment alive, and none of us will raise a bladed weapon against you. We won't even beat the shit out of you before letting you go. But I need a moment with my friend here, and Magos is going to make sure you don't do anything stupid."

I looked expectantly at Andrei. He stared at the struggling vampire for another moment and walked over to me.

"You need to make a decision, wolf. I've dumped a lot of shit on you today. You and your sister came to this town to get away from all the supernatural drama. I dragged you into it, and I'm sorry for that. But shit's going down in the next two days, and there's no getting you out of that now. But after this blows over, you can walk away." I kept my tone calm and light.

I didn't want him to walk away. He made me smile and laugh and balanced out all the other crappiness in my life. But if he wanted to leave, I would let him. Part of me knew I should insist he leave after this, but I was too selfish to act on that.

He didn't say anything, and I couldn't read the expression on his face, so I pushed out the next part. "You have two choices. You can go down that hallway and wait in my bedroom. Jinx will seal it, so you don't hear anything. Then you and your sister can skip town in a couple of days. Or you can stay, and we can continue doing whatever it is we're doing. And I'll try to keep my world from bleeding into yours as much as I can."

"And if I want to stay in this room?" Andrei asked.

"If you stay, you'll have to keep what you see to yourself. You cannot tell anyone. Not your sister. Not the pack. No one."

"Okay," Andrei said slowly. "I won't tell anyone."

"I need you to understand what you're promising," I said each word slowly and clearly. My mouth went dry, and I hated myself for what I had to say next. But I had been selfish in keeping Andrei in the dark for so long, and now I was paying the price. "In the human world if you break a promise, most of the time it just results in hurt feelings and some relationships ending. That is not how it works in my world. If you tell anyone what you see here today, I will kill you. I will kill your sister. I will wipe out your entire pack. And the wolves that sent you here."

The words felt like poison on my tongue, but I needed him to understand the gravity of this situation. I knew he would never betray me intentionally.

But I knew better than anyone that a person could change over the years.

Once upon a time, I would never have thought Sebastian would be capable of betraying me. People changed. I'd learned that lesson.

Besides, even if Andrei never willingly betrayed me, he might do so accidentally. With his limited knowledge about my world, he would be so easy to take advantage of. He needed to know and understand the cost of my secret.

Because I would kill him if he betrayed me. Intentionally or not. I meant every word that I said. He needed to know that I was just as much a monster as the rest of them.

He recoiled from me, and the look on his face couldn't have hurt me more than if he had stabbed me in the heart. "How can you say that so casually?"

"Because that's how it is." I kept the pain off my face and out of my voice. "It's how it's always been. The secret you would be keeping could get me killed if it gets out. It could get my friends and family killed. We play for keeps in my world. I need you to know the stakes before you agree to anything."

Andrei looked away from me and stared at Ryder, who had finally given up on trying to get out of Magos's hold. I waited patiently for him to come to a decision.

Honestly, I wasn't entirely sure what I wanted him to decide. If he stayed, it would bring him further into my world, which meant I would have to hide less from him in the future. I could actually be honest with him about everything. But I couldn't help but feel like I was burning away his innocence, and I didn't know who he would be when it was gone.

"I'm staying," he said flatly and walked over to stand beside Magos. He still didn't look at me.

"All right then. Let's wrap up this party." I pushed away the guilt and walked over to join them. Ryder tensed at my approach, and I smiled at him. He paled a bit. I stood over him across from Magos and Andrei and stretched my hand out to the right. Magic burst from me and a ripple formed in the air.

"No!" Ryder screamed and frantically tried to get away.

Magos lifted his foot off the other vampire's neck and yanked him up by one arm. As soon as Ryder was on his feet, he sunk a vicious punch to the vampire's stomach, causing him to double over in pain. Magos didn't give him a chance to recover before twisting Ryder's arm behind his back and kicking the back of his legs. The vampire fell to his knees in front of me.

The gateway tore open a couple of feet in front of Ryder, and the light of the full moon lit up a grassy plain. I couldn't see much, but that plain went on for miles with no shelter in any direction.

"As promised," I said casually. "You will leave here alive." I shoved him through the gateway. He crashed to the ground, and I stepped through after him.

I held my hands up. "No swords or blades as promised."

Ryder jumped to his feet and snarled, "I'm going to kill you, bitch!"

He launched himself at me. I held my hand out and let the rest of my magic loose. My ability to shift to my feline form or open gateways was magic I had to purposely draw out and use. But this magic was different. The effort was never in using it. The effort was in keeping it contained or directing it at a particular target.

The magic practically sang as it ripped out of my hand in a stream of light crystal-blue fire and crashed into the vampire. Ryder flew backwards and crashed to the ground. I laughed as magic poured out of me. It'd been straining to get out for hours, and this felt so good. I could do so much more with it, but I didn't even try. I simply let it devour Ryder for a few seconds before pulling it back.

"Please," Ryder croaked.

The blue fire hadn't burned him. His normally tan skin was pale with a bluish tint. He tried to push himself off the ground but only succeeded in rolling onto his side.

"I'll do anything. I'll find out more about the warlocks. I'll get you inside information on the Council," he pleaded.

I knelt down in front of him, and he looked at me with a face full of terror. "Even if I did trust you not to betray me at the first chance you got, which I don't, I still wouldn't accept your offer." A cruel smile spread across my face, and I bared my teeth at him. "You tortured me for a year. You broke every bone in my body. You fed from me. You *broke* me. Did you really think I was going to let you walk away from that?" I shook my head at him and rose once more.

His expression shifted to one of defiance as he accepted his fate. "You deserve whatever they have in store for you. I hope you suffer."

"Such is life," I said indifferently and let my magic out once more.

His screams echoed across the grassy plains as the fire consumed and devoured him. I reined my magic back in, and it coiled up inside me again, happy with its meal. I turned my back on the pile of ashes, a perfect ring of frost around it, and walked back through the gateway. Magos and Andrei had been waiting on the other side watching everything with a wary expression.

Magos simply said, "I ran into Ryder while I was out running that other errand. I'm going to take care of that now. I'll be back in an hour." Translation, he still needed to find some humans for the vampire kids to munch on.

I glanced at the clock in the kitchen. Two hours until sunrise.

Andrei walked into the kitchen and started jerking cupboards open, a pissed off expression on his face.

I watched him for a few seconds before asking, "What are you doing?"

"Whiskey," he replied and kept looking.

"Oh. Middle cabinet under the island. Just bring the bottle over." Gods knew we'd need it as I explained what the hell had just happened.

Chapter Fifteen

ANDREI and I sat next to each other on the couch in a comfortable silence for a few minutes passing the bottle of whiskey back and forth. Gradually, the rage slipped off his face, but his expression remained guarded.

"Care to explain what the hell you did to that vampire?" Andrei finally asked.

"I ate his magic," I said simply, taking a long pull from the bottle.

Andrei frowned at me. "Like . . . a devourer? And the flames?"

"I don't know," I said with a strained voice. "Fun bonus unique to me."

"Oh." He sat rigidly, staring at the bottle in my hand. I couldn't tell what he was thinking.

"Do I scare you?" I whispered. The pain in my chest that had struck when he'd looked at me with such revulsion earlier was still pulsing.

I never should have let things go this far between us. It wasn't fair to him, and it would only cause me pain.

Gentle fingers touched my chin and lifted my face. I met Andrei's beautiful hazel eyes and held my breath.

"You will never frighten me, kitten," he swore. The ache in my chest eased. "You might piss me off. Scratch that, you definitely piss me off." The corner of his lips quirked up. "But you won't scare me away."

I should, I thought. *For your sake and mine.* But couldn't bring myself to say the words out loud. Instead, I merely nodded and enjoyed the feeling of his fingers against my skin.

"If the fae or daemons learned about my ability to open gateways to any realm regardless of the protective spells in place, they wouldn't be happy, but they would likely find a use for me. If they learned I could consume magic like a devourer,"—I shrugged with an indifference I didn't really feel—"they would kill me."

My magic stirred inside me, sensing my discomfort. I pushed against Andrei's fingers one last time before leaning back into the couch.

"But earlier you said that devourers were always a predatory species and that they weren't capable of speaking." Andrei gave me a scrutinizing look. "You've got the predatory part down, but unless I've been imagining things these past few months, you're more than capable of talking."

"I don't know what I am," I admitted. "Am I a devourer? Part devourer? Some type of hybrid like you? I don't know."

"Your parents . . ." he trailed off. Family was one of those things we'd never really discussed. I knew he had a sister, but that was all I knew about him. And he knew I had a brother because I'd mentioned Cian in passing once.

"My parents died when my brother and I were teenagers. As far as I know, they were both shifters. They never hinted that I might not be their child or that there was a devourer in our family history." I stared blankly at the bottle of whiskey. How many times had I wondered about my family history to myself? My brother was adamant that our parents were just that, our parents. But it was easy for him when he fit neatly into the shifter category.

"Does your brother have magic like you?"

"No. Not as far as I know anyway. He took after our mother, who was a powerful necromancer. The only thing I received from her was the ability to read souls. But I'm nowhere near as powerful as she was. My mother always knew exactly the type of person she was dealing with within seconds of meeting them. For me, everyone's soul just smells a little." I made a face.

Andrei laughed and crooked a grin at me. "Smells? What does my soul smell like?"

I breathed in deeply. "You smell like the deep woods. Like fallen pine needles. There's a wildness about it. It feels primal." I thought more about how it felt. "It's more than just the way you smell. I inhale your scent and let my magic sample it. And then . . . I don't know how to explain it. It's just a feeling I get."

"Huh. Can't decide if I would want to have that ability or not."

"Me neither. Like I said, it's not that powerful, and most of the time I just ignore it. Sometimes I'll get a feeling about people. It's hard to describe, but I'll feel a pull towards them. My mother was far stronger, and even her ability to read people's souls so well didn't *save* her," I said, my voice turning bitter.

"What was your father like?" Andrei asked gently, not missing the shift in my tone.

"Nothing like my mother." I huffed a laugh. "My mother had this quiet fierceness about her. When other magical beings bothered us, or if human bandits thought we were an easy target, my mother would shift into a lion and frighten them off. Or pick up a sword and slaughter the lot depending on what type of danger she thought they posed."

A soft smile played across my lips.

"My father was sweet. His magic was mostly earth-based, which he used to farm the land around us. He had an affinity for plants and would talk to them as if they could listen and respond. Maybe they did because every type of plant grew for him. He even had a small section of the greenhouse dedicated to plants from other realms."

"So, he was the damsel, and your mother was the knight?" Andrei teased.

"Definitely," I agreed. "Both of them knew about my magic. I had an incident when I was a child, and it scared the hell out of them. They told me I had to keep it hidden and never use it. As I grew older, I learned about devourers and asked them about it. They said I was nothing like a devourer, and that was the end of that conversation."

I'd played back every conversation I'd ever had with my parents about my magic over and over since their death. Nothing ever came out of it.

If my parents knew what I was, they'd withheld that information from me. Old anger flared to life, followed quickly by a wave of guilt. My parents had loved me. I had no doubt about that. But I was equally sure that they had lied to me, and I didn't understand why.

"I know that look," Andrei said. I glanced at him and arched my eyebrow in question. "You hate your parents for not telling you more. They could have spared you so much pain if they'd been more honest with you. Then you feel guilty for hating them because you also know they loved you and probably did the best they could."

"Yes," I breathed, surprised he'd identified my mixed emotions when even I had trouble deciphering them.

He rubbed the back of his neck as a somber expression spread across his features. "My parents died when we were young. I was six when it happened, so I only remember them a little bit, but Stela barely remembers them at all. They'd arranged for a friend of theirs to raise us in case anything ever happened to them. With instructions to never tell us about our heritage."

Andrei's eyes flashed yellow, and he took a deep breath.

"He kept his promise to them, and we had a happy childhood and spent most of our time living in the mountains in various cabins. He was a real off-the-grid kind of guy," he said fondly. "He died a few years ago and left us a cabin in the Sierra Nevadas. Stela was in college at the time.

"I was living further south and picking up odd jobs here and there to stay afloat. We hadn't seen each other in a while, so we made some time in our schedules to spend a week at the cabin. We'd been there for two days when I got bit. We were out hiking, and this wolf came out of nowhere and nipped my leg. It freaked us out, but the damage was minimal. Didn't even require stitches, and I'd had a rabies shot recently. It was after sunset, so we couldn't see that well. We thought maybe we saw wrong, and it was just somebody's weird-looking dog that got loose."

I passed the bottle back to him, and he took a swig. "Let me guess. There was a full moon that week?"

Andrei looked at me, eyes full of sorrow and anger. "Yes." He swallowed. "It was three days after I was bitten. My sister and I were making dinner when my leg went from being a little sore to feeling like it was on fire. It kept getting worse and worse. Until the moon rose."

"And then you shifted and attacked your sister." A hint of horror crept into my voice. I remember what it felt like to lose control of magic and the time I'd hurt my brother. Werewolves completely lost themselves during the first shift; it was the most dangerous time to be around them.

"I had no idea what was happening. There was just pain

and my sister screaming as I convulsed on the floor. That's where my memory of that night ends," he said numbly.

"So, the local pack knew about you?" I asked, puzzled about how they had let this happen. "And they let your first shift go down like this?"

"No. Only *he* knew," Andrei growled. "He kept the information from the pack. Apparently, my parents were the alphas of the pack before they died. They didn't want me or my sister to be involved with the werewolves, which was why they'd asked their friend to take us if anything happened." He stopped as he wrestled with some other part of the story. "Even if nothing had happened to them, they'd planned on sending us away."

I nodded but kept quiet. That was the least surprising part of this story so far.

"Some of the wolves in the pack weren't happy about that and wanted us to be brought back in." Andrei's voice became deeper and rougher as the words poured out of him. "I know my parents loved us and thought they were doing what was best, but they had no right to make that decision. Had we known what we were, I would have known what was happening to me after I got bitten. I could have protected my sister. It could have been her choice about whether or not she was turned."

I gripped his hand and held his wolf-yellow eyes with my gaze. "I'm sorry, Andrei. I know that doesn't change anything, but I'm sorry for what you and your sister went through."

Maybe he and his sister would have chosen to become werewolves had they known about their heritage. But that choice had been taken from them.

I added, "When it became clear that the vampires were winning against the werewolves, rumors started that werewolf parents were giving up their children. Before your wolf side is awakened, you can easily blend in with the humans. I know that doesn't make it right, especially considering what happened."

"Yeah." The yellow gradually faded from his eyes, but a few flecks of yellow still shone in the hazel. "So, I know what it feels like to both love and hate your parents."

He shifted slightly and wrapped one arm around my shoulders, pulling me closer to him.

It was an odd feeling for me. Between the two of us, I was far stronger. I could protect myself. Hell, I could protect him. But this closeness . . . it was nice. I'd forgotten what it felt like to be held by someone like this. I leaned into him further and rested my head against his shoulder.

Jinx lifted his head and looked at us from his chair. He met Andrei's eyes, and a low growl rippled out from him.

"Umm . . . should I be worried?" Andrei whispered in my ear.

A soft chuckle broke from my lips. "You'll be fine. He's just not a fan of canines."

"What is he?"

"Grimalkin. They're from the fae realm."

"They have magic?" Andrei asked. "Things go a little fuzzy for me sometimes when I'm in wolf form, but I remember being pinned to the ground."

"In general, it's safe to assume anything from the fae realm has magic," I said dryly. "Grimalkin magic, like most fae, is difficult to explain. Fae magic tends to be more elemental based. They're very connected with nature. But they also have a much closer . . . relationship with magic? Understanding? I don't know what the right word is. But they can see and feel magic, and some of them can manipulate it in odd ways.

"Grimalkin, for example, can turn magic into a physical force. Jinx was able to pin you down by gathering the magic in the air surrounding you and forcing that on you. He basically dropped a ton of magical bricks on you. That particular use of magic is somewhat limited. He couldn't do it to another fae, for example. And even daemons and other magically gifted species could probably get out of it. But it's pretty useful against werewolves." I huffed a laugh, and Andrei pinched my arm.

"What else can he do?" he asked as he studied Jinx curiously.

All sorts of things, a sly voice said in my head. By the way Andrei jerked, I knew he'd heard it too.

Andrei tore his gaze away from Jinx and looked at me, wide-eyed.

I smirked. "Forgot to mention they're telepathic."

"He can read my mind?" Andrei asked with a touch of panic.

There's nothing in that head worth knowing.

"That's not an answer!" Andrei snapped.

A deep laugh rumbled through my head.

"He can definitely read minds to a certain degree. Surface thoughts are easy for him to pick up. The rest of it he has to work for, and he's a lazy asshole, so he doesn't normally bother."

Jinx growled at me from the chair but didn't disagree with my assessment.

"How did you two meet?" Andrei asked.

"He's actually been with me since I was born," I said, looking at the grimalkin fondly.

We'd been each other's constants throughout life. The longest we'd ever been apart was when Sebastian had captured me. Being separated from Jinx had been its own brand of torture.

I continued, "He was barely past the kitten stage then. I didn't realize until I was older that it was unusual for a grimalkin to live outside a fae realm. And to become bonded to someone who wasn't fae is even rarer. Him always being there was just normal to me."

"And you don't know why the two of you were bonded?"

"Nope. You can add that to the list of secrets my parents kept from me."

Andrei grunted. "What about the grey one?"

"Luna." I gave the lilac-eyed grimalkin an affectionate look. "After I was captured by the vampires, Jinx searched everywhere for me, including the fae realms. While he was looking, he came across Luna. She was severely wounded, and he was barely able to save her. Later, Jinx tracked me and Magos in the mountains, days after we escaped. Luna came with him. She doesn't remember anything from before Jinx found her. And her magic hasn't come back either.

"It's not unheard of for grimalkin to travel on their own, but it's not exactly common either. Usually, they stay with their family or bond with a fae. We're hoping as she continues to heal, she'll get some of her memories back."

"You keep strange company, kitty cat," Andrei pointed out, and I couldn't exactly disagree with that assessment.

I lifted my head and nipped at his neck, causing the arm he'd slung around my shoulders to tighten. "You're part of that strange company now, wolf," I whispered into his ear before leaning back against the couch.

Andrei gave me a heated expression that went straight to my core. He stroked my shoulder, and the tension between us went up a notch.

I do believe we have more pressing matters than your hormones. You should take this time to rest. You likely won't have another chance to do so today, Jinx said wryly in my head.

Andrei's finger froze where it'd been trailing down my arm. He looked at the grimalkin and growled.

By all means, dog, try and do something about it. Jinx flicked his tail a few times.

Andrei tensed beside me, and I put a hand on his arm. "He's right. I've thrown around a lot of magic today. Especially that last bit. Even napping for an hour will help me recover." I moved away from him and stretched out on the couch with my feet in his lap.

After a few seconds, the tension slipped away from him. "Move up a bit."

I scootched forward, and Andrei shifted to lie behind me, with his back against the couch and his chest against my back. He wrapped an arm around me, and I leaned back into him.

"I'm glad to be a part of the weird company you keep," he said softly.

I smiled. "Me too."

Andrei fell asleep in a few minutes. His breathing was soft and even as it lulled me to sleep as well. As I closed my eyes, I loosened the chains I kept wrapped around the part of my magic I hid so deeply. After munching on that vampire's magic, it felt content and was no longer pushing to be let out.

It wouldn't last. I knew from experience I had only a few hours before it would be straining to be set free again.

But for now, I could let it out a little, which felt nice. It felt right. It settled around me like a warm, heated blanket. Between it and Andrei at my back, I felt safe and drifted off into darkness.

Chapter Sixteen

In what seemed like seconds after falling asleep, the scent of burnt flesh hit my nostrils. Dread filled me as I recognized the agonized screams that filled the air and knew without even looking around where I was. And I knew what I would see if I turned to face the source of the screaming.

So, I didn't.

Instead, I looked at the crowd that had gathered in the center of the village and scoured the familiar faces. He had to be there. I'd fallen into this dream too quickly for it to be natural.

"Apologies for that. Didn't expect you to join me here so quickly," Sebastian said smoothly as he stepped to the front of the crowd.

He snapped his fingers, and everyone stopped moving. No more screams of pain. No more jeers from the crowd. The smell of burnt flesh unfortunately remained.

"You're really playing through all the greatest hits of my life, aren't you?" I asked, keeping both my tone and my expression calm even as my blood boiled. "I'm curious which one you'll choose next. My favorite pony died on my sixth birthday, if you need some ideas."

Sebastian ignored me as he continued moving through the crowd of people who had come to watch my parents burn.

He paused in front of a few people who wore cloaks and peered at their faces before moving on. "As I told you previously, I wasn't responsible for the dream about the mermaid's death. That was all your doing. I was just stopping by for a chat. I do admit to bringing this dream up, though."

"Why?" I bit out.

"Just a hunch I'm following up on."

His tone was light, but I knew him well enough to know he was up to something. Why would he care about the day my parents died? What was he looking for?

I tracked his movement through the crowd, occasionally looking away to study those gathered. They were nothing special. Just humans rejoicing in the cruelty they so often inflicted on others.

All of them had died beneath my blades. It hadn't brought my parents back. And it had done nothing to quench the rage that simmered deep within my soul. But it had brought momentary satisfaction.

My only regret was that I hadn't made them suffer more.

"Do the rest of the warlocks know about whatever 'hunch' it is you're following up on?" I asked. "You know, since *you* told them about my magic and now the Circle is after me."

Sebastian paused at the edge of a crowd and shot a quick glance my way. "Ah. So you know."

"I do." I sank a lot of rage into those words.

He walked away from the crowd and over to a small building where two lanky teenagers were on their knees. Hands bound. Knives held against their throats.

My heart froze as I stared at the younger versions of me and Cian. My brother's face full of grief and disbelief. Mine twisted in rage and fear. I lifted my gaze from where we had been forced to kneel and saw Jinx perched on the roof of the building in his smaller feline form, eyes closed in concentration. He'd been young then too. We'd all been so young.

Sebastian followed my gaze and saw Jinx. "Ah. I was wondering how you'd kept your powers in check that day. I see you had help."

I didn't say anything. If it had been only my life at stake, I would have let my magic free that day and destroyed all those villagers. My parents had left Ireland shortly after having us. We'd traveled through various villages throughout Western Europe, eventually settling in southern France. We'd always lived in the countryside but made regular trips into that village. Most of those people had known me and my brother since we were toddlers.

And yet they'd been so quick to turn on us. A lot of them had wanted to see me and Cian burn alongside our parents. Some of the town elders had argued against that and given us a chance.

If my parents were indeed innocent, they would burn in the purification fire, and we would be free to go. If my parents were the "spawn of hell," they would surely break themselves free from the fire and save themselves. That was why they'd held knives to our throats in plain view of our parents. Seeing the knife at my brother's throat had been the only thing holding me back that day. And even then, it required all of Jinx's power to help me hold my magic back.

"It's odd, don't you think, that your parents were captured? And how all this played out?" Sebastian looked around. "They must have been powerful. And yet they couldn't save themselves. How very interesting."

He studied the men who had surrounded Cian and me. He looked to the right at another small building and the lonely person who stood underneath its overhang. Their face was hidden by a deep hood. Sebastian's eyes narrowed, and he started to walk over to that person, but I moved to block his path.

"Be careful how you describe the murder of my parents," I said quietly, but I knew he understood the promise of violence in my voice. "We both know this was the work of the warlocks. Of the Circle you claimed to hate so much. Speaking of which, why did you tell them about me? Given all that you've gone through over the years, I thought you wanted me all to yourself."

He reached out to brush my hair back, but I leaned away. He dropped his hand and gave me a sad smile. "When you and I were together, I was on the outs with the Circle. I had made a bid for power and lost. Despite my scheming over the years, I never found a way back in."

Surprise flickered through me. "I didn't think you wanted a way back in. You hated them."

That was the only reason I had overlooked Sebastian being a warlock. He'd seemed to hate the witches and warlocks as much as I did. We had even hunted them together for decades.

"I hated the individuals who had been involved in my fall from power," Sebastian corrected. "I never hated the warlocks as a whole. And I believed in our cause. I still do. At the time, I disagreed with those in power. They knew that, which is why they tried to have me killed after they orchestrated my exile."

I went completely still at his admission. "Those warlocks and witches we hunted and killed," I said slowly. "They weren't random targets. They were the ones responsible for your exile."

"Some of them, yes," Sebastian said with a casual shrug. "Some of them were simply relatives of those involved. A way for me to send a message to them. You were so bloodthirsty back then,"—he gave me a sly grin—"you didn't even question who they were or if they deserved it. All that mattered to you was that they were a witch or a warlock."

"You used me." I was surprised at the feelings of hurt and betrayal that welled up.

I hated Sebastian. He'd murdered the love of my life and had made my life a living hell for the past few decades. But I'd always thought our relationship had been real and had turned into something rotten. Not that it was a lie from the start.

How had I been so blind?

"Oh, come now. We had fun." He winked at me. "And it's not like they were good people. All of them had a part in stirring up the hatred among the humans that led to things like this." He waved a hand at the crowd frozen around us, their faces locked in sneers and scowls as they jeered at my parents. At me and Cian on our knees.

Even if that were true, I didn't like to be used. I let the rage settle over me and used it to clear my head. Sebastian owed me answers, and I couldn't waste this opportunity. He may know me well enough to push my buttons, but I could do the same.

"Doesn't seem to me like your position within the Circle has changed all that much," I drawled. "I mean, you captured me and had me all that time, but instead of handing me over to them, you lied about having me all so you could desperately try to get me to agree to a binding. And now here you are. Trying to capture me again . . . for them. Like a good little errand boy."

Sebastian narrowed his blue eyes at me, a muscle ticking in his cheek. Point to me.

"There was a bit of a coup in the Circle. Emir is now in charge. He was part of the Circle back when I was, but he was the least powerful among us," he seethed. "I haven't figured out exactly how he's managed to gain so much power, but he's now the strongest warlock to have ever existed. He agreed to end my exile in exchange for bringing you in. I may have implied that I only had you for a short amount of time and had been planning on handing you over prior to your escape."

I snorted. "And he believed you?"

"He had no proof otherwise. And the fact remains that I'm the best suited to capture you."

"Emir is a fool to trust you, even a little. You'll stab him in the back the first chance you get."

"You still know me so well." He chuckled and walked around me towards the figure hiding in shadows under the building. "I will get you before they do. And I will bind you to me. Together, we will be unstoppable."

"That will never happen. I'll kill you first or die trying," I promised.

"It's either me or them," Sebastian replied simply, not at all concerned by my threat.

Given that I'd hunted him for decades only to be captured by him, I understood why. But I wouldn't fail again.

He paused in front of the cloaked figure, and whatever he saw under the hood brought a satisfied smile to his face. I wanted to know who it was and why Sebastian was so pleased, but Sebastian controlled everything about this dream. If I tried to walk over there, he'd simply make the person disappear. I stared at the figure, but that damn cloak hid everything about them. My gaze dropped towards their hands. Olive toned skin. Looked male.

Sebastian traced my gaze and waved his hand. The person vanished from sight.

"The Circle's reach has expanded further than you can imagine." He straightened the collar of his shirt. "They're no longer content to work among the shadows of the human realm. Things are going to change. And you will be part of that. You can do that from my side. Or as a slave to the Circle. Those are your only options."

"Or I can kill you all. You might have magic, but you're still only human." I smiled sharply, imagining his blood running down my throat as my fangs tore into his flesh. It wasn't often that I killed with tooth and claw, but damn would it be satisfying.

Sebastian laughed deeply as if he knew every thought that had just run through my head. "I think you'll find those in the Circle have become much more powerful than you realize. They've made some interesting new friends."

"What do you mean?" I tilted my head in question.

Like the vampires and werewolves, the witches and warlocks were largely isolated from the rest of the magical community. Their powers weren't strong or unique enough to be of interest to anyone else. I had no doubt the Circle could find mercenaries among the daemons and some of the other groups to do occasional jobs for them. But that hardly qualified as "interesting new friends."

Instead of answering my question, Sebastian looked around at my parents and the younger versions of me and Cian kneeling in the dirt. "Your dreams have been pretty dark as of late, and I apologize for adding to that."

Before I could push him more about who was helping the Circle, he snapped his fingers. Between one blink and the next, the village disappeared, and I was standing in a heavily forested valley with mountains in the distance. The sound of laughing and splashing came from behind me, and I turned to see the source of the sound.

"Our lakeside cabin," I murmured.

Sebastian said nothing as he stood beside me and we watched our younger selves playing in the lake. The younger me was scrambling up some boulders that rose out of the lake with Sebastian trying to keep up.

"What's the matter, warlock? Can't make it up a few rocks?"

The younger Sebastian swam in circles around the boulder trying to find a way up. He was strong for a human, but I'd only been able to climb up because my claws had found purchase in some of the rock crevices.

"Looks like I'll be sunbathing all by myself," the younger me said with a laugh. "Such a shame."

"Not a chance, my love," the younger Sebastian said, his French accent much thicker than it was now. He pushed off the boulder and spoke a few words, and the water shot up and carried him with it. He made it to the top of the boulder but drenched me in the process. "Oh . . . um . . . oops?" A shy and somewhat embarrassed grin slid across his face.

I glanced sideways at the current Sebastian standing on the shore with me. I'd forgotten about that shy smile he used to have. Had that even been real? Or merely a tool he'd used to charm me? There was no point in asking him. I'd never trust anything he told me again.

I turned my gaze back to the younger versions of us standing on that boulder. That grin had looked real.

"You're kind of a shitty warlock, you know that, right?" The younger me laughed and shook out her soaking wet hair.

"Let me make it up to you," the younger Sebastian replied and held out his hand while speaking a few more words. A blanket appeared in his hand. "Why don't we soak up the sun and nap for a bit? Then we can head back and make some dinner. Maybe tomorrow we could hike up the mountainside and see if we could find those hot springs we've heard rumors of?"

The younger me took the blanket and laid it on the boulder, stretching out on it and tilting her head back, enjoying the heat of the sun. It was a little unsettling to watch young me doing that since I still did the exact same thing. Lying in the sunshine soaking up the heat always calmed me and brought a quiet joy. The younger Sebastian lay down next to her and stared at her face. His expression held love and contentment.

It had to be a lie. Given what he'd told me, he'd been using me from the start. In between these trips to the lake, we'd been hunting witches and warlocks which had been all part of his plan.

Before I could demand he get us out of this dream, the younger me spoke.

"I thought you wanted to leave tomorrow?" she asked, her eyes still closed and face tilted towards the sun.

Young Sebastian didn't answer right away, but his expression changed slightly. He seemed torn about something. But maybe I was imagining it. Or maybe the real Sebastian was manipulating this dream to make me see what he wanted me to see. My jaw clenched. I hated dreamwalkers.

"It can wait," young Sebastian told her softly. "Let's just stay here a while longer."

I turned away from the lake and stalked further into the trees. "It wasn't real."

"Seemed real enough," Sebastian called from behind me.

I flipped him off and kept walking. I'd wake up eventually. I leaped over a fallen log and stopped abruptly when Sebastian appeared in front of me.

"You can't run away from me forever. But for now, I have to go, so we'll have to continue this discussion another time. But don't worry. I'll see you soon." Sebastian raised his hand and snapped his fingers once again.

He disappeared, and the dream of the lake slid away, taking me once more back to that damn village. My hands flew to my ears to try to block out the sounds of my parents screaming. I kept myself from turning around to see them, but I couldn't stop from looking at my younger self.

The teenage me had knelt in the dirt screaming and looking not where my parents burned but at the knife digging into my brother's throat. At the man who stood next to us holding an ax. If we demonstrated we had magic and tried to save our parents, they would slit our throats. That wouldn't kill us, but it would weaken us enough for them to cut off our heads.

I still remembered my rage at my parents being murdered in front of me. And the terror I'd felt at seeing the blood swell where the blade cut into the flesh at my brother's throat. My magic was thrashing to be let out, but I knew it wouldn't be fast enough to save us. I had spent years keeping it chained and smothered. I had no idea how to use it.

"I can't. I can't. I can't." The words had stumbled over and over from my lips as I desperately tried to keep the chains in place.

If Jinx hadn't been there that day, my magic would have erupted. I had no idea how that would have changed the events that unfolded. Maybe I would have saved my parents, or maybe I would have devoured them and Cian along with every human in that goddamn town.

My magic was a wild, uncontrollable monster. I would never trust it around those I loved.

Besides, even if I had managed to save my family, the fae or daemons would have hunted me down. And my family would have died protecting me.

Still, as I stared at the blood dripping from the cut on my brother's throat, I felt the sharp sting of guilt. I should have done more.

A scream tore out of my mother.

The pain and anger in it felt unending. I'd had this dream often enough to recognize it. It was the last scream she'd made before passing on. My father had died moments before.

I tried to stop from turning around, but I couldn't. My body moved of its own, and I fell to my knees exactly like my younger version. Then a scream ripped out of me. Unlike my younger self, my magic had no chains. It poured out of me as I screamed over and over again.

"It's okay," a voice said.

My eyes flew open. I blinked, trying to focus. My throat felt raw. Living room. Apartment. Our apartment. Magos. Everything snapped into place.

Magos was kneeling in front of me but not touching me. Jinx was standing on the coffee table, eyes closed in concentration. An arm was wrapped around me. Holding me tight against a strong chest. Andrei.

My magic was raging around me. Frost covered most of the furniture, but it hadn't turned on anyone yet, of which I was grateful. I'd been foolish to let it out earlier, but keeping it locked down all the time was so godsdamned exhausting. I glanced at Andrei over my shoulder. He stared at me wide-eyed but seemed fine.

I can't hold it back much longer, Jinx said to me, voice strained.

I concentrated on breathing and pulling in my magic. Slowly. So slowly it coiled back up inside me, and I wrapped the chains around it once more. I nodded at Jinx once I was sure it was contained, and he dropped his magic.

"Are you all right?" Magos asked, concern written all over his features.

"Yeah." I rubbed my face. "Sebastian has been messing with my dreams the last couple days. I didn't get anything all that useful out of him."

"You didn't tell me Sebastian had been in your dreams." Magos's jaw hardened in reproach.

"It's nothing he hasn't done before," I said defensively. "Besides, the one from the other day was a quick appearance. Not really worth mentioning."

I could still smell burnt flesh, and my soul hurt from watching and listening to my parents die. I'd relieved that nightmare so many times. It never got any easier.

Magos gave me a look that said he clearly didn't agree with me but didn't push it. I moved to sit up on the couch, and Andrei did the same.

"I need you to keep an eye on Andrei," I said.

Magos narrowed his eyes at me. "And what will you be doing?"

I glanced at Jinx, who jumped off the coffee table and trotted over to the door with a smooth feline grace. "Jinx and I are going on a witch hunt."

Chapter Seventeen

ANDREI WASN'T happy about being left behind, but he caved pretty quickly, which made me suspicious. The innocent smile he gave me after the quick goodbye kiss ratcheted up that feeling. But I trusted Magos to handle whatever the wolf was scheming.

After loading up on weapons, I stopped at the apartment on the second floor. As much as I wanted to track down the witch, I needed to check in with Kaysea and Pele first. Plus, I didn't exactly know where to find said witch, and there was a chance Pele had heard something that could point me in the right direction. I could have made these calls from our living room, but that would have led to Andrei asking all sorts of questions I just didn't want to answer right now.

The door was unlocked, so I let myself in. Jinx followed and leaped onto one of the couches. Like the apartment on the first floor, this one was also furnished, although no one had ever lived here to my knowledge.

I walked over to the mirror on the living room wall that was the twin to the one in our living room.

It was made of four pieces of glass. One large body-length

piece in the center was surrounded on the top and along both sides with three other narrow pieces. Thick wood carved with glyphs framed all of it.

Since no one lived in this apartment, the side glass pieces were empty, whereas mine had glyphs running down the side. I could tap one of those glyphs and it would reach out to the mirror, matching that glyph. Mine had glyphs for Pele, Kaysea, Cian, and a few other regular contacts. Since this one didn't have any glyphs stored, I drew the glyph for Kaysea on the top glass panel. The glyph glowed a gentle blue while I waited.

A few minutes later, the center piece of glass glowed with a similar gentle blue and rippled slightly, revealing Kaysea. Her long green hair plastered down her naked body. Clearly, she'd been swimming and had bounded back up to answer my call. The merfolk were like the shifters in that they didn't really care about nudity. It was hard to be bashful when you regularly stripped down to change forms.

"Hey," she said breathlessly as she grabbed a towel and dried herself off quickly, wrapping the towel around her hair. "Just a sec."

I watched in amusement as she threw clothes and blankets around the room. Kaysea was quite possibly even messier than me.

Finally, she found a light pink robe and wrapped it around herself, plopping down on the large cozy chair in front of the mirror. I knew she only bothered with the robe because she didn't like how the fabric of the chair stuck to her damp skin.

"I'm glad I was able to reach you." I filled her in on everything that had happened since we'd last spoken. "So my problem has gotten considerably more complicated."

"You always did have a gift for understating things," Kaysea responded absently. Her face held a look of concentration, and I let her think through whatever was bouncing around in her head. "I need to see you." Her expression changed to one of focus, and her light green eyes fell on me. "Today."

"No." I shook my head violently. "Absolutely not. You can't come here today with everything going on."

And I can't go there.

I left out those words but knew she would understand. It wasn't safe for me to go to her realm.

Connor wasn't the only one who blamed me for Myrna's death. The ruling king and queen of the sea fae had loved their daughter deeply.

Without Kaysea's intervention, they would have called for a blood debt which likely would have required my death. As it was, somewhat of an unofficial blood debt was going on. If I set foot in Kaysea's realm, I would be targeted. I didn't want to have to kill any of Kaysea's relatives, so I stayed away.

"I had a vision," Kaysea argued back. "Several, actually. It's been the same vision over and over again. But it's vague, and I don't understand it. I don't see anyone. I don't hear anything. Just intense flashes of gold . . . gold wings, I think. And this overwhelming feeling that it's connected to you."

"Fantastic," I said dryly. Just what I needed in addition to dealing with my clusterfuck of a life. Vague vision nonsense. "Do you think it's connected to my current problem, or is this a future problem? Because if it's the latter, I can probably just put it off for a day or two. I might be dead by then and not have to worry about it."

"That's not funny," Kaysea snapped, her green eyes flashing with anger. "I need to see you," she repeated, force-fully this time. "This vision is important. I'm getting it more frequently, and I still don't understand it. I think being near you will help. Please."

I exhaled in frustration. "Fine. I'm going to check in with Pele, but I'll leave for the beach right after that. Should only take a few minutes."

"Okay." Kaysea breathed out in relief, and some of the tension drained from her face. Whatever this vision was, it was clearly getting to her.

"Bring your asshole brother with you," I said begrudgingly. Connor was a prick, but I had no doubt he would do whatever he had to do to protect Kaysea.

"Fine," Kaysea agreed quickly. "I'll see you soon." The mirror rippled, and my reflection appeared once again.

I didn't waste any time and drew Pele's glyph across the top. The glyph glowed once again along with the main mirror and rippled almost immediately to reveal Pele sitting at her desk.

"There's a witch in town," I said by way of greeting.

Pele didn't look up from whatever she was working on at her desk. "Interesting. I haven't heard that. But I did hear that the werewolves got into it with some vampires last night. That you were involved in this little scuffle. And apparently, I now have a bunch of vampire brats living in *my* extremely nice apartment." She glanced up at me. "Care to explain?"

Damn. I was hoping to carefully broach the subject of the vampire kids. But of course, Pele already knew.

I eyed my friend suspiciously, wondering what types of spells she had woven into this place.

Pele only cared about privacy when it was *her* privacy. For everyone else, she just viewed it as a suggestion. If I survived this, I'd have to figure out exactly what type of invasive spells she'd left behind here and negotiate with her on removing at least some of them.

That was a future problem. For now, I quickly gave her the same recap I'd provided Kaysea.

"So that's everything that's happened," I finished. "The vampire brats are housetrained, I promise."

The corners of Pele's mouth curled down in distaste. "They'd better be," she muttered.

"Have you learned anything?" I asked.

Her brow furrowed together as she pondered her answer. Pele was always careful when it came to information. She didn't like to speculate, and she never passed off gossip as good information.

"Bits and pieces," she said. "The warlocks are clearly plotting something big, but what exactly that is or their plan to accomplish it is unclear. They can throw some strong magic, but they would need greater numbers and more offensive power to be considered any threat." She shrugged and didn't sound the least bit concerned about this information.

"The vampires would help with that," I mused. "But even allied with the vamps, they could never go against the fae or daemons. Either could wipe them out."

Pele hummed in agreement. "Either they have something else planned that we don't know about, or they're incredibly naive in thinking the vampires can give them the power boost they need. I've made a recommendation to the Assembly that we look into it further, but nothing seems particularly urgent about it. The warlocks have made minor power plays like this in the past, and they never amounted to anything."

"Aside from wiping out most of the witches and a few of the other supernaturals," I countered with a grimace.

Pele nodded and waved a hand in acknowledgment. "Fair point."

"Anything else?" I asked.

Pele pursed her lips but didn't say anything.

I narrowed my eyes at her. "Out with it."

She sighed. "I've received some new information, but to be clear, I have not been able to confirm this, and my only source on the matter is sketchy at best."

I held up my hands in a placating manner. "I'm totes good with sketchy."

"Fine. Never tell anyone I gave you this unverified information or I'll never help you again." She paused, reluctance clear in her turquoise eyes. "I've noticed an increase in the daemon youth coming through this gateway these last couple months. They usually prefer to hang out in the major human cities where they can cause more trouble.

"A couple groups came through last night, and I asked what brought them to this town. They said someone in town was selling some sort of potion that, and I'm quoting here, 'caused whoever took it to trip balls for dayyysssss.'" She drew out the last few syllables in a perfect imitation of a wasted demon teenager. "In light of the information you've discovered, it would seem this person could be our mystery witch."

I stood up straighter as my interest piqued. "Did they say anything else about the person?"

"The kids who came last night to score some of this potion came back to the bar empty-handed. She told them her uncle was in town, so she was shutting down business temporarily."

"Did they know her name? Or what she looked like?"

"They never got her name, and they met her in the public park in the center of town. They were already pretty drunk when they went to see her, so they couldn't tell me what she looked like beyond a white woman with brown or red hair. One of them said blonde hair, so who knows?"

"Gotta be fucking kidding me," I growled in frustration.

"I told you this information was sketchy. More than likely it's a loki messing with them," Pele said in distaste. "They remembered one thing. She apparently smelled like rosemary and lavender. One of the kids is allergic to rosemary, so he kept sneezing while they were talking to her."

Jolie. No fucking way. A snarl ripped out of me. I should have trusted my instincts all those times she felt off to me.

Pele tilted her head and gave me an inquisitive look. "I take it this means something to you?"

"Yes," I spat. "Anything else?"

"Nothing concrete, but I did check-in with the local herb shop. The owner owed me a favor. He's delivered a few odds and ends to a cottage on that frontage road just outside of town. Probably worth checking out."

"Thanks, Pele. I've got to go, but I'll check in with you soon."

"Be careful, Nemain." She disconnected from the mirror.

You know who the witch is? Jinx asked.

Andrei's sister Stela has been dating a human woman for the last few months. She always smells like lavender and rosemary. It took a little more effort to communicate mind to mind, but I didn't want to take any chances on Andrei overhearing us.

Are you going to tell Andrei?

No, I said after a long moment. *I'm going to get whatever information out of her that I can, but the witch has to die.*

That's going to cause problems for you.

I rubbed my face and let out a deep breath. *I'll deal with the fallout.*

Andrei hadn't run away screaming after I told him my secrets or after watching me kill Ryder. But he didn't know Ryder, and his only reference was that he was one of the vampires that had captured and tortured me. His sister was head over heels in love with Jolie. And Stela's happiness meant everything to him.

Somehow, I didn't think Andrei would take this in stride like he had everything else. But Stela was a threat, and I couldn't afford to let her live. I'd just have to hope that Andrei understood. And accept it if he didn't.

The thought weighed heavily on me as I left the second-floor apartment. I jogged down the steps and headed to the front door but paused.

I'd barely checked in with the vamp kids since dumping them in the apartment. It was unlikely, but they might know some useful information about the alliance between the vampires and warlocks. If they knew anything, I could ask the witch more specific questions when I tracked her down for a nice little chat.

I spun back around and knocked on their apartment door. The movement I'd heard inside stopped, and I got the impression all the vampire kids were holding their breath.

"It's just me." I rolled my eyes and shook my head.

"Oh. Right," Elisa said through the door. "Come in."

I'll wait out here, Jinx said. Apparently, he wasn't in the mood to deal with vampire teenagers.

I let myself into the apartment and met Elisa in the kitchen. The layout of this apartment was similar to ours. I looked her over quickly, noting a little more color in her cheeks than had been there before. "Guessing your parents weren't big on the knocking before entering thing?"

Snorts came from the couch. I glanced over and saw the two boys on the couch with Isabeau passed out between them, her riot of brown curls spread over the cushions. One of the boys, Damon, was trying to move some of the curls off her face without waking her up. The other boy got up and walked over to stand beside Elisa.

I hadn't noticed in the alley, but standing next to each other, the resemblance was uncanny. Same dark hair and porcelain-white skin. Both had identical dark blue eyes.

"We don't have parents so much as vampires who donated their genetics," the boy said. "Who those particular vampires were . . . we have no idea."

"You don't know who your parents are?" I frowned at them.

"Not exactly," Elisa cut in. "Based on our abilities, we know what bloodlines we're descended from. But we've never actually met our parents. Or if we have, we didn't know it. The Council keeps the identities of the remaining Apex vampires a secret when they can. Even from other vampires."

"Are you two related?" I asked, looking back and forth between them.

"We don't know for sure." Elisa waved a hand between them. "Based on appearances, we've always assumed so. But our powers are different, so maybe we're half-siblings or cousins."

"Misha, right?" I asked, and the boy nodded. "What can you do?"

He grinned at me. In a blink, he disappeared and reappeared right beside me. He yelped as the blade I'd pulled out bit into the skin underneath his chin. "A little warning next time, yeah?" I said simply.

Misha swallowed, and I lowered the blade. "Right. Sorry about that."

Elisa shot me an apologetic look. "He likes to show off."

"The way he teleports—"

"I'm not related to them," Misha said quickly. "To Magos or Mikhail, I mean. They don't teleport. Not exactly. They can turn themselves into mist which allows them to travel to a different spot quickly or just hang out in mist form. My magic is true teleportation. From one place to another in seconds. No mist. No stopping along the way."

"All right." I nodded towards the other vampire boy on the couch. "Telepathy, right?"

Yes, a voice said quietly in my head. *Not quite as flashy as their magic. But I can connect minds together telepathically, even those who don't have much in the way of telepathic ability. That's how we planned our escape. The Vampire Council didn't know I could do that.*

"Nice," I said, impressed not only by his magic but at the clever use of it. "And the little girl?"

They all fell silent.

"We don't know." Elisa chewed her bottom lip. "She turns five next month. Her magic should start manifesting any day now. We were worried that if we delayed our escape for much longer, her magic would manifest, and they would separate her from us."

"Are there others like you? Other Apex vampire kids?"

"Yes, but we don't know how many," Elisa replied. "Me, Misha, and Damon have been together almost our entire lives. Another girl grew up with us, but she . . . left."

A haunted look passed between Elisa and the boys. There was more to the story, but I'd have to get it out of them later.

"After that, it was just us three for a while until Isabeau came along." All three of them were staring at the sleeping girl, and they wore the same protective look on all their faces. "We couldn't let them take her from us."

Of course they couldn't. They may not be related by blood, but it was clear they all loved each other like siblings. And Isabeau was their baby sister. I figured it was only fair to tell them what was going on.

"I don't know if the Council is in town, but the Circle definitely is, and they have at least some vampire support."

Elisa turned her head sharply to look at me.

"The good news is I'm pretty confident that I'm a higher priority to both the Council and the Circle than you guys."

"They'll send someone after us." I could see the panic in her eyes even as she fought to remain calm.

"They already did . . . sort of. Mikhail volunteered for the job."

All three vampire teens stared at me with their mouths open. Misha recovered first. "Mikhail?" he squeaked. "They sent the fucking assassin after us?"

"Language," Elisa snapped and smacked him on the back of the head.

Misha rolled his eyes. "She's sleeping. And I think the assassin being after us is a good enough reason for me to drop an f-bomb."

"You don't have to worry about Mikhail. He only used

looking for you as a cover to come to town and have a nice little chat with me and Magos," I said dryly. "I'll deal with Mikhail."

Honestly, I had no idea how I would accomplish that. But that was a problem for future me. One of my many, many future problems.

Three skeptical looks answered me.

"Magos and I will deal with Mikhail," I clarified, and they looked a little more confident with that reply.

Apparently, they viewed Magos as way more of a badass than me. Whatever.

I added, "A lot of shit is probably going to go down in the next twenty-four hours. The owner of this building, Pele, is my friend. She's a daemon and not exactly a fan of vampires, but I told her the situation. She's fine with you guys staying here for now. If something happens to me and Magos, she will help you."

Technically, Pele hadn't agreed to that, but I knew she would. Pele would never say no to a child in need. No matter what they were.

"We could help—" Elisa stopped when I raised a finger.

"I already have one overeager werewolf who wants to help. I can't handle a bunch of teenage vamps on top of that."

Misha chose that moment to teleport out of the room. A second later, a loud crash came from down the hallway that led to two of the bedrooms.

"I'm okay!" he yelled.

Elisa rubbed her forward. "Yeah. That's probably a good call."

Chapter Eighteen

As I walked down the beach with Jinx perched on my shoulders, I tried to ignore the guilt growing over not telling Andrei about my suspicions of the witch's identity.

But he'd tell his sister, and then they'd want to confront Jolie themselves. And if she did indeed turn out to be the witch, they wouldn't like what I'd have to do. I'd explain it to him later.

After I did what had to be done.

He'll leave you, a voice whispered in my mind. *Once he sees you for the monster you truly are, he'll leave.*

I swallowed as the numbness I kept wrapped around my soul slipped a little. Who would I be if I didn't have Andrei to distract me? Would I go back to being nothing but rage and violence? Since coming to Emerald Bay, I'd been able to piece together some semblance of a life. This was my home.

I'd never had a home that hadn't ended in pain and suffering. My parents had died. Sebastian used and betrayed me. And then there was the cottage I had shared with Myrna. Where we'd built a life together . . . and she'd paid the price for it.

Maybe I should leave Emerald Bay, I thought with a hollow pang. Leave before Andrei or someone else paid the price for my selfish desire to be happy.

A tingle over my skin alerted me that I was passing the fae ward. A quick glance at the wooden gazebo told me Kaysea wasn't there yet.

Jinx leapt down to railing, his golden eyes shadowed with concern. I'd kept my thoughts to myself, but Jinx understood me better than anyone. Despite his gruff exterior, he loved me and was every bit as devoted to me as I was to him.

"I'm fine," I said, giving him a weak smile.

Liar.

"No," I said sadly. "I'm all kinds of fucked up. But survival comes first."

Survival comes first, he agreed. *But we will talk about what's going on in that head of yours once the threat has passed. If I have to hold you down while I rip through your pathetic mind shield, I'll do it.*

"My mental shield isn't weak, and you know it," I said without any real heat. I was a weak telepath, but mental shields were more dependent on one's will. And my will was fucking iron.

I grabbed the wrap-style dress Kaysea left draped over one of the benches and turned to head back down the stairs. I froze mid-step.

Andrei stood at the bottom of the stairs, a sheen of sweat covering his skin.

"What part of stay in the apartment was unclear to you?" I growled in frustration. Jinx snickered in my head.

"That was magic, right?" Andrei pointed to the part of the beach where the fae ward was located, his eyes alight with curiosity. "You walked right through it, but when I approached, I got this overwhelming urge to turn around and walk away. It was a bitch to get past. So, what are we doing?" He wiped some of the sweat off his forehead and plopped down on the gazebo stairs.

"*We* are doing nothing." I walked down the steps over to the water.

As soon as I was done catching up with Kaysea, I'd be marching his cute ass back to my apartment where he'd be safe behind the wards and with Magos watching over him. Speaking of Magos . . .

"How the hell did you get away from Magos?" I turned slightly so I could keep an eye on him and the water.

Andrei shrugged. "Behaved myself after you left and started to make some breakfast. He went downstairs to check on something, and I took the opportunity to see what happens when a werewolf jumps out a three-story window." He grinned at me. "Turns out we land on our feet."

"Andrei—" I stopped when I saw movement in the water. I scanned the surface, trying to find the source of the movement. Kaysea wouldn't play games like this, especially not now. "Go back to the gazebo and stay there."

"Why—"

"Now," I snarled.

Andrei pursed his lips tightly but did as I said, moments before Connor's head popped out of the water. "Oh joy. It's you," he sneered as he bopped just above the surface ten feet away.

I knew from experience that you could wade out about ten feet from the shore during low tide before the sea floor dropped and you were in deep water. I wasn't sure if it was a natural occurrence or if the fae had something to do with it. It was pretty common in the area to have those steep drop-offs. Between that and the strong undercurrents, swimming was generally ill-advised on these shores.

I looked at him warily. "Where's Kaysea?"

I rested my hands casually at my sides and shifted my body, so I was slightly angled towards Connor. Within seconds, I could either grab a throwing knife or reach over my shoulders to pull out my swords. I didn't think he'd try anything, but until I saw Kaysea, I wasn't going to let my guard down. I was fairly confident she was the only reason he hadn't seriously tried to kill me ages ago.

He watched me adjust my stance and raised a cocky eyebrow. "Someone's on edge today."

"It's been a rough couple of days," I said in a measured tone.

"So I heard." A sharp smile spread across his face.

"Where is Kaysea?" I asked again, shifting anxiously from foot to foot.

"She'll be here shortly. Given the mess you've created and insisted on bringing her into, I wanted to scout the area first."

"Oh, shut the fuck up, Connor."

The merman narrowed his eyes at me and drifted slightly closer.

"Kaysea was the one who insisted on this meeting. And *I* insisted on her bringing you for protection. Although now that I think about it, I probably should have made sure you weren't the one who sold me out to Sebastian."

I didn't actually think he'd done it. And all the evidence pointed to a witch who had informed Sebastian of my whereabouts. But still . . . Connor really did hate me.

"If I wanted you dead, I would kill you myself, not pawn you off to someone else," he promised.

I snorted. "Good to know where I stand with you. Now, how about you sit there quietly while we wait for Kaysea?" I wasn't in the mood to bait him right now. I just wanted to meet with my friend and help her out with the vision so she could get back to the safety of her home realm.

Sand crunched behind me, and a moment later Andrei stood beside me. Every part of me went on high alert. Why couldn't he have just stayed back, damn it?

"Who's the boy? Your new pet? Pretty low to go from a fae to a human mutt. Why don't you just fuck a human while you're at it?"

Part of me was impressed at the malice Connor had kept up all these years. He held onto his hate the way I held onto my rage. It really was amazing we hadn't killed each other yet.

"Andrei, go back to the gazebo and wait." I glanced at Andrei.

His eyes had turned yellow, and I could see the wolf calculating how far it would have to leap to reach the fae bobbing in the water and rip its throat out. This was so not good.

"I'll introduce you to a nice mermaid later. This one bites." I grabbed his arm and turned to walk down the beach.

"Tell me, Nemain. How long did you wait to find a new toy after Myrna died? Or were you out whoring around while she screamed your name?" Connor sneered. The water around him started to swirl.

Nemain, Jinx said in warning from where he'd crouched beside me.

I didn't heed his warning. Something inside me snapped at Connor's words, and the old Nemain who was nothing but rage and fury sprang forward. The water was up to my waist before I even realized what I was doing.

I had entered the domain of a sea fae who wanted to kill me. He'd baited me, and I fell for it hook, line, and sinker.

Shit.

Before I could turn around, the tide pulled my feet out from under me, and I was off the ledge in the deep water. I kicked until I burst through the surface and took several deep breaths.

Connor was on me before I could recover and pulled me under again. The water slowed me down, making it impossible to hit him, but I scratched at his face. He pulled back a little, and I shoved my thumbs into his eyes. He screeched and let go of me, swimming away into the dark, murky water. I hadn't done any real damage, but he wasn't done with me yet.

GET OUT OF THE WATER! Jinx screamed in my head.

My lungs burned for air as I pushed back to the surface and greedily gulped air before throwing myself forward and frantically swimming towards the shore. Jinx was prowling back and forth at the water's edge. Andrei had entered the water and was standing waist deep screaming at me. Idiot. Now we were both in the water.

I was close to the shallow area when Connor resurfaced and leaped out of the water between us. He flipped, and his tail struck Andrei so hard he was launched backwards. I had a moment to hope that he made it to shore or that Jinx would pull him out so he wouldn't drown before Connor pulled me under again.

My back was pressed against his chest and his arms were pinning mine to my sides. He held me just below the surface. My lungs screamed for air as I thrashed around trying to get out of his grip.

Nemain! Jinx's voice was full of panic and frustration. His magic was strong, but fighting other fae was always challenging. And the water was Connor's domain. Jinx's magic didn't stand a chance.

It had never before occurred to me that I could drown. I was usually more worried about being burned alive, beheaded, or drained for some magic spells or by vampires. But drowning would definitely do the trick, I thought, as my lungs fought to breathe. Fuck. This was a shitty way to die.

I struggled against him but found no give. I couldn't reach

any of my weapons, and I had nothing to push off to give me some leverage. My magic pulled against the chains I'd wrapped around it, and I started to let it out, knowing I'd probably pass out before it could save me.

Something appeared in front of me but was gone before I could see it in the murky water. Or maybe it was the fact I was seconds away from losing consciousness. I dug my nails into Connor's arms and put one last effort into getting free. His body spasmed behind me, and we were both jettisoned from the water.

I managed to twist in the air so I landed on my feet in a crouched position. Still in the water but close enough to shore that it was less than a foot deep.

Without waiting to catch my breath, I pulled out one of my throwing daggers and pounced on Connor, who was flopping around trying to get back to deeper water. It would have been smarter of him to lose the fins and shift to legs, but Connor hated taking that shape.

"You fucking bastard!" I screamed.

He groaned as my knee rammed into his stomach and froze as my knife pushed against his neck.

I smiled as I shoved the blade harder against his throat. His eyes were still full of hatred, but I saw something else flicker there. Fear.

My magic swirled around me and nipped at him. He'd never truly seen this side of me before. When he and Kaysea had found me on the beach the day Myrna died, my magic had been raging for hours and had dwindled down to almost nothing. And he'd been so caught up in grief at his sister's death that he hadn't looked at it too closely.

Now my magic sensed his fear and found it intoxicating. It wanted a taste. Part of me wanted to let it; it would be so easy to give into it. The chains around my magic loosened a little more.

A blue fire flickered briefly across the surface of the water. Connor's eyes went wide.

"Stop, Nemain."

Kaysea's voice brought me back from the abyss. But I still wanted blood.

She knelt beside me but made no move to take the blade away from her brother's neck. "Connor is a fool. And I will have words with him about what he did today. But please don't take him away from me. Come back to me. Don't take this path."

I couldn't bring myself to pull the knife away from Connor's throat, so instead I shoved myself backwards and landed on my ass in the cold water. Not very graceful, but it worked. I pulled my magic back and after a few moments slipped the dagger back into the sheath on my arm.

The bastard had almost drowned me. Like I didn't have enough nightmares already.

Connor started to push himself up, but Jinx was on him in a flash. He'd dropped his glamour and held the merman down in his fae form. Golden eyes met light green ones and they glared at each other.

Whatever Jinx told Connor made the merman raise his head in a snarl. Jinx swiped lightning fast with his claws stretched out and left bloody scratches down Connor's pale cheek. The grimalkin leaped away and landed back on the beach out of the water. Connor raised a palm to his cheek and grimaced as he pulled the hand away and studied the blood on his fingers.

I pushed myself up and took a few staggering steps before collapsing on the sand. At least I was out of the water. My hair had come loose during the struggle and hung around me with bits of seaweed tangled in the clumps. My swords were still on my back, and my daggers were still in place.

I looked around for Andrei and saw him lying on his back,

twenty feet from the water's edge. I jumped up and ran to him, but I could see his chest rising and falling. He was alive. I knelt beside him and looked him over for damage. His lip was split, and he had a nasty bruise on the left side of his face, but it was already fading. He would be good as new in a few minutes.

As I walked back towards Kaysea and her prick of a brother, I tried to ignore the worry that ate at me.

Andrei had been in my world for less than a few days, and I'd already dragged him into a fight with vampires and he'd gotten knocked out by a fae. Connor easily could have killed him.

I worried about all of my friends, but Magos, Pele, and even Kaysea were no lightweights. They weren't easy targets. Andrei was far out of his weight class, and he didn't seem to realize that.

Despite the emotional unease, I was already feeling much better physically and was reasonably sure I could be close to Connor without decapitating him.

Or turning him into sushi.

"Put the sword away, Nemain."

I glanced at the sword I'd apparently pulled from its sheath while I'd walked back over to Connor and Kaysea.

"Right." In one smooth motion, I put the sword back, holding back an eyeroll. "My bad."

Connor had moved into deeper water. Kaysea stood on the beach, her long hair covering her breasts and most of her stomach. I swiped the dress I'd dropped on the sand earlier and tossed it to her. She wrapped it around herself.

"Would someone please explain to me why I just had to break up a fight between my best friend and my brother?" she asked very calmly in a way that almost sounded like she was singing softly. It creeped me out when she did that. It also meant she was incredibly pissed.

"He started it," I said at the same time Connor said, "She started it."

Kaysea let out a long sigh. "You are both too old for this shit. And how exactly did you end up in the water?" she asked with a touch of exasperation.

"I told him to be quiet while we waited for you. He decided to say some nasty things instead. So, I decided to find out how well he could swim with half a flipper," I offered.

Kaysea didn't have to ask what he said; she just turned to glare at her brother. Connor had been digging at me the same way for decades, and today I just let it get to me. I swallowed the anger back down before I did something stupid like jam my knife in his throat.

The blade in my boot had a high iron content. It wouldn't kill him, but it would hurt like hell. The thought alone brought a smile to my lips.

"We're going to have a little chat later. For now, wait for me there," Kaysea said to Connor, and her tone left no room for argument.

Connor shot me and Jinx one last murderous look before diving under the water. I knelt on the sand, and Kaysea moved to sit next to me.

Jinx walked over to us and lifted one paw. Then the other. An expression of pure feline disgust came over him as he looked at the sand stuck to his fur. *I'll be in the gazebo. And you're carrying me back when we're done here.*

"Is your wolf okay?" Kaysea asked as I stared out to sea.

I could feel her concerned gaze on me. Such a simple question. Those were often the type that got me in the most trouble. This was one of those pesky questions where my body language was more important than any verbal response. And Kaysea had spent the past two centuries learning my tells.

"He will be better when he comes to his senses and gets the fuck away from me. At the risk of sounding trite, he's a lover not a fighter." So far so good. Just a nice, calm conversation with my BFF.

"So was Myrna." She whispered the words so softly, the tide almost carried them away.

I squeezed my eyes shut and tried to think nice, calming thoughts even though my magic raged as it remembered that day.

"You're right. Myrna wasn't a fighter. And your brother was right, too. I should have forced Myrna to return to the water so she could be protected. But I didn't. And she got her heart ripped out because I was too weak to send her away." Despite all the time that had passed, I couldn't keep the raw pain out of my voice. "I won't be weak again."

Kaysea moved until she was kneeling in front of me. She reached out with her hands and pushed my hair back, gently tilting my face up. "No one could have made Myrna leave you." Her words were gentle but firm. "She loved you with every part of her soul. It was her choice. Just like it is the wolf's choice to stay by you."

"He doesn't understand what he's getting into, Kaysea." I let out a long breath and pinched the bridge of my nose. "Myrna at least knew and understood how our world works. Andrei knows almost nothing. He's still playing human most of the time. Even if I could protect him, it won't work." I thought about the Jolie problem that I still needed to take care of. "The version of me that he knows and cares about is a lie. I've been using him to keep myself from falling apart. It's not fair to him."

"It's not fair to either of you," she countered. "Don't think we haven't noticed the difference in you since you've been back. It's okay to not be okay," she said gently as she stroked my hair. "I will never leave you. Neither will Pele or Magos. You should give Andrei a chance to know the real you; I don't think he'll be as scared as you think. But you can't keep shutting people out, Nemain."

"To know me is to know death. It doesn't matter what I want. All that matters is keeping others safe, which means keeping my distance."

I'd barely been keeping it together when Sebastian had been leaving the hearts of strangers or people I only knew in passing. If I ever found Kaysea's heart, or Cian's, or anyone who truly mattered to me, left for me on my birthday . . . my soul that was already so bruised and broken would shatter beyond repair.

"Look, I understand the decisions you made for how to deal with Sebastian. I know these last few decades have been hell. But obviously things have changed. Sebastian has to die."

My eyebrows crept up slightly at the violence in her words. So odd to hear the need for violence coming from my kind-hearted friend.

Her seafoam eyes were serious as she looked at me. "He's coming here, Nemain. You spent decades trying to kill him but never being able to find him. This is the chance you've been waiting for. Let us help you, and then this can all be over. You can truly move on."

"And then what?" I asked. "Even if I kill Sebastian, it won't be over. The warlocks and vampires aren't going to forget about my existence."

"Then we'll deal with them next," she replied calmly. "But you can't keep pushing people away forever. Tell Andrei everything. Let him decide for himself if he wants to be with you, knowing all that entails."

Kaysea opened her mouth to say something else but stopped as the blood drained from her face. Her eyes were locked on something behind me. A moment later, I felt a strong rush of magic behind me and what felt like a gateway opening.

In one smooth movement, I pulled a dagger free and spun around but froze before finishing the throw.

Sebastian stood on the beach with Andrei kneeling rigidly before him. Panic and fear competed in my mind, but I shoved them away as best I could. I needed to stay calm if I was going to get Andrei out of this alive.

Sebastian beamed. "Hello, my love. Are you ready to come back to me?"

Chapter Nineteen

I BIT BACK my snarl and instead asked, "Given that you just opened up a gateway, it doesn't seem like you need me anymore."

"Oh, that? That was nothing. Just a gateway from one part of the human realm to another. Your talents are still very much in demand." The touch of sultriness to his voice turned my stomach.

As far as I knew, warlocks weren't capable of opening gateways within a realm. True, it was easier than opening a gateway between realms, but it still required a lot of power and skill that warlocks simply didn't have. Someone was helping them. And it definitely wasn't the vampires.

"How'd you find us?" I slid my throwing dagger back into my sleeve but took a small step forward, hoping the one movement would cover up the other.

"Ah, ah, ah," Sebastian chided, and I froze. "I know that move of yours. No closer, my love."

Andrei's eyes were wide open, and the muscles on his arms bulged as he strained to break free from whatever holding spell Sebastian had cast on him.

"You can't get to me before I kill this pretty little wolf," Sebastian crooned.

He was right. The distance between us was far too much. Sebastian brushed some sand off his light blue button-down shirt. I wanted to know how he had tracked us here, but it seemed unlikely he would tell me. This was a well-known meeting spot for the fae, so him figuring out where I would meet Kaysea wasn't surprising. But something or someone had alerted him to me being here *now*. Argh, I was so tired of being surprised by warlocks and vampires.

I tried to spot where Kaysea had gone, but she wasn't in my peripheral vision, and I wasn't about to turn my back on Sebastian. "I'll never serve you or the Circle. I didn't break all that time the vamps had me. You will *never* break me."

"While it's true I wasn't able to get you to accept the binding, I think we both know that you broke." He tilted his head, sending a curl of hair tumbling over his shoulder. "You were broken the moment I tore out that weak mermaid's heart."

A growl rumbled out of my chest as my body quivered with barely contained rage. A gasp of pain slipped through Andrei's lips, and I realized I'd taken two steps forward. I forced myself to stop, and Sebastian's eyes glittered in satisfaction at having me under control.

"I set certain rules during your stay with the vampires to make sure some lines weren't crossed. There will be no lines this time," he promised. "And if that doesn't work, we'll see how well your resolve holds when you have to watch your little mermaid friend being tortured. Or perhaps your brother."

My blood ran cold as fear gripped me.

"Magos, of course, is too powerful to be left alive. He'll be hunted down and killed," he said, airily waving a hand.

The fear faded a bit, and a savage grin spread across my face. "Magos will slaughter all of you, and then he'll come for me."

Sebastian shrugged and played with a lock of Andrei's hair. "He is quite strong, there's no doubt about that. But the old warrior has failed before. And his people died because of it. He will fail again. And you won't be there to bring him back this time." He gave me a small knowing smile.

My hands twitched, aching to reach for my blades, and my skin felt like it was on fire from my magic raging beneath the surface.

I had no good options in front of me and couldn't think of any actions that resulted in Andrei still being alive at the end of this encounter. I assumed Kaysea was back in the water, which meant she was safe. Connor would care only about Kaysea's safety. He'd happily stay in the water and watch this unfold. I flicked my eyes over Sebastian's shoulder and saw Jinx crouched at the bottom of the gazebo. If he could have done anything, he would have by now.

"The Circle will be extending an invitation to you to meet with them tonight. Your time has run out," Sebastian continued. "You have what remains of today to decide whether you want to surrender yourself to me or to them. I can make your imprisonment as pleasant as possible. After all, we had some good times, you and I."

My stomach churned at the idea of him capturing me again. The echo of the pain I felt as bones were broken over and over again rippled across my skin. The memory of having my flesh carved up with dull blades. I'd never told anyone just how close I'd come to breaking and accepting the binding before. Those moments had been rare and over in a flash.

But I couldn't go through it again, and I wouldn't last long if Sebastian got a hold of anyone truly important to me.

"I know you're not going to come willingly with me now. It's just not in your nature." Sky-blue eyes looked thoughtfully down at Andrei. "So consider this a taste of what's to come."

Before I could reply or move, he whispered something so

softly I couldn't make out the words. Andrei clutched at his chest and fell, arching his back. Sebastian clapped his hands together. I flew backwards and landed in the water. I leaped to my feet just as a gateway opened and slammed shut.

Sebastian was gone, and Andrei was lying where he had fallen. I ran towards him and collapsed to my knees at his side. Small, desperate gasps were coming out of his mouth as I ran my hands all over his body. I could see no injuries, but he clearly couldn't breathe.

Kaysea crashed on the other side of Andrei with Connor right behind her. She calmly but quickly looked Andrei over.

"He can't breathe! Help him!" I screamed.

Magic poured from Kaysea and wrapped around Andrei. "It's a hex!" She concentrated on Andrei.

Seconds passed and my magic started to leak out of me.

Kaysea's magic withdrew, and she looked at me bleakly. "I can undo it, but it will take too much time. I can't save him, Nemain."

"You have to!" All of my magic ripped free of its chains and raged around us.

Connor tried to pull Kaysea back, but she yanked out of his grasp.

"Nemain!" Kaysea said frantically. "There's nothing I or anyone can do. I'm sorry. I'm so sorry. You have to pull your magic back." She looked over her shoulder at her brother, who was staring at me with open suspicion and fear.

"No, no, no." I repeated the word over and over again and looked down at Andrei. His eyes found mine, and he reached out a hand and gripped mine. I gently stroked his face with my other hand. "I'm so sorry." Tears streamed down my cheeks.

Andrei gave me one small smile and gasped one last time, falling still.

I sat there numbly, not wanting to process what had just happened. This morning, Andrei had been safe and protected in my apartment. And now he was dead. I should have taken him back to the apartment immediately instead of waiting. His death was my fault.

My magic wrapped around me as if trying to comfort me. I didn't put it away. Not yet. I couldn't bring myself to care what Connor thought.

"Wait." Kaysea sprang into action across from me.

I looked at her in confusion as she tilted Andrei's head back.

"Spells on the living expire at their death," she said hastily as she began chest compressions. "That means the spell is no longer in effect."

My body shook as I processed the meaning behind her words and a small hope kindled to life inside me. Kaysea knelt down to breathe into his mouth before resuming chest compressions. I could feel her magic working on his body as she tried to breathe life back into him.

"Is his soul still there?" she asked.

My brows bunched together, not understanding what she was asking.

"Nemain! Check to see if his soul is still here." She said each word slowly and clearly, showing no signs of being out of breath despite what she was doing.

Understanding clicked, and I leaned over his body and breathed in. Of all my magic, I considered my ability to read souls the least useful. I'd never think that again. My magic searched and searched but found nothing. Hope died, and my chest clenched.

"It's gone," I squeezed out.

"Figure something out!" Kaysea barked. "Without his soul, my magic can only do so much."

I frantically tried to figure out how to retrieve his damn soul. My brother? He'd never done anything like this before, but he was my only shot. Was he a strong enough necromancer to pull this off? I tried to think of anyone else who might be able to pull this off when the answer to a question I'd had for years finally came to me.

"That son of a bitch." I breathed and started laughing. Kaysea shot me a look. She probably thought I was losing it. Which I might be.

But something told me this was right. He was a necromancer. He was powerful. He was hiding from people. He had a secret. And I knew what it was.

I stood up and threw my right hand out. A gateway ripped open, revealing my brother's living room. My brother was nowhere to be seen, but that was fine. He wasn't who I needed.

"Hades! You get your fucking ass over here now!" I yelled.

"Hades?" Kaysea squeaked.

In less than ten seconds, the man I'd known as Dante appeared before me but made no move to walk through the gateway. He looked a little pissed, which I expected. I didn't think I'd ever seen him not look at least a little pissy, but I wasn't expecting the look of bemusement.

"Well, you're not quite as dumb as I thought you were." He glanced at my surroundings and stiffened when he saw Andrei. "I take it back. You're exactly as dumb as I thought you were."

"Bring him back."

Hades snapped his gaze back to me and narrowed his eyes. "That's not the way it works," he said coldly.

"Bullshit. I know the stories, and even if they've been embellished, that doesn't change anything. This is within your power," I said, my voice hard.

"I'm not risking people finding out I'm still alive just because your toy is broken. You don't get everything you want, Nemain. Deal with it and move on like you always do." His tone said he was done with the conversation.

"I don't have time for this." I reached through the gateway and grabbed him by the shirt and pulled. He broke my hold but not before he had fallen through the gateway, which I promptly closed behind him.

"I can open another one. I may not be able to walk all the realms like you, but the death realms are mine to wander," he growled at me. I wasn't surprised my brother had told him about my abilities.

Hades rose from where he'd fallen, but before he could speak another word or open a gateway, I moved. And punched him right in the face. He snarled at me, and I threw another punch, which he blocked and spun me around pinning my arm to my sides.

"Are you finished?" he seethed.

"Bring. Him. Back."

"No."

"Then I'm not fucking finished!" I slammed my head back, and Hades hissed as I broke his nose and pulled free. I whirled around to face him. "If you don't bring him back, I'll tell everyone who you really are and where they can find you."

My voice was even and my expression hard so he wouldn't doubt my words. I felt like an asshole for doing this. And I wouldn't actually go through with it. I'd never jeopardize my brother like that. I didn't like Hades, but I never once doubted he loved my brother. But Hades had a pretty poor opinion of me, so hopefully he wouldn't call my bluff.

Hades stilled. "You wouldn't. If you do that, your brother will be in danger. They'll use him to get to me."

"I can protect my brother," I said coldly. "But bring back Andrei's soul, and I'll never breathe a word of who you are. I swear it."

He looked at me, calculation taking place behind those dark eyes. He was probably debating killing me, Kaysea, and Connor and dumping all of our bodies somewhere. Connor moved in a flash to stand between Kaysea and Hades, two wicked daggers drawn. My magic erupted once more, and blue fire spread up my arms.

"Looks like I'm not the only one keeping secrets," Hades said softly as he studied my magic.

Apparently, my brother hadn't told him everything. Interesting.

Finally, he growled. "You are such a fucking pain in the ass. You're lucky I love your brother. Otherwise, I'd just kill you all and be done with it." He stalked over to Andrei.

Connor moved out of his way at the last second but kept his daggers drawn. Kaysea had continued with chest compressions this entire time but still managed to give Hades a weary look. Hades raised his left hand, palm down over Andrei's body. His right shot out, and a ripple formed in the air. His head tilted back, and a burst of power shot out from him. His right hand reached into the ripple and pulled out a faint silver ball of light. Hades's eyes glowed white, and cold power radiated off him. It was no wonder humans had worshipped him as a god.

The ripple in the air closed, and in one movement Hades knelt and slammed that silver ball of light back into Andrei's body. Kaysea moved back, and we all stared at Andrei. His chest rose and fell, and I heard him take a breath on his own.

Relief slammed into me, and I would have fallen to my knees if Hades hadn't turned to face me and gripped me by the throat. I grabbed his arm as he lifted me off the ground. His magic tried to seep into me, but mine lashed out, and his withdrew quickly.

"You will speak to no one of my true identity. Nor will you ever call upon me again to do such a task. I have no interest in being hunted again." The energy pulsed from him as a gateway opened behind him. "And we will speak soon about this magic you've been hiding."

He shook me once and dropped me before striding through

the gateway without another glance. It shut a second after he passed through.

"You truly do have a talent for pissing people off, Nemain," Connor said flatly.

Ignoring him, I looked at the spot where Hades had opened the gateway. I suspected he was going to fill my brother in on what had just happened. And then ask why he hadn't been informed about all of my magic. Did he know what it was? He was thousands of years old; perhaps he'd come across something like my magic before.

Shaking my head, I ran back to where Andrei was still lying. Questioning Hades further would have to wait.

I knelt by Andrei. He was breathing easily but still unconscious, although I could feel the lingering traces of Kaysea's magic as it healed the last of his injuries.

He was alive. I didn't lose him. A deep, shuddering breath tore out of me as I rested my hand on his chest, marveling at the feeling of it rising and falling.

But then I glanced at Kaysea with a perplexed expression. "When did you learn CPR?"

Chapter Twenty

"He'll probably need a few more minutes to wake up. In the meantime . . ." Kaysea held her hands out to me.

"Right. Your vague visions which may or may not be related to the current problem at hand." I kneeled in front of her and held her hands in mine.

Kaysea closed her eyes and went still.

I chewed my bottom lip and glanced at Andrei, still not entirely convinced he was okay. I wanted to shake him until he woke up and get him the hell out of there. But visions could be tough on a seer. The fae had a unique relationship with magic. They interacted with it on a level none of us came close to, which made them powerful but came at a cost. It was almost like they had a partnership with magic, and if they failed to hold up their end of the bargain, they were punished for it.

Seers were supposed to interpret their visions and act accordingly. If the magic behind the visions felt the seer wasn't getting it, the visions would become more and more intense. Seers were rare among the fae, and most went insane eventually. If sitting here with Kaysea and letting her hold my hand could help her figure out these visions, I'd sit here all day regardless of my troubles.

"Stop being so antsy," Kaysea murmured as I shifted around again.

"Sorry," I said. "If it turns out this is more bad news but doesn't directly relate to the current reason my world is blowing up, can you maybe not tell me? Lie to me about it for a few days?"

The mermaid opened one light green eye and gave me a chiding look before closing it again. I sighed and sat there in silence for a few minutes, trying not to move around or disturb her. My nose was itching, and I was trying very hard to ignore it when Kaysea rocked forward and gripped my hands more tightly. Her nails dug into my skin and drew blood as her eyes opened wide.

"Here we go." I stared into my friend's pure white eyes. We'd done this song and dance before, so I knew how it went.

Before long, the words poured out of her. "A change is coming carried on wings of gold," she said distantly, head cocked to the side in a very non-Kaysea move. "I see a cliff. You're there. Others are with you, but I can't see them. There's a girl. No, a young woman, I think. I can't make out her face. You're the only one I can see in full detail. She's crying and bleeding. I-I think she's dying. She stumbles back to the cliff, and you grab her before she tumbles over. You tell her, 'Some must fall in order to rise' . . . and then . . . a young boy runs out and grabs onto her. You pull the boy back and shove the woman off the cliff! SOME MUST FALL IN ORDER TO RISE."

Kaysea's voice boomed the final words in a tone that sounded nothing like her, before her eyes rolled back and she collapsed.

I gently pulled my hands away and stared at my friend. I

hated when she went into seer mode. It was always weird. "Great. That vision was a real joy," I muttered to myself.

The only young woman who had come into my life recently was Elisa. Could this vision be about her? No young boy, though. Kaysea said she couldn't see everyone's face in full detail, so maybe she'd mistaken Isabeau for a boy.

I chewed on my bottom lip. It would be strange for Kaysea to have a vision with them, though. I'd been part of her visions before, but the other players involved were always fae. It didn't make sense for Kaysea to have a vision about me and the vampire kids.

I let out a long-suffering breath. Kids weren't really my thing. The vampire kids were bad enough, and I didn't even know what I was going to do with them long-term. Another set of kids in my life was so not what I needed.

"That should be enough to appease her magic." Connor swooped his sister off the ground. "We'll be leaving now."

I didn't bother to argue as he turned and walked back into the sea with his sister. Kaysea and I could chat later about what the hell her vision could mean. It was clearly about something taking place in the future, which seemed to imply I would survive my current problem—but maybe not. Visions weren't set in stone. It was still possible I could die, and the vision would change.

As I continued to ponder the vision, Andrei finally stirred. He groaned and tried to sit up but settled for resting on his side. "What happened?" he croaked.

"You died." I couldn't keep my voice from cracking. The memory of Andrei's lifeless body was still too fresh.

He stared at me for a moment. "I'm going to need a little more info than that."

"Sebastian tracked me here. I don't know how exactly. He got to you when we weren't looking and . . ." I swallowed and looked away from him. "I couldn't stop him from hitting you with a hex. He took away your ability to breathe, and we couldn't do anything about it. I watched you die."

My voice strained at the last words. My chest tightened as my breathing, too, became shallow.

I'd been too slow. Once again, I'd been too fucking slow and weak and someone close to me had died because of it. I squeezed my eyes shut and took some deep breaths. My breathing evened out, but the tightness remained.

"But I'm here. I'm alive," Andrei said soothingly before pausing and then asked in somewhat of a panic, "I am alive, right? I'm not a ghost? Or a zombie?"

My eyes snapped open. "Zombie? Really? No, you're not a zombie. Or a ghost."

"Don't act like that's not a reasonable question!" He threw his hands up in the air. "You were talking to mermaids before a warlock showed up and hexed me! And then you brought me back to life! Asking if I'm a zombie is a valid fucking question!"

I shook my head. "You're just you. Not a zombie. Not a ghost. Just a werewolf. I . . . called in a favor to get your soul brought back."

"Yeah, I'm going to want a little more info on that 'favor,' but I can tell you're not going to tell me now." He lifted his shirt up a bit and sniffed it. "I want to shower and change clothes. I can smell that asshole on me."

"You can do that at my place. Magos has some clothes that will fit you." I walked over to Andrei and helped him to his feet.

He winced a bit as he stretched his arms out. "Actually, I'd prefer to go to my place. No offense to Magos, but I don't really like wearing clothes that smell like a vampire. Besides, I need to check in with my sister and the rest of the pack."

"Do I really need to repeat the fact that you *literally* just died? You're going straight back to my place." I gave him a hard stare and crossed my arms across my chest.

Andrei bared his teeth at me, and his eyes flashed yellow. "Look, I'm a little pissed and freaked out about having just died. You are still in danger. I'm not leaving you alone. And if you try to force me back to your apartment with the mood I'm currently in, it's not going to go well between me and Magos. Especially if he tries that vampire magic on me again. Do you really want us ripping into each other?"

He has a point. Jinx got up from where he'd been lying in the gazebo. He wasn't a fan of sand or water. He rarely came with me to the beach to visit Kaysea and clearly had only come today because of the seriousness of the situation. *Sebastian thinks he's dead. He has no reason to look for him further. The wolf can meet us at the apartment later. We have things to do.*

Right. Things to do. Witches to kill.

"You guys are talking, aren't you?" Andrei looked back and forth between me and Jinx. "Is the cat on my side?"

Call me a cat again, and you'll be picking up your entrails from where they lie scattered on the sand.

Yellow flashed in Andrei's eyes again, and he opened his mouth to retort, but I cut him off. "Fine. We'll go to your place."

I turned and walked back up the beach without waiting for a response. I'd get Andrei back to his place and get him to agree to stay there until he was ready to meet me at my apartment later. I couldn't have him running all over town in case one of Sebastian's cronies spotted him. I also couldn't have Andrei following me when I went to confront the witch.

My heart clenched in my chest. I might have been able to bring Andrei back to life, but there was still a very real chance I'd lose him by the end of this.

Chapter Twenty-One

BY THE TIME we made it back to the parking lot, Andrei was walking with his standard lupine grace. Werewolves always did bounce back fast. But I still found myself scanning his body, looking for any signs of injury. One moment I'd feel okay, and the next I'd be remembering what it was like to feel the soul absent from his body.

He'd parked his Bronco next to my bike, and I waited for him to pull out of the parking lot before I followed him.

Andrei had offered Jinx a ride in his car, which led to Jinx once again threatening to disembowel him before bounding off down the street. He blinked out of sight a few seconds later, which meant he'd switched to his fae form. Given how fast he could move in that form, he'd likely make it to the lodge long before us.

Fifteen minutes later, I parked in front of the lodge. When I pulled my hands off the handlebars, my fingers started to tremble.

"He's alive," I whispered to myself. The shaking didn't stop completely, but it eased a little. I swung my leg over the bike and clenched my hands into fists at my sides as I looked around for Jinx.

He was nowhere to be seen, so I paused and faced the woods to the side of the house. *I take it you're staying out here?*

Yes. If you make me wait long, I'll ensure you have bad luck for a week once this is over, he grumbled. I saw a flash of black fur high up in one of the trees.

I snorted. "Not sure my luck could get any worse."

Andrei didn't comment on the exchange from where he waited by the front door. He was clearly getting used to my mental conversations with Jinx. I followed him into the house, and we headed straight up the stairs to his apartment on the third floor.

"I'm going to take a shower. Make yourself at home." He walked into his bedroom, and the shower turned on a minute later.

I took a deep breath in and out as I unclenched my hands and stared at my trembling fingers.

This didn't seem real. Despite Andrei being alive and well, I could still feel what it felt like for him to die, and that grief wasn't letting go. My breathing soon turned ragged, and I clutched the back of a chair for support.

Distraction. I needed a distraction.

My feet carried me over to the small kitchen, and I set about making coffee. What I really wanted was to down an entire bottle of whiskey, but that wasn't a good idea right now. Caffeine would have to do instead.

As soon as Andrei was out of the shower, I'd get him to agree to stay here while he got things straightened out with the pack and then head straight to my place. Hopefully he'd learned his lesson about following me after the events at the beach.

I had just taken a sip of coffee when Andrei stepped out of the bedroom. His damp hair was tousled and still dripping a little bit of water. A towel hung around his hips. "So, what's next?" he asked.

I sucked in a breath, and it caught in my throat. The coffee cup trembled in my hands as I set it down on the counter.

Before I could think, I'd moved in front of him and placed my hands on his chest. A strong heartbeat pulsed beneath my fingertips, and I closed my eyes. A soft sigh slipped out of my lips. I opened my mouth slightly and inhaled his scent.

Alive. He was alive.

My eyes flew open and met his stare. Flecks of yellow golden in the hazel.

"I thought I lost you," I breathed. "I did lose you."

"But you brought me back." Large, warm hands closed over mine.

I should go. He was safe here. Sebastian thought he was dead. I had a witch to track down, plus I needed to come up with a plan for dealing with the Circle, assuming they really did plan on meeting with me.

I might die tonight. I had no guarantees of coming out of this alive.

My hands trembled beneath his. Slowly, he lifted them off his chest and kissed the back of my fingers. I shuddered as his warm lips touched my skin and his eyes flashed solid yellow before bleeding back to hazel. I saw the same need burning in them that I felt.

We moved at the same time, our lips crashing against each other's. Andrei nipped my bottom lip before slipping his tongue inside my mouth. I groaned at the taste of him.

Rough hands ran down my back before cupping my butt and pulling me up. I wrapped my legs around his waist, and he took a few steps forward until my back was against the wall. He tore his lips from mine and kissed my neck.

One of his hands worked its way up my shirt, and he

teased my nipple with his fingers. I groaned and ground into him harder.

Alive, the word chanted over and over in my mind.

"Clothes," I breathed. "Too many clothes."

Andrei nipped my neck and stepped back. I unwrapped my legs and dropped them to the floor, then unstrapped my weapons, along with my silver bracers. The shirt and bra went next. I tried kicking off my lace-up combat boots but had to kneel and unlace them first.

Standing, I ran my hand up Andrei's leg and the front of the towel, feeling the hard length of him. He groaned and leaned into me.

I wrapped my arms around him, pulling him tightly against me. My breasts pressed against his chest, and I kissed him harder. His mouth opened, and my tongue darted in, tasting him. Fuck. I'd never get over how delicious he tasted.

His hands quickly undid my jeans, and he broke our kiss to pull them off while I snatched away his towel. He looked me up and down hungrily, and I returned the look. We crashed back into each other, and he lifted me up on him. My legs wrapped around him once more as he walked us into his bedroom.

He lay me on his bed and kissed my neck, working his way down to my breasts. He kissed and sucked, and I gripped his hair with a moan. He gave my left nipple one final kiss before moving down further to kiss and lick the inside of my thighs.

"Fuck," I swore. I wanted him now.

He seemed to sense my impatience but only teased me more as he slowly kissed and licked his way up my thigh before doing the same on the other side.

"Andrei," I hissed in warning.

He chuckled, his warm breath tickling my thighs. Before I could swear at him more, his tongue ran straight up my center. My hips thrusted up as I almost came right then and there—I was wound so tightly. He wrapped his arms under my thighs and gripped me hard as his tongue drove deeper into my pussy.

"Yes!" I breathed as I arched my back, feeling the pressure build and build. When his fingers flicked over my clit, I came completely undone and screamed as an orgasm ripped through me.

I fell back on the bed, my body still trembling in pleasure as Andrei moved over me. He sucked a nipple into his mouth while he pinched the other one hard. Another moan slipped out of me, and he laughed before saying in a satisfied voice, "You taste fucking delicious, kitty cat."

He kissed me deeply, and I groaned into his mouth, the taste of myself on his lips making me even hotter.

I reached down and stroked his hard length, smiling as he stiffened above me and growled. When I raised my hips up in demand, he trailed the tip of his cock against my entrance before pulling it away.

A growl rumbled out of my throat as my fingers dug into his back. He laughed huskily in my ear.

"So impatient."

In response, I sank my claws into his flesh until I was sure I drew blood. He groaned and in one move thrusted inside me.

"Fuck yes!" I screamed as his cock filled every inch of me, only to hiss at him a second later when he pulled out.

A wicked grin spread across his lips as he slowly pushed back in. My patience finally wore out, and I jerked my hips up and twisted until I had him pinned beneath me. I slammed down, enjoying the feeling from this angle.

"Nemain," Andrei groaned.

I smiled wickedly at him as I pulled his hands off my hips and pinned them above his head.

"You were taking too long," I said silkily as I shifted my hips a little. His eyes flickered back and forth between yellow and hazel, and it sent a thrill up my spine. "This is the price you pay for not giving me what I wanted."

He raised his head and languidly licked the slope of my breast before sucking a nipple into his mouth. My body went taut, and I arched my back to give him better access. He smiled against my skin before releasing me.

"I think I'm okay with this position," he said.

The raspy quality to his voice was hot as hell, and it fucking undid me. My hips thrust forward, and I set a fast and brutal pace as I rode him. He tore his hands free, and I was too far gone to care as one gripped my hip and the other flicked my clit.

I threw my head back and screamed, my pace faltered as pleasure rippled through me. Andrei gave me a few seconds to enjoy it before he flipped me back over and raised my legs over his shoulders.

With one thrust, he slid back inside me, and I moaned as his thrusts became harder and more frantic. I'd barely recovered from the last orgasm as another shattered what remained of my mind.

"Fuck!" Andrei barked as he climaxed after me.

We both lay there panting, and I enjoyed the feeling of Andrei draped over me. The sensation of his skin against mine and his heart beating in his chest. I savored all of it.

A large part of me wanted to stay in the bed and just ignore the rest of the world. But that wasn't how life worked. Sebastian was coming for me. The Circle was likely coming for me. It was time for me to deal with reality so I could protect myself and everyone I cared about.

Plus, Jinx only had so much patience, and if I didn't get my ass outside soon, he'd make me pay for it.

Andrei shifted until he was on his side and peered down at me. "What's the difference between warlocks and witches?"

"Are you serious right now?" I couldn't help but smile at

him even as I dug my head further into the pillow. "What even brought that question on?"

"I figure this is a rare moment when I have your undivided attention and you're probably not quite back on point yet, so I might as well take advantage of it." He grinned at me, and I just shook my head ruefully. "Never really gave them much thought until I was killed by one."

His tone was light, but I still stiffened at his words.

He leaned down and kissed me deeply before whispering across my lips, "I'm here. I'm fine."

I jerked my head in a nod and let him pull me a little closer. His fingers traced patterns on my stomach, and I allowed myself to enjoy the contact. Just a few more minutes and then I'd get up.

"Are witches always female and warlocks always male?" Andrei asked, clearly not willing to let this topic drop.

"No." I shook my head and rearranged myself until my head was resting in the crook of his arm, and I stared up at the ceiling. I pursed my lips as I tried to think of the easiest way to explain.

"You and I both have innate magical abilities. We can both shift into our animal forms and have some other magic that is associated with shifters. Like our ability to heal. But neither of us can cast a spell because we're limited in our ability to interact with the magic around us. We can't take the magic that is there and turn it into something else, like a ward or protection charm. With me so far?"

Andrei nodded, so I continued.

"Witches and warlocks can pull magic from their surroundings and use it for spells. How they interact with magic, though, is quite different." I paused again, trying to think of the right words so as not to confuse him more.

I didn't even remember the last time I'd had to explain magic to someone, and I was probably screwing this up.

"Witches are all about balance," I said slowly. "Witchcraft is unique and can be quite powerful, but it requires a lot from the practitioner. Witch covens guard their grimoires with their lives, and some of their spells are never written down and only shared verbally within the coven. The first humans to practice magic were witches. Some of them rebelled from the witches' way of doing things and called themselves warlocks."

"So, witches good. Warlocks bad. Got it." Andrei nodded. "Given it was a warlock who killed me, I'm good with that."

A frown twisted my mouth, and I turned my head slightly to face him. "I did a poor job of explaining it. And we don't have time for me to get into the whole history of witches and warlocks. But believe me when I say neither of them are good."

"You said witches were all about balance." Andrei raised an eyebrow at me. "That sounds like a good guy thing."

"Full disclosure." I sank back into the bed and returned my gaze up to the ceiling. "I hate them both. But my brother regularly points out to me that I might be unfair in my reasoning, so I'll give you a more complete answer. In theory,"—my voice dripped with sarcasm—"either could be good or bad. Morality is determined by the individual, not how they practice magic."

"Okay," he drew out the word, "but the warlocks are after you, and witches practice magic in a balanced way. Still not seeing why warlocks aren't bad and witches aren't good."

I refrained from bringing up that a certain witch was very much working with the warlocks. I needed to explain enough so Andrei wouldn't think all witches were the good guys.

"You're really hung up on this balance thing," I said as I furrowed my brows. This really wasn't my expertise when it came to explaining things. "Here's an example. Let's say a witch wanted to cast a spell that would extend her life. Keep her young for another few centuries. She would need to balance the scales. Any guesses on what would be required to balance out extending a human lifespan by several centuries?"

Andrei thought about it for a moment and narrowed his eyes at me. "You mean human sacrifice?"

"Bingo." I pointed my finger at him. "They could go about it in different ways. They could sacrifice a group of adults. Centuries ago, it was common practice for a witch to sacrifice a small town for a spell like this. They'd either travel to the town or use a local one and then move. Something like that would draw attention. If they wanted to avoid traveling, they could use children instead. The younger the better. Then they'd only need two or three to complete the spell."

"You're serious." Horror and disbelief flickered in his hazel eyes.

"There's a reason humans have so many tales cautioning children to avoid the witch in the woods." I gave him a dark look.

During my time hunting witches, I'd come across the aftermath of more than one dark ritual. The sight had haunted my dreams for years, and even Jinx had been freaked out.

"How would the warlocks do it?"

"They're not above human sacrifice either," I said with a shrug as I shoved the wicked memories of those human sacrifices aside. "But they also like to collect objects of power and use those in their spells. The witches don't believe in using objects like that because they think it upsets the balance. Causes a lot of strife between the two factions."

I gave Andrei a quick kiss and rolled out of bed to shower before he could hit me with more questions. I'd delayed long enough and needed to get a move on.

Just as the hot water hit my face, I heard Andrei enter the bathroom.

"The fae are more powerful than warlocks, right?"

I peeked around the shower curtain. "Seriously? I can't even shower in peace?"

He shrugged. "Just trying to catch up."

I scoffed and let the curtain fall back in place. "Generally, yes. Power varies among the individual."

"Then why didn't your friends help more at the beach?"

I paused, scrubbing myself with the minty-smelling soap. "Kaysea's magic isn't combat magic. She can be dangerous as hell with her water magic, don't get me wrong. But she's not trained to be a fighter. With Sebastian so far from the water, there wasn't much she could do."

"What about the mean one?"

"Connor?" I snorted. "He only cares about protecting Kaysea. He would have happily watched Sebastian slaughter the rest of us."

I waited for another question, but instead Andrei responded, "I don't like him."

I laughed. "Join the club."

Turning the water off, I pulled back the curtain and saw Andrei standing with a towel outstretched. I smiled and stepped out of the shower. He wrapped the towel around me and kissed me. I leaned into him and returned the kiss. In an instant, the towel was on the floor, and he picked me up. I wrapped my legs around his waist and slipped my tongue in his mouth.

A second later, the rod holding the shower curtain crashed to the floor and knocked over the soap and shampoo bottles on the way down.

Andrei glanced at where it landed on the floor. "That was weird."

"No." I sighed and unwrapped my legs from his waist. He set me down on the floor but kept an arm around me. "That was Jinx."

"He's moving stuff around from outside?" Andrei frowned

and looked past me at one of the windows facing the front of the lodge.

"Not exactly." I grabbed the towel off the floor and finished drying myself off. "Grimalkin possess a lot of magic. But they can also cause bad luck. This was a warning that he was tired of waiting. I need to go before he causes all the plumbing in this place to fail." I sighed and headed into the bedroom to collect my clothes.

"Give me fifteen minutes to shower and check in with Stela and I'll come with you." Andrei grabbed clean clothes from a dresser.

I shook my head. "Werewolves aren't welcome where I'm going."

"Is this like the bar from the other night?"

"Something like that," I lied.

Andrei's eyes flashed yellow for a second. His wolf knew I was lying, but his human side hadn't quite caught on.

I kept my face carefully blank. "Can you find your way back to my apartment?"

He studied me for another moment. "Yes."

"Good. Promise me you'll stay here to speak with your pack before heading to my apartment. I'll head back there once I'm done taking care of a few things and fill you and Magos in. Then we can plan for tonight. Promise me, Andrei."

"All right. But don't even think of sidelining me tonight. Whatever happens, I'm going." The determination in his eyes meant there was no way of convincing him otherwise. Just another problem for me to deal with later.

"Of course. I'll see you back at the apartment." I left before Andrei started paying attention to what his wolf side was trying to tell him.

That I was lying.

Chapter Twenty-Two

TEN MINUTES later I was parked on a dirt road just outside of town. Jinx appeared by my side, and we jogged up the road in silence, giant trees looming on either side of us.

I was still getting used to the forest in this area. I'd never lived near a temperate rainforest before, and I was pretty sure the fae had left some things behind that caused the trees in this area to grow even taller than they naturally would.

After about a quarter mile, a driveway appeared on the left. We followed the driveway around a bend that revealed a cottage in a small clearing. Spruce and hemlock trees were scattered all around it, making it feel like it was a part of the woods. Jinx and I paused as we studied the area.

"This has to be it. You feel anything?" I inhaled deeply but couldn't smell anything beyond the surrounding forest.

Just the ward around the cottage.

"Let's head around back."

We moved quietly through the trees to the back of the cottage. A large garden filled the space full of flowers and herbs. A witch's garden. It looked peaceful and welcoming. Stela probably would have loved it. But Jolie had claimed to have a place in Seattle, so she always stayed at the werewolf lodge when she was "in town."

Jinx walked up to the garden and paused. He had shifted to his fae form on the way over here. His jet-black coat that seemed to swallow the light was a stark contrast to the bright and colorful garden. I stepped next to him and reached my hand out to feel the ward in front of me.

"Not bad. She's clearly packing some power. Can you bring it down?"

Jinx sat back on his haunches. *I could. But you should do it as practice.*

I shot him an annoyed look, which he ignored. "Fine," I muttered.

My skin tingled as I pushed against the ward, I could feel its firm resistance beneath my fingers even though I couldn't see it. Letting my magic completely loose was relatively easy once I unraveled the mental chains around it. But focusing it to accomplish specific tasks like this was far more challenging.

My jaw clenched as my magic tried to surge out, but I held it back and directed a small amount of it directly to the ward in front of me.

Blue fire flowed out of my hand so light it looked almost translucent in the sunlight. I pushed it towards the part of the ward my fingers were pressed against, and my magic took a small nibble before rearing back like a snake and diving into it. Brow furrowed, I let my magic devour the ward slowly, so it didn't explode and cause a scene.

Bit by bit, the ward weakened, and its magic poured into me until it was gone. As if it had never existed.

You're getting better at that. Jinx studied the air where the ward used to be.

"Yeah, I still don't know what to do with the magic I consume, though. I can feel it moving around inside me, and it just sort of merges with the rest of it."

I shrugged and rubbed my hands together to try to get rid of the tingling sensation. I'd attempted over the years to figure out what to do with the magic I'd consumed, but so far it was a tingling sensation that lasted for a few minutes to an hour depending on how much magic I absorbed. It was annoying more than anything.

"Stay out of sight, okay?" I walked up the stone path to the back door. I didn't anticipate having any problems dealing with the witch. But Jinx and I had long ago established this system of him glamouring himself invisible when we entered hostile situations. It was always nice to keep your backup a surprise to your enemy.

The doorknob turned under my hand. I wasn't surprised it was unlocked since most of us didn't bother physically locking doors when we had wards in place. It's not like a physical lock would keep any of us out anyway.

On silent feet, I stepped through the threshold into a quaint kitchen. Empty. Clippings of lavender hung across one wall. Apparently, Sebastian had passed on his tendency of using lavender in potions to his supposed niece. I recognized other herbs commonly used in witchcraft. Interestingly, she still chose to walk the path of a witch instead of becoming a warlock like her uncle.

The sound of movement from the next room drew my attention. I moved quietly and quickly towards where it came from. Sunlight poured through a large window onto a brown couch and a coffee table. Jolie stood between the couch and table, her eyes wide in alarm. Her curly red hair was in a messy bun on top of her head, and she wore casual clothes instead of the pretty dresses she usually wore around Stela. A grimoire and knitted blanket had been hastily cast aside on the couch.

"How did you get past my ward?" Magic pulsed from her. "What did you do to my ward?" Her brows shot up and she moved back a step, bumping into the couch.

"Well, I'm glad you're not going to feign ignorance or try and spin some story about how 'you're a good witch who was just too scared to tell the truth.' I am surprised your opening question wasn't about how I found you, though."

She still looked alarmed, but annoyance flickered across her delicate features. "You're here now, so what does it matter how you found me?" she snapped.

"Wow, you're never this testy around Stela. Must have been hard for you to act all sweet and innocent these last few months." I glanced at the grimoire on the couch. "Why would a witch work for a warlock? You do know what they did to your ancestors, right?"

"My ancestors were idiots," she sneered. "They spent all that time and energy hunting down warlocks when they should have been hunting down *your* kind."

"Like the warlocks hunted down my kind?" A chill crept into my voice.

She didn't answer, but she held my stare, and I knew she agreed with them. I narrowed my eyes at her. She was being awfully cocky to someone who had broken into her home. A glint of green caught my attention, and I gave the ring on her left middle finger a quick glance.

A protection amulet. I recognized it immediately as Sebastian's work. He must have given it to her recently or she took it off whenever she was around me so I wouldn't recognize it. My lips curved into a cruel smile. She thought it would protect her from me.

"If you despise your ancestors so much, why still practice witchcraft?" I tilted my head, actually a little curious about the answer. "Why not become a warlock?"

"Plenty of witches from my generation and older ones agree with the Circle but still choose to practice witchcraft." She swiped a wayward red curl behind her ear. "My uncle never had a problem with it. In fact, he encouraged me to remain a witch."

"Is Sebastian really your uncle?" He'd never mentioned any family when we'd been together, and I tried to ignore how much it hurt that I had bought all his lies. I hated him now, but I had loved him then.

"Yes. My mother died shortly after I was born, and he saw to it that I was raised well. My uncle is a brilliant man, and you were an idiot to leave him." She straightened, and a haughty expression spread over her face. "He was always too good for you."

I laughed softly. "Sure. Let's go with that." I made a show of looking around. "Doesn't look like your precious uncle is around to protect you."

"You can't kill me. You care about Andrei. And you know how important his sister is to him. And she's in love with me," Jolie said confidently. I didn't miss that she twisted the ring on her finger.

"Why her? You two were dating before I met Andrei. So you didn't start dating her just to get to me."

Jolie shrugged. "Had to do something to pass the time. Besides, she's not exactly hard on the eyes. Great in bed. She's very conflicted about being a werewolf, which can get tiresome to listen to."

Distaste flashed across her delicate features, and I had to force myself to stay still and let her keep talking. I wanted more answers, but I'd make her pay for using Stela.

She continued, "You starting to date Andrei was just a lucky coincidence. Truth be told, I'm glad this is coming to an end. I've had my fun with her, and it's time to move on."

"Sounds like I'll be doing Stela a favor in getting you out of her life," I said flatly.

"She'll never believe you. And putting Andrei in a position to choose between you and his sister won't go well." Jolie paused and gave me a calculating look. "It's pretty obvious how much you like Andrei. Bad move for someone in your position to go for someone like that. He's a liability."

"I do care about Andrei," I agreed. "Hell, if we're being honest, I'm pretty sure I'm falling in love with him. But I have survived centuries by being ruthless and violent. I'm hardly going to go soft and change who I am over some guy I've known for only a few months. Regardless of how I feel about him." I stretched out my hand, and a ripple shimmered in the air a few inches in front of my hand.

Jolie looked at the opening gateway. I had to give the witch credit; her expression was calm and her voice steady as she spoke.

"Going to use that fancy magic of yours to throw me into one of the devourer realms and leave me to die? Sebastian said that was a favorite trick of yours. You know, when you were killing any witch he told you to kill? Does Andrei know how much blood stains your hands? I bet he has no idea. Poor, sweet, innocent Andrei," she crooned.

I tried my best to keep my expression neutral and not let her know she'd scored a hit with her words. "He is quite innocent, isn't he? I'm not really sure what I'm going to do about that." I kept my tone even and continued, "But fortunately for him, I'm ruthless enough for the both of us."

My magic lashed out and ripped through the power of the protection amulet, swallowing it down in one gulp. It was a minor drop in the bucket compared to what I'd gotten from devouring the ward minutes ago. One of my throwing daggers was flying through the air a second later. It sank into Jolie's left shoulder, and she screamed.

"Bitch!" she spat out as she grabbed the knife and tore it from her shoulder. She stared in shock at the knife and then at the ring on her finger. My magic hummed in satisfaction at her confusion.

For the first time since my arrival, genuine fear shone in her eyes. A merciless laugh rumbled out of me as she shakily held the knife between her fingers. I studied her for another minute before pulling my hand back from the gateway I'd been opening. It snapped shut in an instant.

"You're right. Let's try something else. A friend has been pushing me to practice some of my other magic." I raised my fingers towards the ceiling. The light blue flame erupted around my hand and spread down my arm.

Jolie gasped, her expression wide in absolute terror. I flung my hand out towards the coffee table in front of her, exploding it into hundreds of frozen pieces. She screamed and leaped to the side away from the couch, dropping the knife in the process. She scrambled back until she was against the wall. Her only way out of the room required her to get past me into the kitchen or scramble over the wreckage of the coffee table to a hallway that I was guessing led to the bedroom.

"Your uncle didn't know about this." A savage grin played across my lips as I twisted my hand around and watched the flames dance. "He had his secrets, and I had mine. I call it cold fire. Not the best name, I know, but I was a kid and it just sort of stuck. It's accurate enough, though. Looks like fire. And it does leave ash behind. But it's quite cold and as you can see"— I gestured at what remained of the broken coffee table—"it tends to leave frost behind as well. The frost will last for a while too. Weird, right?"

Jolie remained plastered against the wall and said nothing. She gaped at me as she looked at me like I was the monster from her childhood nightmares come to life.

"I've never encountered another soul who has this magic. And I've traveled to plenty of realms."

The terrified witch whimpered as I moved towards her, eyes frantically looking around for a way out. I stopped in front of her and stroked a finger down her cheek. She jerked her head away.

"That's not the best part, though."

The flames reached out and licked Jolie's cheek. She screamed as my magic tore into hers. My power surged as it feasted. I pulled back after a few seconds.

She collapsed to the floor, sobbing. "That's devourer magic . . . What the fuck are you?"

I made a tutting noise and shook my finger at her. "Were you not paying attention when I said I had no idea? I've been to devourer realms. I've seen all sorts of devourers, and none of them have magic like mine. I have no idea what I am," I replied coldly. "Can't ask my parents more about it since the warlocks you respect so much had them burned at the stake."

"I can give you information about the warlocks!" Jolie looked up at me as tears ran down her cheeks. "My uncle has told me all kinds of things about the other warlocks."

"That's the second time someone has promised to betray their own to get me information. You guys certainly aren't big on loyalty," I said in mock disappointment. "But I don't believe you anymore than I believed him." I raised my hand towards her. "Plus, I don't like you. Sebastian likely would have found me at some point. Or the Circle would have. But that doesn't change that you sold me out this time around. My brother was always so forgiving of the witches. I was always more the suffer not a witch to live type."

Blue flame shot from hand and covered the witch, and she screamed. Her magic rushed into me as the flames devoured her, and I closed my eyes as it settled. After a few moments, I opened my eyes and looked at the floor where the witch had died. Only ash and frost remained.

I felt no regret about killing her. Well, not entirely true. I felt regret that I'd had to kill her so quickly. Given more time, I could have drawn out her death. She was a loyal supporter of Sebastian, and her death would weaken his position.

Plus, it bothered me that she'd used Stela so callously. Not that I was particularly close to the werewolf; I liked her well enough and being Andrei's sister, I felt a certain need to protect her. But I didn't lie to myself. Finding out just how much Sebastian had lied to me during our relationship pissed me off, and what Jolie did was too fucking similar.

Jinx dropped his glamour and padded over to the wreckage of the table. *I'm surprised you didn't take out most of the living room with that move.*

"So am I, to be honest."

He let out a raspy laugh.

"Can you glamour our scents? The wolves don't know about this place, but just in case, I don't want them finding it and knowing we were here."

Andrei's sister isn't going to let the disappearance of her lover go. She'll search for her. And she'll find this place eventually. What will you do when she starts digging? What are you going to tell Andrei?

"The truth," I said softly. "I won't lie to him. Not about this."

He won't understand.

I swallowed. "I am who I am. And it is what it is. He'll either accept that or he won't."

Chapter Twenty-Three

I WALKED BACK through the kitchen and out the door into the sunny garden. It would take Jinx a few minutes to set the glamour.

Raising my face towards the sun, I closed my eyes. My magic was calm after enjoying a meal, and the warmth from the sun felt nice against my skin. The moments after I let my magic out of its cage were something I treasured. The struggle of keeping it contained and hidden had weighed on me my entire life. Soon, I'd have to lock it away again, but for now I could enjoy this sensation of feeling complete.

The witch's words floated back to me, "*Does Andrei know how much blood stains your hands?*"

I'd never allowed myself to feel guilt or shame for what I'd done in the centuries after my parents had been murdered.

Cian was right. I did view things in a black and white way when it came to witches and warlocks. I'd never really regretted it. But knowing that Sebastian had been pulling my strings and using me as his own personal witch finder and killer made me feel unsettled.

I had believed Sebastian when he had told me all the

witches and warlocks we targeted had been responsible for the deaths of other nonhumans. Had been responsible for stirring up the hatred that led to so many deaths. And maybe some of them had. But maybe some of them had been completely innocent. And I'd killed them anyway.

My stomach churned slightly, and I started to take some deep breaths. It helped, and I took in another deep breath and then froze when *his* scent hit my tongue. My eyes snapped open, and I looked to my right.

Standing in the shade of a large pine tree was Mikhail. He stood with his hands clasped in front of him and a patient look on that exquisite face.

"It's a bit early for your bullshit, don't you think?" I raised my hand, letting my fingers play in the sunshine. "I'm guessing your ability to walk in the sun is related to whatever magic you inherited from your father? Since your mother's magic was similar to Magos's."

Mikhail pushed off the tree and walked into the sunshine until he stood ten feet away from me. At first glance, he didn't look anything like Magos. His brown skin was several shades lighter. They both had black hair, but Mikhail's barely had any curl to it. Magos kept his head practically shaved, but I knew his hair had a thicker, coarser texture to it and was curly. I tried to look for any physical resemblance and just didn't see it. But then again, most people would never guess Cian was my brother; looks could be deceiving.

"I see Magos filled you in on our family history." Mikhail gave me a sly smile.

My magic drifted towards him almost lazily. I tried to pull it back, but it ignored me and instead wrapped around Mikhail like it was embracing him. What. The. Hell.

At least I managed to keep the blue flames from manifesting, so Mikhail was completely unaware of my magic feeling him up. I was silently grateful that vampires didn't have the ability to see or sense magic. With one strong tug, my magic reluctantly pulled back and curled up inside my chest.

"He did," I answered him, barely managing to keep my voice even after being freaked out by whatever the hell was going on with my magic.

It'd never reacted to anyone like that before. It usually just wanted to destroy and consume magic.

He tilted his head with a predatory awareness. "You killed the witch." It wasn't a question.

"She's the reason they found us. Her death was necessary," I said flatly.

"I don't disagree. Simply surprised you came to that conclusion and followed through. Based on the screaming, I'm guessing it wasn't a pleasant death."

"Death is rarely pleasant."

"True enough. Still, you could have killed her quickly. Witches don't have our healing. A snap of the neck would have sufficed. But you made her suffer." He paused and looked at me carefully, as if searching for something. "Magos understands ruthlessness and the occasional cruelty when it comes to protecting those he loves. But will that wolf you run around with understand why you tortured and killed his sister's girlfriend? Will he look at you the same way, I wonder?"

"That is none of your concern." My nostrils flared. I added Mikhail's perceptiveness to the growing list of things I didn't like about him. "Why are you here?"

He shifted slightly, and a flash of discomfort appeared on his face before he settled back into his pleasant mask. "Why did you aid the vampire children?" he asked.

It took my mind a second to process the change in topic. "What makes you think I did?" I asked lightly and gave him a bored look as I clasped my hands in front of me, mirroring his position.

"They have disappeared. I caught their scent in an alley

along with yours. You walked out of that alley. They did not." His weight shifted ever so slightly as the fingers of one hand moved further into the sleeve of the other. "Quite a risk to use your magic to help some vampire kids you don't even know. They could betray you. Or someone could have seen what you did. So, I ask again. Why did you help them?" Those dark bluish eyes looked at me curiously.

I shrugged one shoulder, my fingers brushing against the release for the dagger tucked away in my silver bracer on my forearm. "I wouldn't expect the notorious assassin of the Vampire Council to understand."

Before he could respond, I threw my dagger at him and slid to the side on liquid joints. The dagger he'd thrown at my face missed by less than an inch. He'd moved a fraction too slow, so my dagger had sunk into his shoulder. I'd been aiming for his heart. Even by vampire standards, he was fast.

As soon as I'd released my dagger, I'd pulled my swords free and attacked. Mikhail leapt back, pulling a short sword from his back and a long dagger from a sheath on his thigh. He parried my strike for his side and thrusted the dagger at a downward angle, aiming for my inner thigh. I blocked the dagger with my other sword, and Mikhail twisted the blade so that the ornate handle caught my sword and yanked it to the side.

Rather than get pulled off balance, I released the sword, letting it and the dagger tumble to the ground.

Mikhail didn't give me a second to recover. Stepping forward, he swiped his blade across my chest. I parried and snapped my leg up in a kick. He blocked my kick but left his other side open. I swung my sword, and it bit into his side. Without a pause, he hammered a punch to my jaw.

I staggered back a few feet and brought my sword up just in time to block his blow to my chest. We traded blows for another minute, both of us scoring minor hits but neither gaining the upper hand. I had no doubt he was holding back to see how good I was and what Magos had taught me. I backed up a few spaces, and mist swirled around him.

I trusted my instincts as he disappeared and reappeared a moment later in front of me. Both of us had our swords pressed against each other's throat. Mikhail smiled and leaned forward, pushing himself onto my blade. Blood welled where my sword bit into his neck. My heart sped up, and the pull I'd felt towards him that night in the forest when the vampires had attacked flared to life again. I needed to get the hell away from Mikhail and figure out what the hell this was and how to make it stop.

"Not bad. I was wondering if you'd make the first move. You're really quite violent," he purred.

"What do you want, Mikhail?" I bit out.

He studied me for another second and pulled his blade away from my neck, taking a step back. "Actually, I came to apologize for my behavior last night. My uncle and I have walked different paths, but that doesn't mean I don't care about him. He is the only family I have left. I acted last night out of frustration and fear for his safety. You are not a safe person to be around and definitely not to be friends with."

"The world isn't a safe place." I gave him a flat stare. "And last I checked, you weren't there when Magos was sitting on that rock waiting for the sun to rise all those centuries ago. So you don't get to question our friendship or my devotion to him."

"You don't know anything about me or my history with Magos," Mikhail said, his voice icy.

"I know enough," I retorted. "You poured yourself into the war with the werewolves. But I know from experience that revenge only gets you so far. After a while, it just becomes meaningless. And now you don't even have that. The war is over. You don't have any interest in working for the Council anymore, but you don't know anything else. So you volunteered to track down a bunch of teen vampires so you could do what? Check in with Magos and hope he could set you straight? Or were you just desperate to pretend like you still mattered? Former grand assassin and war hero, now errand boy for the Council."

The words had barely left my mouth before my back was against a tree with Mikhail's blade once again at my throat.

"Careful," he hissed.

I looked into those twilight eyes and saw rage. Despair. And possibly a touch of insanity.

Probably shouldn't have baited him like that.

My magic rumbled to life, but I got the distinct impression that it wanted to curl around Mikhail again instead of defending me. *Traitor*, I growled at it as I shoved it back down.

"I admit I find myself at a bit of a crossroads these days. But you and I are not friends," he said in a silky-smooth voice that made me shiver for reasons I refused to think about. "You don't get to speak to me that way. The only reason I don't cut your tongue from your mouth is because Magos would take offense to that."

"I accept your apology for being an asshole last night." I ignored the blade at my throat. "Now get the fuck off me so I can continue going about my day trying to figure out a way to save myself and Magos from the assholes *you* work for."

Mikhail pulled the blade away quickly but made sure to slice my throat a little. Couldn't really blame him for that. I remained against the tree and watched him warily as he took a couple of steps back and shoved the sword into its sheath.

"Why don't you have a sword you can summon from the mist like Magos?" I asked without really thinking. "You have his ability to travel in the mist. Why not the sword?"

"Is it the feline in you that makes you so curious?"

"Is it the asshole in you that makes you refuse to answer any questions?"

Can we move this along? Jinx appeared between us.

Mikhail tried to hide it, but he flinched slightly. He had no idea Jinx was there. My lips curved into a small smile.

"Stay out of my head, fae," Mikhail growled softly and glanced at me. "I've been told to pass on a message. The Council figured I had the best chance of speaking to you without being killed on sight. You are to come to the woods tonight at midnight. Alone. The Circle will be waiting for you in the clearing of the fae tree. You are guaranteed safe passage."

I stared at him incredulously. "And why the hell would I trust them? Or want to make a deal with them, for that matter? We could split town again and go somewhere they can't find us."

"True. You and Magos could run." Mikhail nodded. "Perhaps you could convince your werewolf lover to go with you, as well. But I am not the only assassin on the Council these days, and the warlocks have their own methods. This is no longer just Sebastian after you. The Warlock's Circle and the Vampire Council are working together. You are being hunted by all warlocks. By all vampires. You can't hide in the shadows any longer. If they can't find you, they will target your friends and family. All of you can't run forever."

I grimaced at his words. At the truth in them. He was echoing my thoughts, and I hated him for it.

They might know where my brother was, but they were in for a shock if they thought he would be easy to capture. My brother wasn't a pushover. And he was in his element in the death realm. Not to mention, they had no idea my brother's lover was Hades.

Still . . . if something happened to my brother because of

me, I'd never forgive myself. "And you? Would you come after us if the Council ordered you to?"

He looked at me for a long moment, and I wasn't sure he would answer. "The Council would never give me that order because they would not trust me to follow through with it." Not exactly the answer to my question but close enough.

"All right. Message delivered." I raised my hand and made a shooing motion. "You can leave now."

Mikhail nodded and mist gathered around him.

"Wait!" The word slipped from my lips before I could stop myself. The despair I'd seen in his eyes earlier reminded me so much of the first time I'd met Magos, I couldn't let it go. The mist swirling around Mikhail seemed to pause.

I took a few steps forward, closing the distance between us. "I know what it's like to lose everything. At first you have the rage and sorrow to latch onto, and that pushes you forward. But eventually that fades, and you're just left with this emptiness. And part of you misses the misery of grief because at least that was something." I stumbled through the words and took a quick breath. "You'll never forget the loss and you shouldn't. But you can let it coexist with who you become after it. We get to heal and move on," I said softly but firmly.

Mikhail looked at me for another moment. A storm raged in his dark eyes, and the mist swirled around him once more before he vanished.

I stood silently in the garden for a long moment. Something told me that Mikhail was going to be a complication in my life going forward. I'd need to get a grip on my magic and whatever this weird pull was between us. I could also accept that I had loved every second of that fight between us, and when Mikhail had me pinned with that blade against my throat, it wasn't fear I'd been feeling.

Fuck. I squeezed my eyes shut. My list of problems to solve was growing faster than I could resolve them.

What you said to that vampire applies to you too, you know.

I opened my eyes and turned my head to glance up at Jinx, still sitting in the tree.

"I know," I said softly. "I didn't mean to say all that, but the way he looked . . ." The hollowness in those twilight eyes flashed in my mind again. "The words just came out, and I felt the truth in them. Only took me a few centuries to learn how to process grief and loss." I gave Jinx a wry smile.

Well, your brother always was the smart one.

I flipped him off and headed back to my bike. If I was going to try and take my own advice and truly move on, I needed to make sure I survived the next twenty-four hours and remained free.

A plan started to come together in my head. It was a crazy idea. And it basically went against everything I'd been doing my entire life.

But Mikhail was right. I'd been hiding in the shadows, and that clearly wasn't working.

Where are we heading now? Jinx asked.

"Back to The Inferno. I've got a plan, but it requires Pele's cooperation."

I'm not going to like this plan, am I?

"No." I grinned at him. "You're really not."

Chapter Twenty-Four

Jɪɴx and I walked through the doors of The Inferno less than ten minutes later. I made him drop his glamour as soon as we entered. The first time he'd come with me to the bar, he hadn't dropped his glamour and almost got stepped on by a young daemon.

That led to me getting in a drunken brawl with the daemon. And all of his friends.

For some reason, some lokis stepped in and started fighting with everyone, which got more of the bar involved. By the end of the fight, I was nursing a swollen lip and my ribs hurt like hell.

Jinx and the lokis had left the fight early and were watching it unfold from a table across the bar. I'd been pissed. Jinx had been amused.

I told him I was never going into the bar with him again with his glamour up.

I waved towards the bartenders chatting with some locals as we moved through the bar. I paused outside the heavy curtain leading to Pele's office. What I was about to do would change my relationship with Pele forever. I knew there was a very real chance that Andrei would walk away from me by the end of this. That would hurt . . . badly . . . but I would recover.

I wasn't sure if I would recover from Pele turning her back on me, however. Aside from Jinx, she was my oldest friend.

"Pele? We need to talk," I said before I lost my nerve. My plan was crazy, but it was the only play I could think of that might actually work.

The curtain shifted to the side a few seconds later, allowing me and Jinx to pass through. Jinx prowled around and looked over some artifacts Pele kept on one of her shelves. I plopped down into a chair in front of her desk.

"Something's happened since we spoke this morning?" Pele tilted her head as she looked at me from behind her desk.

"Yeah." I huffed a laugh. "Sebastian showed up when I was meeting with Kaysea at the beach. He killed Andrei. I brought Andrei back. Don't ask for details on that one. Killed the witch who sold me out. She was the human dating Andrei's sister. He doesn't know, so that's a mess I'll have to deal with soon. Magos's nephew Mikhail is the assassin of the Vampire Council. I think he's having what passes for a midlife crisis for vampires and is around town being generally annoying.

"The Circle has 'requested'"—I made some air quotes—"my presence tonight in the woods. If I don't show up, they're going to start targeting my friends and family. Obviously, I could run, but I can't run forever, and I can't expect everyone to stay on high alert for the rest of their lives. Sebastian wants me to surrender to him so we can play house again and he can use me to secure his place in the Circle."

"Is that all?" Pele quirked a perfectly sculpted eyebrow at me.

I waved my hands in the air. "Eh, Kaysea is also having visions, all of which seem to imply some big change is coming to the fae, and I am somehow involved." I frowned. "I'm probably going to have to avoid hanging around cliffs for the foreseeable future."

Pele tensed for a moment before catching herself. Most people would have missed it, but I'd known Pele for a long time.

I narrowed my eyes at her. "I told Kaysea that was a problem for another day since nothing implies it's connected to my immediate problem. Anything you want to add to that?"

"You are correct that it's not connected to your immediate problem," she said evenly, her words slightly clipped.

I knew that tone. Whatever Pele knew, she was keeping to herself for now. My frown deepened, but I decided to let it go. Pele could fill this room with things she knew and I didn't. While I did my best to avoid daemon and fae politics, Pele lived for them. Whatever Pele knew or suspected about Kaysea's vision apparently wasn't related to my current problem, and that was good enough for me.

"I don't want to run." Even though I'd decided on this plan already, I was still surprised to find that my words felt true.

After centuries of moving from place to place, I was done with running. I wanted to find out what happened if I called a place home again.

"I'm going to make it clear to the Circle tonight that I will never voluntarily go with them," I explained. "And even if they succeed in capturing me, they will have to deal with the wrath of the fae and daemons."

Pele's bright turquoise eyes met mine, and I saw the concern and wariness in them. "How will you convince them the fae and daemons as a whole would become involved? Over one shifter?" she asked cautiously.

We stared at each other for a few seconds. I could feel the tension rolling of Jinx from across the room. He had not been a fan of this plan at all. But I wasn't going to back out now. My heart thumped wildly as I held Pele's stare and slowly stretched my hand out.

"Don't," Pele said sharply as she sat up straighter in alarm. It occurred to me that this might be the first time I'd ever seen true panic on her face. "Think about this, my friend," she said in an urgent, almost pleading tone.

"I'm sorry to put you in this position," I said softly. "I know we've danced around this so carefully over the past couple centuries. But it's time for that dance to change." Magic flowed out of me, and a gateway opened, revealing one of the daemon realms.

Pele let out a long breath and closed her eyes.

"That's not all," I said sadly and let the gateway close.

That was the easy part. Pele had always known I had some way of easily getting to different realms. While she'd never seen me use my magic, I regularly took jobs from her that required going to realms that most people couldn't travel to. I hadn't volunteered how I was doing it, and she'd never asked. I'd just blown up that unspoken agreement and now was going to dump kerosene on it and light a match.

Pele's eyes snapped open, and she looked at me in confusion. "What do you mean?"

"Do you have any magical artifacts you don't care about?" I asked. Showing would be easier than telling.

Pele opened one of her desk drawers and slowly pulled out a wooden figurine and handed it to me. It was a carving of a dragon. Crude, but I could feel the power in it. It was probably some type of fire spell.

I stretched my left hand out, holding the wooden figure, and let my other magic loose. It was still full from devouring Jolie's magic, so it was more sluggish to respond than usual. It needed some prodding for the blue fire to coat my hand and the figurine. I concentrated on holding it back, so I didn't destroy it completely. After a few seconds, I pulled my magic back and put the figurine back on the desk. It was covered in a light coat of frost, but at least it wasn't a pile of ash.

Pele slowly reached out and picked up the wooden dragon. She dropped it instantly and pushed back in her chair. I didn't say anything as I let her gather her thoughts.

I didn't know what I would see in her eyes when she looked at me again. Would she still be concerned for her friend? Or would I see only fear and suspicion?

After a few moments, she reached forward and picked up the wooden figure again. Without looking at me, she asked, "Are you even a shifter? Or are you pure devourer?"

"I don't know," I said truthfully, and a sharp pain struck me as she continued to avoid my gaze. "For obvious reasons, I haven't let anyone besides Kaysea study my magic. There aren't many shifters left since they scattered when their realm fell. The few I've encountered don't have magic like mine. I've been to dozens of devourer realms. None of them possess magic like this. Their way of consuming magic usually involves physically consuming flesh or blood. Even the ones that can consume magic from a distance don't use a blue fire to do so. And they don't leave frost behind. I shift into a feline. The same type of feline as my brother shifts. And I remember our parents shifting. I'm obviously at least part shifter.

"The rest . . . I don't know. Kaysea says my magic also tastes like fae magic. But I've never encountered a fae who can do what I can." I looked at Pele, but she was still staring at the wooden dragon figurine.

"Is there anything else?" she asked, her expression and tone still unreadable.

"I have a minor talent for reading souls. That's it," I said quietly, trying to keep the angst out of my voice.

She wouldn't be able to accept this. The gateway magic

was one thing, but Pele's father was the leader of the Assembly. She would take over as leader of the daemons one day. I was asking her to choose me over her unfaltering loyalty to her father and the Assembly. A crack started to form in my chest, and I didn't think I'd be able to fix it.

"Fuck." Pele rubbed her forehead and finally looked at me. All the tension that had been building as I told her the truth fled when I saw no fear or anger in my friend's eyes. Only desperation and concern. "Who else knows? I'm assuming Magos and obviously Jinx."

Obviously, Jinx replied.

"Andrei knows," I said.

Pele frowned at that but didn't say anything.

"My brother. Cian is probably filling in his lover on everything as we speak so we should probably include Dante on this list. And I'm pretty sure Connor suspects but probably can't prove anything." I bit my bottom lip, still not sure what Pele was thinking.

"Connor could prove to be a problem. He wants you dead, Nemain," Pele warned.

"Trust me, I know." The memory of almost being drowned by him hours earlier was still too vivid for my liking.

"The Circle cannot be allowed to have you," Pele said firmly, her gaze taking on that distant look when she was thinking through a problem.

"I would never voluntarily help them. When I meet them tonight, I'm going to tell them that. And that I've taken steps to inform both the daemon and fae of my abilities if they take me by force. Whatever they're up to, they're not ready for the daemons and the fae to come after them. Taking me will ensure that happens."

Turquoise eyes locked on mine, fury brimming within them. "This is a foolish plan."

"Foolish doesn't always mean terrible."

"You have to know that if the warlocks take you, the fae and daemons won't be mounting a rescue mission. They will kill you, Nemain." Her tone was harsh, but I saw the panic in her eyes. "They will probably kill you just for existing."

"I don't think there is any probably about it." I laughed.

"This isn't funny!" Pele snapped.

"Sorry. I know it's not funny." I held up my hands in a placating gesture. "It's been a really long fucking day, Pele. And I'm holding it together by the barest of threads. I know I've put you in a terrible position." I swallowed, not wanting to ask my next question.

But Pele heard the unspoken question between us anyway. "I won't tell anyone. Not until I have to."

"Your father . . ." I didn't know how to continue. As the leader of the Daemon Assembly, his power wasn't absolute but pretty close. And Pele was his eldest daughter. Everyone knew he was grooming her to take his place one day.

"My father likes you," she said softly. "But that doesn't mean he wouldn't kill you."

"Well, hopefully it won't come to that. The Circle might decide to be smart about this and back off rather than face a possible fight with the fae or daemons over me," I said.

"Let's hope so." Pele didn't sound all that confident in that outcome. "Survive this and we can come up with a plan for the future. You won't be able to hide this forever. Keeping the secret of your ability to open gateways has been challenging enough. This will eventually get out. You need to form some powerful alliances before it does."

"Fuck." I rubbed my forehead. I was terrible at playing politics. Jinx's low laugh rumbled through my head, and I shot him a dirty look. "Back to the immediate problem of surviving tonight. I need to make sure Magos and Andrei stay behind. Do you have a KO ball?"

Pele frowned. "No. They're not particularly common since they only work on humans or human hybrids. And they take an annoyingly long time to make, so few bother to make them."

"I was worried you'd say that." I chewed on my lip as I thought of other options. The KO balls would have made several parts of my plan easier. Andrei would be easy to confine. Magos . . . not so much.

"The warlocks will likely be protected against them, but a strong KO ball could weaken them a little. Maybe knock out some of the less powerful ones. And if they had any vampire backup, it would take them off the table." Pele tapped her long fingernails on the desk. "I know someone who might be able to help."

She stood and I followed her out to the bar with Jinx trailing behind me. Pele stopped at a table where a lone figure sat.

Mischievous amber eyes met mine, and a grin spread across Eddie's face. "Well, hello again."

I narrowed my eyes slightly at him. I felt like I'd seen him a lot the last couple of days. He'd been with those fae who had a problem with the job I did for the loki. Then he'd been at the bar chatting up Pele. It wasn't unusual exactly. Eddie had moved to town a few months earlier and ran a shop down the street that specialized in rare books and artifacts. He *did* conduct a lot of business at the bar. I was probably just being paranoid.

It didn't help that I had no idea what he was. He reminded me a little of a loki, but I knew he wasn't one. Eddie always looked harmless in his ripped-up jeans and band t-shirts. His long dark blond hair was shaved on the sides and usually slicked back from his face or pulled into a ponytail. He looked human. But I was pretty sure he wasn't.

"Want to join me for a drink?" he asked, kicking out a chair for me to sit in.

I crossed my arms and remained standing. He glanced at where Jinx was sitting next to me, and I got the distinct impression they were talking to each other telepathically. Interesting. Outside the fae, most people had odd reactions to grimalkin. They either treated them like animals or were weirded out by their presence.

"Nemain has a question for you," Pele replied. "You two have met before, right?"

"Oh, yes." Eddie responded before I could. "Nemain and I are the best of pals."

I raised an eyebrow at him. He merely smiled at me.

I cut to the chase. "Do you have a KO ball, or can you get one on short notice?"

He frowned. "A knock-out ball? That's random."

"Kind of need a yes or a no on this, Eddie."

"I can help you out." He gestured towards the chair. I let out a sigh and took a seat.

Pele rested a hand on my shoulder. "I'm sorry I can't help you tonight. I have to go back to the daemon realm for a meeting with the fae. My appearance would be missed. And if they found out I missed this meeting to help you . . . they would ask questions."

I rested my hand on top of Pele's. "You've done more than enough. Thank you." I squeezed her hand one more time before pulling mine away.

She removed her hand a second later. "Leave a quick message for me when it's done so I know you're safe?"

I read between the lines. If I didn't leave that message, Pele would tell her father about me. There'd be no going back from that.

"I will."

Pele nodded and walked back to her office. Eddie threw back a shot of whiskey and grinned at me. Something in that grin had me worried.

"All right. Do you want the good news or bad news?"

I sighed. "Let me guess. You don't have a KO ball on hand, but you know where to get one?"

Eddie raised his eyebrows as his eyes lit up with amusement. "Up for a quick trip to one of the Seelie realms?"

Chapter Twenty-Five

WE HEADED to Eddie's place from the bar so he could determine where exactly we needed to go. I glanced around the living room. I didn't know Eddie all that well, but Pele vouched for him, and she wouldn't do that lightly. His apartment was above his shop, and there wasn't much to it aside from some furniture and empty beer bottles.

"Mind if I use your mirror while you get ready?" I asked.

Eddie waved a hand and headed down a hallway. "Go for it."

I swiped my glyph across the top of the mirror, and Magos answered from our living room. I gave him the quick version of my run-in with Mikhail and the Circle's request that I meet them tonight in the forest. I informed him about heading into one of the Seelie realms with Eddie to pick up something for tonight.

He wasn't happy about me going to one of the fae realms without him, but bringing him with me would ruin my plan. He would recognize a KO ball immediately and get suspicious. After assuring him we'd leave directly from Eddie's place and return to our apartment, he reluctantly agreed.

With that taken care of, I headed down the hallway where Eddie had gone. I stopped in the doorway at the end as I took in his office. "Oh," I breathed out.

Jinx curled around my legs so he could get a look. The room was pure chaos. Boxes were stacked against one wall. Maps and papers were taped or tacked to the opposite wall. More papers and artifacts were piled on what I was assuming was a desk, but I couldn't actually see it. My eyes roamed over everything, stopping on a painting that hung behind the desk. A woman stared out from the painting with bright green eyes and fiery red hair.

Eddie moved some papers around on the floor and snatched a rolled-up map. His movement drew my eyes away from the woman in the painting, and I stood next to the desk where he had stretched out the map. He didn't say anything about the painting, and I didn't ask even though I was dying of curiosity.

Jinx reared up on his hind legs and rested his front paws on the desk so he could look at the map. His movement caused a stack of papers to slide, and I slammed my hand down on them before they tumbled over. I gave Jinx a dirty look, but he was busy staring at the map, and I felt his uncertainty.

Before I could question him about it, Eddie pointed to a spot on the map. "Have you ever been to Mag Ildathach?"

I looked at the area he was pointing to, some plains stretching between mountains on the map. I studied the area and tried to think about all the places I'd been in the various Seelie realms.

"Yeah, it's been over a century, though. A friend of mine is from Tír fo Thuinn, so I've spent most of my time there and in Mag Mell and a few other places in the Unseelie realms. I've only been to the Seelie realms a handful of times, one of which was to Mag Ildathach." I tried to remember what it had been like. An image of a field of wildflowers and trees with bright purple blossoms floated to the surface of my mind.

"We need to go here." Eddie pointed to a northwest section of the plains. "Can you open a gateway there even if you haven't been there before?"

I nodded. "It may not be precisely where you have in mind, but I can definitely open a gateway in that area. We might have to travel a couple miles to get wherever we need to be."

"Good enough. There's a building used for storage there. Mostly cheap or commonly found artifacts and amulets. Last time I was there, I saw a box full of KO balls. They're not really a high demand item, but since they take a few days to make, the owner of this place makes sure to always have some on hand just in case," Eddie said. I noticed he carefully didn't say the name of the owner.

Something was bothering me about this. Something I wasn't remembering was skirting around in my mind just out of reach. I frowned at the map as I tried to remember. "Eddie, who exactly is the owner we're going to be stealing from?"

"Just some prick who shorted me on a deal. I hate dealing with the fae." Eddie flashed a smile at me. "It's not like KO balls are used all that often. They probably won't even notice they're gone."

Somehow, I doubted it, but I didn't have another choice. I needed KO balls for my plan and didn't have enough time to have someone make them. "If this goes sideways, I'm blaming you." I sighed. "You ready to head out?"

Eddie slung a bag over his shoulder. "Yeppers."

I arched an eyebrow and glanced around at the papers, boxes, and random items cast about the office. "Let's do this in the living room."

Eddie shrugged and walked out of the office.

Before following him, I turned to Jinx. "Everything okay?"

Why wouldn't it be? He trotted out of the room, deliberately sending papers flying everywhere.

Annoyance and concern flickered through me. Something about going to Mag Ildathach bothered him. I followed him to where Eddie waited for us in the living room.

I pulled a large blue gem wrapped in silver wire out of my pocket. "A good friend of mine is fae, and she's well connected to the royal family." Not a lie exactly. Kaysea was a fae princess. So technically she was well connected to the royal family. "Because I've done a lot of jobs for them in the past, they gave me this artifact so I could easily travel back and forth between the fae realms."

An absolute lie. Such artifacts existed, but they were only gifted by one of the fae queens. And they always came with a limited number of uses and other strings attached. But it was one of the many cover stories I used when I had to open gateways in front of people. Usually, I only opened gateways in dire circumstances; people were less likely to question my magic when I was saving them from being killed by a devourer or some other creature.

"Nice friends you have. Convenient you have such a gift for this endeavor." His tone was friendly enough, but I saw some calculation flickering in his eyes.

Something about Eddie left me uneasy. Like he knew more about me than he was letting on. But I was sure I'd never met him before moving to Emerald Bay, and he'd never specifically done anything to deserve such suspicions. It was just a feeling I couldn't shake.

"I am indeed fortunate to have such nice, *powerful* friends."

Eddie just grinned at me. I didn't like what I saw in that grin, but it was too late to stop now.

I held the blue gem out and pushed my magic through it. It caused the gem to light up in an impressive way even though that lighting was only for show. The gateway opened and revealed a wooded area on the other side. I stepped through, and Jinx and Eddie followed me.

We looked around to get our bearings as the gateway closed behind us. The trees in this area were small and planted in rows. The trees didn't have any fruit, but this was clearly some type of orchard. No one was around, which wasn't surprising. From what I remembered of this region, it wasn't that populated. A small village sat to the south of the plains and was the only way in or out of this region that didn't involve going over the mountains.

"Good. We're actually pretty close. Our destination is at the end of this row." Eddie gestured north and moved forward. Jinx and I followed.

I concentrated my thoughts and pushed them out to Jinx. *I smell sidhe. And recently, too. You sense anything?*

Jinx kept pace beside me, but I could read the tension in his body. *Definitely sidhe. But I can't get much from their magic trail, which means they're probably warriors left here to guard the place. They know how to cover their tracks. And to stay hidden.*

I barely managed to contain my groan. *Fuck. He implied this place wouldn't be guarded. Sidhe warriors will be a problem.*

Both of us narrowed our eyes on Eddie.

Think he's setting us up? Jinx asked.

I don't know. My gut tells me no. I think he was being truthful about being annoyed at fae who stiffed him on something. Maybe he really did think this place would be unguarded?

Maybe. I think we should kill him just to be safe.

That seems a bit drastic, I thought wryly.

Indeed, it does. Eddie cut in with a sense of amusement.

Jinx and I both froze and stared at each other, wide-eyed.

"What the fuck are you?" I blurted out as Jinx said the same thing telepathically.

Eddie just turned around and continued to walk backwards, never missing a beat. "Someone who's quite good at monitoring telepathic conversations," he said with a playful grin. "I didn't tell you about the fae because I didn't want you to freak out. I delivered the supplies they asked for to this house a week ago, and it was mostly vacant. The family they serve only uses it as a summer vacation house, and the workers won't be returning to maintain the orchard for another month. It'll be fine. We'll be in and out with no one the wiser."

"Fine. Next time just tell us everything from the start, okay?" I replied, not entirely convinced by Eddie's assessment, but it was too late now.

"Sure thing." He gave me a mocking salute and spun back around.

Jinx and I glanced at each other with equally annoyed expressions.

We were nearing the end of the orchard, and a two-story house made of wood and stone with vines growing up the sides came into view. Tall trees surrounded the sides of the house that didn't face the orchard. The fae were connected to nature, and it was common for plants to grow on the sides of their houses. In some regions, houses would be built around or even inside massive trees. Or the center of houses were left open so large gardens could be maintained.

"A house in the middle of the woods with magical vines growing up it? I'm pretty sure every folklore tale has warnings about not going into places like this." I paused when I felt the ward surrounding the house.

Eddie held his hand out to me. "You worry too much."

I just arched an eyebrow at him and stared at his hand.

"I can get us through the ward, no problem. I'm assuming the grimalkin will have no trouble getting himself through?"

In response, Jinx's magic sprang to life, and he casually walked through the ward. I tentatively put my hand in Eddie's and tried not to jerk as his magic settled over my skin. My magic twitched underneath my skin, not liking this at all, but I held it in check. It felt itchy. I rubbed at my nose a couple of times and sneezed.

Eddie gave me an amused look. "Felines and their delicate senses."

I flipped him off with my free hand.

"Ready?" he asked.

I nodded, afraid that if I spoke, I'd sneeze again. We took a couple of steps together and walked past the ward. Once we were ten feet past it, Eddie released my hand.

I frowned at my hand, then Eddie, and glanced back at the ward. "I didn't feel the ward at all as we passed through it. What did you do?"

"What can I say? I'm a man of many talents." He winked at me, and I looked at Jinx.

I think he mimicked the magic of the ward. It saw both of you as a piece of it, so it didn't react at all. I don't know how he did that.

Jinx and I looked at Eddie expectantly. He just smiled at us and walked towards the house. Jinx looked at me, genuine alarm in his eyes. Eddie clearly freaked him the hell out. And I was kind of in agreement there.

"There's an entrance to the basement where the supplies we need are stored around the back of the house," Eddie said over his shoulder.

I followed after him but almost slammed into his back when he stopped a moment later. I bit back the rather rude name I'd been about to call him when I sensed magic building up around us. *Shit.*

Eddie spun around and shoved me back just as two sidhe wearing silver armor appeared out of nowhere and unleashed dual bursts of flames that slammed into Eddie's chest.

Jinx! Get the one on the left!

I drew my swords and ran towards the one on the right. My bracers could easily manage one direct hit if the sidhe warrior directed those flames at me. I'd still probably be thrown back a bit, but at least I wouldn't be burned to a crisp.

I'd just about reached the sidhe when they both stumbled forward slightly, their flames sputtering out. I halted but kept my swords raised.

What the fuck is he, Nemain? Jinx growled in my head.

I glanced where Eddie had been standing, expecting to see a charred body but instead saw a perfectly fine and not-at-all charred Eddie. The flames the sidhe had shot at him hovered over his skin.

"Umm . . . you okay there, Eddie?" I asked.

"Oh yeah," he replied cheerfully and made a flicking motion with his fingers. The fire that had been surrounding him moved until he held a small tornado made of flames in each hand. "I'd move back if I were you, shifter."

Not having to be told twice, I leaped back. The magic of the sidhe warriors snapped into a shield as Eddie hurled the fire back at them. It slammed into their shields, and they flew backwards, crashing into the trees. I winced at the sound of several bones breaking.

Jinx trotted over to them as I slid my swords back into their sheaths. *Still alive. They were able to protect themselves against the flames, but they're going to be out for a while to heal and recharge.*

"All right, now that the guards are taken care of, let's get what we came for." Eddie started to head back around the house, but I caught up to him and slammed him against the wall.

"What the fuck was that?" I snarled.

"Me taking care of the guards while you stood there with your swords?"

"Those were sidhe warriors. They're trained in all sorts of elemental magic, and they're not exactly lightweights. You took a direct hit from them and then you . . . took their fire magic from them? What the hell did you do?"

Every part of me wanted to draw my swords back out, but I wasn't prepared to escalate this fight with him. Technically, he'd done us no harm. And Pele trusted him enough to recommend him for this.

Still… he bothered the hell out of me.

"How did you do that, Eddie?" I asked once again, slightly calmer this time.

Eddie raised his left hand and tapped a finger against a simple gold ring he wore on his middle finger. "Picked this up a while ago on a job. Lets me manipulate fire magic."

"Bullshit."

Eddie just smiled and slowly removed my hand from where it still rested on his arm. "My ring is every bit as magical as that fancy gem of yours that lets you open gateways."

Alarms ran through my mind, but I kept my expression neutral as I stared at him, not admitting to anything. He could be bluffing and was trying to get me to reveal more about myself. The funny and harmless appearance that Eddie gave off every time I'd met him in the past was rapidly crumbling. Eddie was a lot more than he seemed, and I wasn't liking this one bit.

I told you we should have killed him, Jinx said.

"That's still an option," I muttered. "Let's just get the KO balls and get out here."

"Sure thing." Eddie pushed off against the wall. Apparently, he wasn't the least bit concerned about Jinx and me discussing his death. I sighed and headed after him with Jinx behind me.

"Anything truly valuable is kept elsewhere in the house. Or not kept in the house at all since they only use it in the late spring and summer." Eddie knelt in front of two sturdy wooden doors. "But they keep the KO balls down here, along with the other non-valuable stuff."

He reached a hand out, putting the palm flat on the door.

A tiny wisp of magic came from him, and a metal clang sounded from the other side of the door. He grabbed the handle of the right door, and I grabbed the other. Together, we heaved the doors open.

I peered into the darkness. "Down we go?"

"Down we go." Eddie smirked and made a sweeping gesture towards the basement stairs.

"Why do I have to go first?" I frowned at him, not loving the idea of him being at my back.

I didn't think he'd actually do anything to harm me; if he was planning that, he could have done it at any time. Maybe he was planning on trapping me down there, but I didn't know what he would gain from that. And even if he did, Jinx or I could break through the ward. Doing so would alert the fae we were here, but we were on limited time anyways.

"Because you've got those fancy kitty cat eyes and can see quite well in the dark. I don't remember where the lights are down there, and I'm scared of the dark." He gave me a wide-eyed innocent look.

I growled under my breath and headed down the stairs. My eyes adjusted quickly, and I walked across the basement towards a lantern that hung from the ceiling. Eddie slowly walked down the stairs and had just reached the bottom when I got the lantern turned on.

"Last time I saw them, they were over there." Eddie pointed to some shelves on the left.

I walked over, letting my eyes skim the objects on the shelves. Mostly dried herbs and some other ingredients used for spells. Another shelf had gems and stones organized by type and size. None of it was particularly valuable. Below the shelves were several boxes Eddie was looking through. I poked through the boxes as well.

"Found 'em." Eddie pulled out a box.

I looked in the box where a dozen glass spheres were rolling around the bottom. I snatched one up and held it in front of me, moving it back and forth between my fingers. "And you're sure these are good?"

"It's not like they have an expiration date," Eddie replied.

He wasn't wrong, so I grabbed the remaining glass balls and tucked them into a leather pouch wrapped around my waist. I tied it shut and headed to the basement doors. "Let's go."

Jinx waited for us at the top of the basement stairs.

"All good?" I asked him once we were back outside.

I'm not sure, he said slowly, and I noticed the tension in the way he was standing. *Let's just get out of here.*

I scanned the area around us, trying to sense what was upsetting Jinx, but nothing stood out. Still, I knew better than to ignore the grimalkin's instincts. We needed to get out of here.

I sighed. "I don't want to open a gateway inside their ward; they'll investigate this area too much once they realize we were here, and I don't want anything traced back to Pele." Or them realizing that some weird ass magic had been used to open a gateway in a realm where that shouldn't be possible. But the Pele part was true, as well. "Let's get past the gateway and go into the woods a bit, then we'll get the hell out of here."

Eddie got us past the ward once more, and we quickly walked into the woods.

The sense of being watched hit me, and Jinx and I stopped abruptly. Eddie went still as well. Whatever he sensed was enough to make him drop the carefree mask he normally wore; predatory amber eyes scanned the woods. We moved until we were standing back-to-back as we tried to figure out what was out there. Unlike the orchard on the other side of the house, these woods were dense, and the sunset decreased visibility. I could still see into the shadows pretty well, but I suspected Eddie couldn't.

Movement to my left caught my attention, and a second later, Jinx appeared and planted himself next to me.

What's out there, grimalkin? Eddie's voice rumbled through my head. His voice was slightly deeper when he spoke telepathically.

Before Jinx could answer, a low rumbling growl came from our right, and half a dozen feline forms leaped down from the trees.

"Shit," Eddie and I exclaimed at the same time.

The largest of the grimalkin stepped forward and looked at us. Given the size, it was a female. Like Jinx, she had a solid black coat, which was somewhat unusual among the grimalkin, who were generally some shade of grey. We waited but didn't say anything. I saw only six of them, but I had no doubt more waited in the trees.

So much effort was spent to keep you safe and out of the fae realms. And here you are drawing attention to yourself, a female voice said in my head. The large grimalkin walked towards me and started circling. *Perhaps it was a mistake to send my son to you. He clearly hasn't done a good job of keeping you out of trouble.*

"He tries, but honestly I make his life hell." The words spilled out of me before I'd fully processed what she had just said. "Wait. Your son? Jinx is your son?" I looked down at Jinx, who had gone utterly still as he stared at the larger grimalkin.

She completed her circle around us and sat down in front of me. Sitting down, her height was only a couple inches below mine. Her light green eyes narrowed at me. *You need to leave. Now. She has always suspected you exist and has been searching for centuries. Stay out of the fae realms.*

She turned to leave, and the rest of the grimalkin followed her.

I started after her. "Wait! I have no idea what you're talking about. Why did you send Jinx to protect me? Who is looking for me?" I asked desperately. I wanted to ask if she knew what I was, but I held that question back.

The grimalkin paused and looked over her shoulder at me. *Leave now, realmwalker. We will cover all traces of your time here.*

Hounds bayed in the distance, and I whirled to face the direction of the sound. What the hell was going on?

"We should go. Right now," Eddie said tightly.

I looked back and forth between the direction of the baying hounds and the grimalkin. I desperately wanted to know what was going on. She knew something about me. She was Jinx's mother. I might never have the chance to find out more about what I was and why I had this magic.

The time will come to give you the answers you seek. But it is not now. YOU MUST LEAVE, REALMWALKER.

The hounds were getting closer, and I got the sense we really didn't want to be here when they arrived. I snarled in frustration and flung my hand out, opening a gateway into my apartment. Eddie jumped through the gateway, and I moved to follow but paused as I looked for Jinx.

He hadn't budged and was staring at the retreating black grimalkin. His mother. Holy shit, his mother.

With a graceful move, she turned and cleared the distance between us with a single leap. She rubbed her head against his, but I couldn't hear whatever words they shared before Jinx turned and went to the gateway.

"Come with us," I told her urgently.

No. I am needed here. Go.

Every part of me wanted to stay. This was the closest I'd ever come to finding out more about myself. "Fuck!" I swore. "This isn't over. I will find you again," I promised.

I have no doubt.

It physically hurt, but I turned and followed Jinx and Eddie through the gateway, leaving behind the answers I'd been seeking for centuries.

Chapter Twenty-Six

THE GATEWAY CLOSED BEHIND ME, and I stood in our living room facing Magos and Andrei. Magos said nothing as he looked me over for any wounds. Andrei just stared at me wide-eyed.

Before I could say anything, Eddie tossed a small object at me. I caught it on instinct; it was the gem I'd used earlier to "open" the gateway when we first went to the Seelie realm. He must have swiped it from my pocket at some point in our adventure. Probably when I'd slammed him against the wall.

Shit. My swords were a heavy weight on my back. Eddie and I weren't friends, but I did like him. The few times we'd hung out at The Inferno he'd made me laugh, and that was something I valued quite a bit these days. The only other person who made me laugh so easily was Andrei, but my relationship with Andrei was complicated and only getting more so.

"Interesting how you were able to open that gateway to get us home without your fancy little gem," Eddie drawled and walked over to the kitchen. "Got any coffee?"

Magos looked at me with raised eyebrows, and I saw the question in his eyes.

"Let's not kill him just yet," I sighed. "Coffee first, then we can discuss the pros and cons of killing him. Pele recommended him for this, and she'd probably be annoyed if we killed him before checking with her."

"Or . . ." Eddie paused from rummaging through the cabinets and walked over to the butcher block and pulled out a knife. "I'll swear a blood oath here and now to never reveal your secret in exchange for you opening a gateway to a realm of my choosing at a later date."

"Which realm?" Magos asked, still focused on Eddie like he was a potential threat.

"My home realm," Eddie replied. That predatory alertness was back in his eyes as he held Magos's stare. "I was exiled. But someone I still care about is there. She's everything to me. I *need* her back."

I thought about the woman in the painting. Those intense green eyes. I didn't know what Eddie was or what he was plotting, but his devotion to that woman was real. Long-term blood oaths weren't something people did lightly. The one I'd done with Ryder had come with relatively low risks because it had a time limit. But even if I took Eddie to this realm he wanted to go to soon, he'd carry his side of the blood oath for the rest of his life. And the longer a blood oath lasted, the more it sank into your soul and the risk of it killing you outright for breaking it became a reality.

Killing him remained the easier option. But I kind of liked him. And my damn curiosity was growing about what the hell Eddie was, and if I helped him with this, maybe I'd find out.

"Fine," I agreed. "Swear it."

Eddie slashed his hand and said the oath. I used a claw to cut my hand and accepted. Magic snapped between us. Hopefully this wouldn't come back to bite me in the ass.

Magos shook his head slightly in disapproval and walked to the kitchen. "Move," he said to Eddie and started to make coffee.

I walked over to the kitchen island and sat on one of the stools. Eddie joined me, slumping on the stool next to me. Andrei was still oddly quiet as he walked over and stood at the end of the counter on the other side of Eddie.

"Andrei, meet Eddie." I gestured towards Eddie and made the same gesture at Andrei. "Eddie, meet Andrei."

They nodded at each other, and Andrei asked, "Is it rude to ask what you are? I'm still learning all the rules."

I spun on my stool to face Eddie and gave him a sly look. "Yeah, Eddie. What are you exactly?"

He laughed under his breath. It was oddly raspy and didn't quite fit in with his appearance and laid-back demeanor. "I'm amazing is what I am."

I scoffed and smiled as Magos slid my coffee in front of me. "That's one word for it."

Magos handed Eddie a cup of coffee, then rested his hands on the counter and looked at me. "What happened in the fae realm?"

"Ran into some minor trouble, but we handled it. Got what we needed and were almost in the clear when some grimalkin showed up." I sipped some coffee. "Their leader gave me a cryptic warning about staying out of the fae realms, made it clear she knew who and what I was, and then told us to get out. Oh, and apparently, she's Jinx's mother."

We all looked at Jinx, who was sitting in front of the window staring out into the night. Luna was sitting between him and us as if protecting him. Jinx turned around to look at us.

I don't want to talk about it, he growled in my mind.

"Jinx . . ." I said with a frown.

No.

There was no forcing Jinx to do anything. I'd have to wait until he was ready to talk about it.

"All right," I sighed. "Let me make sure everyone is up to speed on everything." I left out the role of Hades bringing back Andrei's soul and instead left it at him being revived via CPR. Both Magos and Eddie snorted at that.

"Also, the witch who informed Sebastian about my whereabouts is no longer a problem," I said smoothly, hoping no one would ask any follow-up questions to that.

"Who was it?" Andrei asked.

Damn it.

Nice try, Jinx snickered at me.

Bite me, I thought back at him and flipped him off for good measure.

All the guys were looking at me. Magos was glancing back and forth between me and Jinx. I braced myself for the fight that was about to come, but we might as well get it over with now instead of him learning the truth at the worst possible time.

"Jolie," I ground out. "It was Jolie."

Andrei's eyes turned hard. "What do you mean 'was'?"

"I went to her cottage to talk to her," I said calmly.

Andrei leaned closer to me, and his eyes flashed yellow. "Bullshit. You went there to kill her."

I forced myself not to react even though I really didn't appreciate him getting in my face with the wolf so close to the surface. "Technically, I planned to talk to her *before* I killed her. If she'd told me she'd been forced to work for Sebastian against her will, I would have let her live."

Liar.

I shot Jinx another dirty look.

Andrei went absolutely still. "You killed her." His voice held a raspy edge to it.

"She was the reason you died today!" I growled.

Eddie slowly got up from his chair and moved to stand on the other side of the counter next to Magos so he was no longer between me and Andrei. Couldn't really blame him for that one. Magos kept calmly drinking his coffee.

"You didn't have to kill her," Andrei growled and moved closer to me. I tilted my head up to look at him. "You could have at least held her captive until Stela and I got to talk to her. We could have figured out another way! You can't just kill people!" he yelled.

"Let's recap." I held up a hand and started counting off. "She was Sebastian's niece. She's been working for him for her entire life and was completely devoted to him. She was a witch who practiced some pretty dark magic and was completely on board with whatever fucked-up plan the Circle is working on. Oh, and she's the reason Magos and I were discovered in this town. She *had* to die."

Andrei glared at me and looked to Magos and Eddie for support.

"If Nemain hadn't killed her, I would have." Magos's expression said he didn't understand why we were even having this conversation.

Eddie shrugged. "Didn't know her, but based on what Nemain said, the death was justified."

"What the fuck is wrong with you people?" Andrei demanded, his face a mixture of horror and disbelief.

"This is how it is in our world. I warned you," I said softly.

I hated the way Andrei looked at me. I knew this would happen eventually. But it's not like I could change the way things worked in my world. Doing so would get me killed. Either I would have to let Andrei go, or he would have to adapt to a much harsher world than he was used to. I didn't like either option.

"We'll talk about this more later," Andrei said through clenched teeth. "And no one tells Stela. I'll have to figure out how to explain this in a way that won't have her coming for your head."

"No one will tell her," I agreed. Before we could dive back into the argument over Jolie, I looked at Magos and narrowed my eyes at him. "I saw Mikhail today. In broad daylight working on his tan. You could have told me he had the ability to walk in the sun."

"I thought I implied that in our conversation," Magos replied. "What did he want?"

"To apologize," I said sarcastically. "He was also the one to deliver the message about meeting the Circle tonight. They want to have a little chat by the fae tree at midnight."

"Fae tree?" Andrei asked. He was still clenching his fists in frustration, but his eyes sparked in curiosity.

"The fae don't have as much interest in the human realm as the daemons do. They care about it because they need it as a power source, but they don't have nearly as many gateways here as the daemons. They also prefer to have their gateways in more natural settings. They commonly use a type of fae tree to hold gateways. One of them is in the forest around here. I'm guessing it has some sort of glamour on it so you wouldn't notice it. But I don't know for sure. It's pretty deep in the woods with no paths that go to it," I explained.

"Maybe you'll get lucky and one of the warlocks will try and tap into its power," Eddie offered and smiled at me.

I grinned back at him. "That would be nice, but I don't think they're dumb enough to try it."

He shrugged. "Those daemon youths tried it last month."

"That's because one of the lokis put them up to it. Plus, daemons are forever trying to prove themselves as being better than the fae. And the young ones go about it in particularly stupid ways," I said.

Eddie grunted in agreement.

"What happened to them?" Andrei asked after glancing around at us.

A pang of guilt hit me. He was constantly having to ask questions like this because he didn't know or have any history to go off of. I should have been better about giving him more information up front so he wouldn't constantly have to ask for it. Although, he probably wouldn't like a lot of the information I would have to give him.

"Well, none of them died," I offered.

Only because two out of the three are still unconscious. They had to be put into magically-induced comas because the tree waged a psychic war on them and shredded their mental defenses. It will probably take them years to recover, Jinx said without looking at any of us. I could tell by the way he was positioned he was still rattled from our encounter with the grimalkin and his mother.

Andrei looked at me, a deep crease forming between his brows. "And that's where you're meeting them tonight? Is that even safe?"

"That happened to the daemon idiots because they were trying to channel power from the tree. It's sentient . . . sort of. It was just defending itself. I've been to that area of the forest a bunch. I've even napped against the tree, and it was fine." I shrugged.

"You napped against the fae tree that's capable of shredding people's minds?" Andrei asked incredulously.

"The pup does have a point," Eddie said. "Even I wouldn't go within twenty feet of that tree."

"It likes me," I said defensively. "Moving on." I launched into my simple but probably crazy plan for the night.

All three of them gave a resounding no.

I looked at Eddie. "You don't get a say in this. You're only here because we had to flee that fae realm quickly. You're not part of our group, so you can leave whenever."

Eddie smiled at me and leaned back against the counter. *Argh.*

"This is the only option we have," I said to Magos. "Running is only a temporary solution. Besides, I'm tired of running."

"Going alone is foolish," Magos argued. "You can't count on them to keep their word and grant you safe passage. At least let us go with you and hide out of sight."

"They'll know you're there." I shook my head. "They've had plenty of time to set up wards around the area alerting them to your presence. They need me alive, but they'd happily kill the rest of you. Or capture you and use you to keep me in line."

"I'm perfectly capable of taking care of myself," Magos said in a hard voice. He wouldn't budge on this.

Andrei moved to stand next to him. "So am I."

"Told you so," I said to Eddie. He smirked but didn't say anything.

Magos eyed me suspiciously. Before he could react, I pulled one of the KO balls out of my pouch and threw it on the ground. It shattered into dozens of pieces, and the light that had been swirling around the ball shot out. I closed my eyes to avoid being temporarily blinded but heard two bodies thump to the floor.

I opened my eyes after a few seconds and looked at Magos and Andrei lying unconscious on the floor. "Help me move them?" I asked Eddie and grasped Magos under the arms.

"Yup." He grabbed Magos's feet. We moved him to one of the couches and repeated the process for Andrei.

"How long do you think it will last? A few hours? All night?"

Eddie thought it over. "Assuming that one was from the same batch as the one I used a while back, it'll probably last until the morning."

"Stay here and keep an eye on them?" I asked.

It was probably foolish of me to be this trusting of Eddie. But he already knew about my ability to open gateways. And he needed me to open the gateway into his home realm. So in for a penny, in for a pound.

I sighed, "You may need to move Magos to his room if he's still out when the sun comes up. I don't know if the warlocks know about you, but I don't want to take any chances. Stay inside tonight, Eddie. You understand what you have to do if I don't return, right?"

"Sure. Can't guarantee you'll have any whiskey left when you get back, though." He winked at me.

"Thank you." I looked around for Jinx. He was waiting for me by the door. There was no way of convincing him to sit this one out. But he at least was capable of moving through wards undetected.

"You're absolutely sure about this?" Eddie asked.

"It's the best play." I walked over to where Luna was sitting on the back of the couch. She was staring at Jinx with obvious concern. I gently rubbed her back. "It'll be okay, Luna. He'll come back."

The silver grimalkin looked away from Jinx and up at me. Her light lilac eyes were serious and a little more focused than normal. *You. Too.* Her words were somewhat disjointed but clear enough.

I blinked in surprise at her communicating with me for the first time since coming to stay with us. Her magic must be returning. I smiled, feeling a sense of relief at knowing she was making progress in her healing. At least something was going right.

"That's the plan." I headed towards the door after stroking her head one last time.

Eddie reached out and grabbed my arm as I passed him. "Come back, okay?" he said quietly.

I looked at him and once again saw the predator that set my instincts on edge.

"I come back and you tell me what you are?"

He flashed his teeth at me in a smile. "I'll think about it."

Chapter Twenty-Seven

THE ONLY SOUND in the night was the leaves crunching under my boots as I jogged through the woods. I would have preferred to run through the woods in my feline form, but that would have meant leaving my clothes and weapons behind.

I paused between two exceptionally tall trees to get my bearings. I was likely a couple of miles away from the clearing.

"You're really going to do this?" a voice said from the darkness.

I was pretty sure I jumped five feet in the air. "You're such an asshole," I snarled.

Dante snickered and pushed off from the tree he had been leaning against just off the path in the shadows "So?"

"So . . . what?" I drawled.

"Don't be thick. It doesn't suit you," he said smoothly.

"Why are you here?" I angled my body towards him and readied myself for an attack. He'd been pretty pissed off after our last encounter on the beach. "Actually, more importantly, how did you know I would be here?"

Dante sighed. "I informed your brother about what happened, and he was worried. After a lot of arguing, he insisted on going to your place to check on you. We got there shortly after you left. It took a bit of convincing, but we eventually got the information out of your friend."

Alarm shot through me. "Is Eddie okay?"

"He's fine." Dante rolled his eyes. "He's almost as annoying as you." The former god of the underworld stiffened, and his eyes shot above me.

He must have spotted Jinx, who had positioned himself directly above us. Dante might have gotten the drop on me, but Jinx had gotten the drop on him, and that was satisfying.

"Your brother wanted to come after you."

My blood ran cold. Cian was never much of a fighter, and these woods were crawling with warlocks and vampires. I had no doubt Cian and Kaysea were at the top of their list for people to capture to control me.

Dante must have seen all of that written on my face. "He's not here. I made him promise to stay inside your apartment tonight. I told him I would do all I could to help you."

"I'm surprised you didn't tell him that and then jump on over to The Inferno to have yourself a whiskey while I walked to my probable demise," I said only half-jokingly.

"I may not care for you, but I love your brother. He loves me, but he would never forgive me if I did such a thing. I will not lose him," Dante said coldly, but I heard the hint of desperation in his voice.

Something in me broke slightly at his words and the intention behind them. I wondered if I'd ever find that kind of love and devotion again. Things between me and Andrei had been casual and were now in "complicated" territory. I didn't know exactly where we would go from there.

"I appreciate your offer of assistance. But I won't let you give yourself away. I don't like you anymore than you like me. But if anyone figures out who you are, we both know my brother will be a target. You can't just walk in and rip out their souls. Word of that would spread somehow. A survivor. The echo of that much magic being used. Hell, even that fae tree may give you away. Pretty sure both the fae and the daemons want to have a word with you. Not to mention all your kin. Or at least what remains of them." I smirked.

Dark eyes glared at me as my words struck home. "I'm still more than capable of fighting without using my magic."

"But defending yourself against whatever magic the warlocks are using will be difficult if not impossible without your magic," I replied.

"I'm not leaving." He locked his jaw stubbornly and crossed his arms across his broad chest.

Let him handle the vampires, Jinx said. *Between the extra KO balls and his skills, he should be able to handle any of them out there. And that will allow me to concentrate on helping you with the warlocks.*

"I have a plan that will work for both of us," I said.

It was my plan, to be clear.

Dante glanced up at the grimalkin and smiled slightly. "Fine."

I shifted impatiently. "Jinx came up with a plan to make everyone happy. The warlocks are running this meeting, and representatives from the Circle will be there. I have no doubt they brought vampires for backup who are probably spread out in the woods surrounding the clearing." I untied the leather pouch from my side and handed it over to him. "Take out the vampires for me. Jinx will help me deal with the warlocks if they don't accept my counterproposal."

"Is your counterproposal 'Eat shit and die'?"

"More or less."

Dante chuckled. "That does like your type of plan. All right." He attached the leather pouch to a loop around his pants. "I'll take care of the vampires. I can't promise not to get involved, though, if it looks like they're going to take you."

"Fair enough," I replied with a shrug. "See you on the flip

side." Without waiting for a reply, I took off again towards the clearing.

The thick marine fog had rolled in and blocked the light from the moon and stars, but I knew where I was going. I was close enough to the clearing to feel the power of the fae tree radiating out. I smiled as I thought about Eddie's suggestion about the warlocks making the amateur mistake of trying to tap into the tree's power. Maybe I would arrive at the rendezvous to find a bunch of warlocks writhing on the ground trying to piece their sanity back together. One could only hope.

I was less than a mile from our meeting spot when I heard movement in the underbrush. I opened my mouth slightly and inhaled. Vampires. I should have known the Circle wouldn't keep their promise to grant me safe passage. Maybe I should have let Dante tag along until I made it to the clearing.

"I'm fairly certain the deal was safe passage. Y'all could have at least waited until after I made it to the clearing to go back on your word." I drew my short swords, holding one high and the other low.

Two vamps appeared in front of me. I recognized them both from the other night. One was a tall woman with dark skin and hair braided back from her beautiful but serious face. She held a wicked curved blade. The other was the young vamp who had been behind me for most of the previous fight. His skin was pale, and his dirty blond hair hung limply around his face. I was willing to bet his sneer was permanent.

"I don't give a fuck what Mikhail said," the dark-haired vampire hissed. "You killed Ryder. I fucking know you did."

"Well. Yeah," I said mockingly as I twirled the swords around a few times. "You have to admit he had it coming."

"I'm going to tear your throat out and listen to you choke on your own blood," she growled. The grip on her blade tightened.

"I don't really know much about vamp politics, but something tells me the Council won't be happy about you disobeying orders." I grinned as I tracked the vampires moving in the trees on both sides of me.

"The order was bullshit," the younger vamp spat. "You killed our clan leader, and it's within our right to claim your life for it."

I didn't respond. Instead, I waited. They were trying to bait me and keep my attention on them. I twirled both swords again. It was an obnoxiously showy move. Spin. Wait. Spin. Wait.

As one, they flew from the trees. The twins. They had leaped straight up, and at the peak of their arch, they lashed out with their whips simultaneously. No doubt they intended to ensnare my wrists which had been following a consistent pattern for the past minute.

I dove forward and rolled back on my feet before they even landed. They hit the ground at the same time, and neither had time to react before I had hacked the head off the twin on the right. Blood sprayed across my face as I turned to face the other twin who was less than four yards away and was still trying to comprehend what had just happened. I sprinted towards him.

Vampires were fast. But shifters were faster. And I was especially fast, even for a shifter.

I thrust one sword into his gut and slashed the other across his throat. Blood bubbled out of his mouth, and I yanked both blades free. He collapsed to his knees, and I swung my sword. His head fell to the ground with a soft thud, and his body toppled over.

My attention turned to the two remaining vamps. They stood frozen. They'd been confident with four-to-one odds. But now they weren't so sure of the outcome.

I moved towards them, half expecting them to turn and run, but instead they split apart. My pace slowed so I wouldn't end up between them. I flipped my swords so they ran parallel with my arms, the flat part of the blade resting against me. The vampires moved as one, each attacking from a different side. I blocked their blows.

The younger vampire on the right slashed at my throat, I dropped my swords and ducked under his swing. Grabbing his extended arm with my right hand, I used my left to shove him. Off balance, he fell forward as the other vampire thrust her sword at me.

The young vampire screamed as the sword bit into him. I grabbed his head and twisted. Bones snapped and he fell.

The remaining vampire snarled at me and yanked her sword free from her fallen companion. I swiped my swords off the ground and parried her first blow with both swords. By pivoting and twisting to the side, I caught her blade between mine and pulled it to the side. I ripped my swords free and cut diagonally upwards with my left sword, catching her across the chest.

She screamed and took a step back, still clutching her sword. Spinning, I sliced her head off with my right sword. I turned to face the vampire with the broken neck and cut his head off with one clean strike.

Jinx leaped down from whatever tree he'd been perched in and trotted over to some bushes at the base of a tall redwood.

"You could have helped." I shot him an annoyed look.

You're perfectly capable of taking care of four vampires. Besides, I wanted to see how this played out.

Not entirely understanding what he meant, I walked over to where he was standing and peered into the bushes. Another vampire lay on the ground, a pouch next to him that reeked of magic. A familiar-looking dagger was in the vampire's heart. Jinx lashed out with his paw, and the head rolled away.

Jinx gave me a knowing look but didn't say anything.

"Whatever. I could have handled it." I pulled the dagger

free from the vampire and wiped it off, shoving it into my boot as I looked around for its owner.

But Mikhail was nowhere to be seen. I didn't like not knowing where he was or what he was out to, but there wasn't much I could do about it. I cleaned my swords and put them back into their sheaths. Assuming Dante took care of the other vampires, I likely wouldn't be using my weapons for the rest of the night.

"You ready to do this?" I asked Jinx.

Of course.

I started to move but stopped and looked at him. Golden eyes locked onto mine. "Thanks for coming tonight," I said softly.

He looked at me for another moment. *You're not going to get all weepy on me again, are you? Like you did at that rock in the lake we used to swim at?*

"I was five years old!" I exclaimed. "And that wasn't a rock. It was a two-hundred-foot cliff!"

You still cried. And then you got all mad at me.

"You shoved me off the cliff when I was too scared to jump!" I growled at him.

Do I need to shove you now?

I growled and stalked off to face the warlocks waiting for me in the clearing. Jinx was laughing above me as he returned to the trees.

Chapter Twenty-Eight

NO OTHER SURPRISES met me on my way to the clearing, for which I was thankful. I didn't see or smell Jinx anywhere, but I figured he was somewhere up in the trees. Whatever spells the warlocks had cast in the area probably wouldn't detect him. It was hard to get magic to work effectively around the fae. And grimalkin magic was particularly tricky.

He should be fine, I reassured myself as I exited the trees and entered the clearing.

I slowed my pace to take in my surroundings. Orbs of light hung around the edges of the clearing, illuminating the area. Six warlocks stood shoulder-to-shoulder in the center of the clearing with another two dozen spread out behind them.

I'd never met any members of the Circle besides Sebastian. For some reason, I'd been expecting them to all be in robes or expensive suits. A few were wearing those things, but most were in jeans with hoodies or jackets. Not exactly how I pictured members of the Circle.

The massive, ancient tree rose behind them, its power leaking out and tainting the surrounding air. Apparently, they'd been smart enough to leave the tree alone and not try to tap into that power. Pity.

I closed half the distance between us and stopped. The six warlocks standing in front, who I assumed were the Circle members, said nothing. I returned the favor and scanned each of them before looking over the warlocks who stood behind them.

I stopped when I found a pair of piercing blue eyes staring back at me. Sebastian. He stood rigidly a few feet in front of the others.

Satisfaction ran through me at seeing him trapped by a similar spell to the one that he'd placed on Andrei earlier. This whole thing could be an act to get me to lower my guard, so I remained vigilant.

"Let's hear this offer," I said clearly, unable to take my eyes off Sebastian.

A middle-aged man with light brown skin stepped forward and gave me an affable smile. His black hair was cut short and tidy. He was one of the few wearing a suit but had forgone a tie and instead had the top few buttons of his shirt undone. He looked like someone's favorite uncle.

"My name is Emir. We appreciate you coming out here to meet with us and discuss the path forward." His voice was pleasant with the trace of what I thought was a Mediterranean accent.

I kept my expression blank, giving no indication I recognized his name. This was the one Sebastian had been trying to oust. Given that Emir was speaking to me and Sebastian stood silently fuming behind him, I was guessing Sebastian had lost again to Emir.

"We'd like to put the past behind us and come to an agreement that benefits all parties involved. If you work with us willingly, we will ensure the safety of all your friends and family. And we'll compensate you for all of your work." He finished with a casual hand flourish as if that would just wave all my problems with them aside.

"And what, exactly, is it you want me to do?"

Emir had gone through a lot of trouble to get me here. Whatever he was plotting, I was certain I wouldn't like.

"Well, we can't give you all the details of that right now. Naturally, trust is going to have to be built up on both sides." He flashed another friendly smile. "But in general, we find ourselves in need of a way to quickly and safely travel to other realms. Specifically, the devourer realms."

I went completely still. He said it like he was asking me to take them for a stroll in a nice sunny park. No one wanted to go to the devourer realms except sometimes survivors hoping to find the friends and family they'd left behind. And those ventures rarely ended well. Going to a devourer realm was almost always a one-way trip.

"You can't possibly be that stupid." I narrowed my eyes in suspicion. "What exactly are you hoping to find there?"

He held his hands up in a placating gesture. "I assure you, we have valid reasons, and no harm will come to the human realm."

He chose his words carefully, but I'd had enough conversations with fae to know that what *wasn't* said was just as important as what was said. "But harm might come to the other realms?"

"And if it did, why would you care?" He looked at me curiously. "Your realm was one of many that fell to the devourers while the fae and daemons did nothing."

True. I shouldn't care, and I mostly didn't. The other realms weren't my problem. But Kaysea was fae. And Pele was a daemon. Both had family and loved ones in their realms that they would fight for, which made whatever the warlocks were plotting my problem.

"But we're getting ahead of ourselves." Emir gestured

behind him, and two warlocks shoved Sebastian forward. He stumbled a step and glared at them before walking stiffly to stand next to Emir.

"We're willing to grant you a boon as a symbol of good faith. I also want you to know the actions of Sebastian against you were of his own doing and were not sanctioned by me or any of the others." As Emir spoke, the rest of the warlocks fanned out until they had the three of us surrounded in a circle.

I eyed all of them warily, not liking where this was going.

"Sebastian is yours to deal with however you like. He has proven himself to be an impediment to our cause," Emir said coldly as he looked at Sebastian. Emir raised a hand towards me and said with a smile. "He's all yours."

Emir walked back to join the others in the circle. A push of power from them created a ward that sealed me and Sebastian inside. Well, that was unexpected.

I looked at Sebastian and saw what I'd missed before. His appearance was somewhat disheveled, and he had a resigned look on his face. Sebastian always considered himself smarter than everyone else, including the rest of the warlocks. He hadn't seen this coming and had no plays against it. He sighed and moved towards me until we stood a few feet apart.

I still had no intention of taking Emir's deal, but I wasn't going to pass up on this opportunity. Not as my blood and magic hummed with anticipation at finally getting our revenge.

"Looks like you lost the game, Sebastian." I drew one of my swords and glanced at the two black bracelets on his wrists. I'd only seen them a few times but knew they blocked a witch or warlock from doing magic. "They're really serving you up on a silver platter to me."

Trembles ran through me as my body flashed hot and cold. One way or another, Sebastian had been at the center of my life for almost half my existence. I'd wanted him dead for so long. He'd killed Myrna. He'd killed so many over the years. He'd tormented me for decades. And he had killed Andrei earlier today. But I'd also loved him for almost a century.

My sword moved slightly as my grip on it tightened and loosened.

Sebastian didn't give away a trace of fear. "One way or another, my life is over tonight. You're right. I did not anticipate this." His voice held a quiet, lost quality to it that I'd never heard before. He knew he'd die tonight. "You should learn from my mistakes. The Circle is not to be trusted. Whatever they offer you after this is a lie."

"Oh, come now, Sebastian. This is most unbecoming," Emir chided from outside the circle. "You were the only one who ever acted against Nemain. It was you who killed Myrna, after all. If I remember correctly, her heart sat in a jar on your shelf for years. It was very distasteful."

The magic in me surged at the thought of my beloved's heart wasting away on a shelf. Emir had chosen his words carefully to provoke me, and it had worked. I had to act or risk all of my magic leaking out in front of the warlocks, and I didn't want to reveal all of my cards yet.

"Wait!" Sebastian said urgently, but it was too late.

I thrusted my sword into his gut, and he gasped. He raised his hand to my shoulder and placed his head against it. I twisted my sword, and he screamed in pain. He lifted his head to my ear and whispered four words. Four words that made my heart skip a beat.

"Emir killed your parents."

This was why he'd wanted to search through the dream of my parents' death earlier. He'd been wandering through the crowds looking for someone. He'd known a warlock had been there. Had orchestrated the events. He'd wanted to confirm who.

Rage and disbelief ripped through me. He could be lying.

He probably *was* lying. This could be his last ploy to get revenge against the man who'd outplayed him and arranged his death.

He pulled back and raised his other hand, soaked with blood, and touched my face before collapsing to the ground. I knelt beside him and didn't pull away when he reached for my hand.

"It wasn't all a lie." He pushed the words out between gasps. "The swimming hole . . . in the mountains . . . that was real."

Pain shot through me as I remembered the dream from earlier. The first decade we were together, we'd spent every summer at that lake in the mountains. We even built a little cabin next to the lake.

"That cabin burned to the ground, and we never went back." My voice trembled.

Sebastian grimaced in pain. "I had to. I had to destroy it. Otherwise . . . I wouldn't have left."

Sadness gripped me, and I didn't know how to process that. I'd hated Sebastian for so long. I still hated him. But for a time, I had loved him. And he had loved me. But he'd chosen his pursuit of power over that love.

Grief and anger raged within me, and I didn't know which was winning.

"Loving her was selfish on my part. I should have left. But I was weak and couldn't do it," I whispered the words, and Sebastian's hand gripped mine harder. "You chose power over your love for me. I chose my love for her over everything else. I blame myself for her death almost as much as I blame you. But you tore out her heart and turned her last gift to me into agony." I stared down at him. "I would rip out your heart for the rest of eternity if I could. But this one moment will have to do."

Sebastian coughed up more blood and smiled at me through bloody teeth. "You . . . always were bloodthirsty."

He let go of my hand and reached into his pocket. He pulled out a small glass sphere and shoved it into my hand. I felt the small pulse of magic in it. His body arced one last time and went still.

I waited for a sense of relief or regret at his death. But I mostly just felt numb. It was over. I was finally free of him.

I rose and pulled my sword free from Sebastian's body, turning to face Emir. He strode forward, and the ward around us dissolved with a pop.

"Well, that's settled. I'd like you to come with me so I can go over the first task I have for you. I have a wonderful house all ready for you." His voice was kind, and delight shone in his warm brown eyes. He must have thought my killing of Sebastian meant I was willing to work with them.

He paused as I raised my arm and pointed the sword in his direction. The rest of the warlocks held their hands out in front of them or reached into satchels at their sides, ready to cast spells in my direction.

"That's not how this is going to go," I said firmly. "I will never work with you. The warlocks may not have directed Sebastian's actions, but you were aware of them and did nothing. For that alone, I would never help you."

Emir sighed and snapped his fingers. After a few seconds of nothing happening, he glanced into the woods surrounding the clearing.

I smiled at him. "Yeah, I don't think the vampires you had waiting in the woods will be joining us."

Emir looked at me, the friendly expression he'd been wearing all evening gone. His eyes were hard and calculating.

"No matter," he said calmly. "You're still vastly outnumbered. You will come with us one way or another. It's in your best interest to come willingly."

"I don't know exactly what you're up to, but I do know you've been very careful to not do anything that would attract the attention of the daemons or fae. You're not ready to face them head-on. Instead, you've been operating from the shadows for centuries, moving pieces into place." I swung my blade back into its sheath. "If I don't return tonight, information will be given to both the daemons and fae about my abilities to open gateways. And that you've taken me as a weapon to be used against them. Walk away, Emir. Nobody has to die tonight."

Emir studied me. "You're bluffing. If the fae and daemons learned of your abilities, they would kill you. And if your friends and family tried to protect you, they would be killed as well."

"True. But you would lose," I pointed out. "And that would be enough."

Emir looked away from me as he thought over my words, and some of the other warlocks shifted uneasily. The idea of going up against the fae and daemons clearly didn't sit well with them. Emir was still thinking it over, and I started to hope that I would be able to walk out of this clearing without any bloodshed.

While killing every warlock here would bring me an immense amount of satisfaction, it wasn't worth the risk of exposing my magic if I didn't have to.

But it seemed I wouldn't be walking away so easily as Emir shook his head and focused on me once again. "No. I think it's unlikely you would take this risk. And even if you did, your ability is unheard of. Without proof of your magic, the fae and daemons wouldn't invest that much time into finding you or fighting us. Their arrogance will eventually be their downfall."

He gestured towards me, and the warlocks on each side of him stepped forward and threw two bags down in front of me.

I leaped back but not fast enough. Ropes shot out of the

bag and wound around my arms and pulled. I strained against them but found no give. The magic in the ropes sank into me, and it felt like thorns tearing into my skin. I screamed and fell to my knees. The ropes tightened, pulling my arms apart. More ropes wound up my legs and midway up my body, the magical thorns digging into me.

Trapped. Bound. Trapped. Bound. The words repeated over and over in my head. Memories of the months I'd been bound and tortured flooded my mind.

I tried to reach for my magic, but it slipped away every time another wave of panic seized me. My lungs seized, and I gulped in air. Pulling against the ropes frantically, I felt the thorns dig in deeper and my magic slip further away. I was vaguely aware of Emir walking around me.

"This could have gone so much easier," he said.

This was spiraling out of control fast. My breath was coming in uneven gasps. I squeezed my eyes shut and tried to calm down, but every time I tried to take a deep breath, I just choked back a sob instead.

Jinx, I called out to him. *I can't break free of this.*

His presence settled in my mind. *You can and you will.*

I can't. I can't. I can't. I chanted over and over again.

Nemain. You need to use all of your magic.

I can't! I screamed again as the ropes tightened. *These ropes. They're blocking my magic. I can't reach it!*

Your magic eats magic, Nemain. Jinx's words remained calm and clear, and I latched onto his presence like it was an anchor keeping me from being lost. *Your magic isn't blocked completely. You just need to calm down and reach for it. It will set you free.*

Free. The word clanged through my head and helped push back some of the panic. If I wanted to be truly free. I needed to let my magic be free.

I felt the cool earth beneath my face. At some point in my panic, I'd fallen to the ground, so I was lying curled up in a ball. I needed to get myself out of this. The numbers were too many for Jinx to take on by himself. They would kill him. Dante would step in any moment now. He'd have to use his magic, which would put my brother in danger. Jinx would die and my brother would be hunted. And I wouldn't be there to save him. The panic rose again but not as fast as my rage.

I reached deep for my magic and found it. Most of my magic was completely blocked, but not the part I needed. The part I'd kept wrapped in chains for most of my life. Not anymore.

No more chains, I promised it.

It surged forward and attacked the ropes that bound me. Gasps came from the warlocks surrounding me. The ropes binding my legs fell away, and I pushed myself to my feet. I faced Emir and spread my arms. Crystal-blue fire erupted and covered my entire body. The last of the ropes fell away.

"Well. This is certainly unexpected." Emir's voice was calm, but I saw the uncertainty and fear in his eyes.

Four warlocks moved closer. One pulled something out of his satchel and threw it on the ground in front of me. Smoke rose, and my thoughts turned sluggish. My magic tried to push back against it, but it kept slipping through.

I gritted my teeth and pushed harder as I heard the warlocks move closer. The fire surrounding me shot out to one of them, and he fell to the ground screaming. I absorbed his magic and pushed harder against the smoke still swirling around me. My thoughts became clearer.

I whirled to face another warlock who was chanting a spell. Before I could lash out with my magic, a dark form pounced on the warlock. She screamed, and blood sprayed as Jinx tore out her throat. The grimalkin leaped to my side and snarled.

"Don't just stand there! Get her!" Emir barked.

The warlocks who had been standing behind the Circle

strode forward and surrounded me and Jinx. Some were chanting, while others reached into bags and satchels.

"Can you keep my magic away from the fae tree if I let it loose?" I asked Jinx. "I don't want to piss it off. Or somehow alert the fae to what's about to go down."

Yes. Jinx took off running towards the fae tree, weaving between the warlocks. *Now, Nemain!*

I stretched my arms out and let the cold blue fire pour out from me completely unrestrained. The warlocks around me screamed, and I closed my eyes as their magic rushed into me. I'd never allowed myself to take in this much magic before, and it was a heady feeling. Laughter bubbled out of me as I absorbed more and more.

After what felt like an eternity but was probably only a couple of minutes, the magic feed became a trickle and stopped completely. My eyes opened, and my head swam as I adjusted to all the new magic.

In a haze, I turned in a circle and saw nothing but ash and a perfect circle of frost.

I looked towards the fae tree for Jinx. Dante was with him. They both looked no worse for wear, and the tree still stood.

Mounds of ash fell away as I walked through what remained of the warlocks to where Emir and the remaining members of the Circle had banded together. I stopped at the boundary of the ward they had erected. Blood dripped from their palms. They had joined their magic in a blood spell to erect a ward powerful enough to keep me out. I was pretty sure with more time I could break through such a ward.

I smiled at them, and they paled a bit. One pulled a gemstone out of a bag and chanted over it. A gateway opened, and they quickly stepped through.

All except Emir.

"Don't think this is over, Nemain." He walked over to the edge of the ward. "You were important before when we only knew of your talents for opening gateways. But this,"—he gestured around the clearing—"this is true power. I always get what I want."

"Sebastian thought that too," I said evenly as I looked to where the body of my former lover turned enemy still lay. It didn't feel real that he was dead. That I no longer had to fear what horrors he would bring into my life.

Emir followed my gaze. "I guess we'll see, won't we?" He strode through the gateway.

It closed behind him, and the ward fell away. Slowly, the orbs of light around the clearing winked out, and I stood in darkness.

A warm body appeared at my side. "Thank you, my friend," I said as Jinx leaned into me slightly.

Dante appeared and stood on my other side, and we looked up at the fae tree.

"Do you think it sensed my magic?" I asked.

"Well, we're all still standing here and sane, so I don't think so," Dante replied. "But who knows with the fae? They're a bunch of weird assholes."

Jinx let out a low growl. I laughed and opened a gateway to take us home. "Careful, Dante. I might start to like you. Go on through." I gestured towards the gateway and turned to walk towards what remained of Sebastian. "I've just got to grab one thing."

Chapter Twenty-Nine

THE FOLLOWING DAY, I woke up in the early afternoon and padded into the kitchen. Jinx was stretched out in a sunny spot in front of the windows. I smiled and walked over to the coffee machine to read the note attached to it.

"Just push the button." I obeyed, pushing the button above the arrow drawn at the end of the note, and the coffee machine started making noise.

Both Magos and Andrei had still been asleep when I'd gotten back from the woods. Magos had been the first to wake up. He . . . hadn't been happy. He spoke in a slightly louder than normal voice, which I was pretty sure was his version of screaming, and asked if it "was done."

I nodded, and he'd walked down the hallway to his room without another word. He didn't slam the door. I kind of wished he had.

Apparently, he'd snuck out after I'd crashed in bed to set up the coffeemaker. So he couldn't be *that* mad at me. Or maybe he just didn't want to deal with me trying to make coffee and messing up all his settings. I sighed. It was probably the latter.

Andrei hadn't been nearly as restrained in telling me how

he felt about my little knockout maneuver. Shortly before dawn, he'd jolted awake with yellow wolf eyes. Eddie stood behind Jinx, who threw up a shield to prevent the werewolf from attacking them. Andrei yelled and growled at me for a solid ten minutes before storming out the front door. He *did* slam the door.

Thirty minutes later, I was walking down the beach swinging a spelled cloth bag at my side. I reached the gazebo and sat down on the wooden steps to watch the waves roll in and out.

A large wave crashed in, and when it pulled back, Connor stood in the wake. He'd come far enough out of the water that he'd had to switch his fin for legs, but he didn't come all the way onto the beach. I didn't know how much Kaysea had told him about me after what he saw yesterday. But he clearly wanted to be close to the water in case I decided to throw down. His posture held a wariness that had never been there before. My lips curved up in a predatory smile.

"Should have known you'd survive. Somehow, you're always the one that survives." His eyes fell to the bag at my side, but he didn't ask.

"Not everyone survived last night." I rose from the steps and walked to the water.

I stopped where the waves ended and held Connor's stare as I purposely took two steps forward. The waves crashed just below my ankles. The merman didn't move, but I could feel the tide growing stronger, each wave a little more intense. I tossed the bag, and he snapped it out of the air.

"What is this?" He looked at the bag. It was spelled to block the scent of its contents as well as keep it fresh. When I didn't answer, Connor slowly untied the bag and looked in. His nostrils flared, and his head snapped back up as he looked at me with those odd pale green eyes.

"The heart of the warlock who killed Myrna. My beloved.

Your sister. The youngest princess of Tír fo Thuinn." I raised my chin slightly even as my voice trembled. "Let it be known that I recognized the blood debt owed but never claimed for my part in her death. And I pay my debts."

Connor pulled the bloody heart out of the bag and stared at it. Emotion churned in his eyes and blood leaked through his fingers, dropping into the water. He said nothing as he dumped the heart back in the bag and tied it shut. He started to turn back to the sea but paused.

Without looking at me, he said in a rough voice, "The kingdom of Tír fo Thuinn acknowledges a blood debt was owed even if it was never called. And we thank you for this gift that will finally allow our princess to rest. You are welcome in our kingdom once more." He glanced over his shoulder at me. "I still don't like you, though."

"Likewise." I watched him disappear into the waves.

As I trudged back up the beach, I didn't want to return to the apartment. There was a heaviness that clung to me. I'd finally gotten vengeance for Myrna. Sebastian was dead, and I could move on. Maybe have a life that didn't revolve solely around my need for revenge.

Jinx had informed me that he intended to nap all day and wasn't to be disturbed. Magos would be hiding out in his bedroom until the sun went down. Plus, he was likely still mad at me. I had spoken with Pele over the mirror last night, so she knew she didn't have to deploy the nuclear option. I didn't really have a plan when I got back on my bike and started driving, but I wasn't surprised I subconsciously made my way to the woods. Despite everything that had happened there the previous night, I still viewed the woods as my refuge.

I jogged through the trees and undergrowth until I reached my normal spot. After removing all my weapons and clothes, I piled everything up on a nearby rock.

The glass sphere Sebastian had shoved into my hand fell

out of a pocket. My heart skipped a beat, and my muscles froze as I stared at the small glass ball resting on top of the dry forest bed.

Cautiously, I reached down to pick it up and held it between two fingers. I didn't know what to make of it. It clearly held some magic, but I didn't know what. Given that Sebastian had given it to me, I doubted it was anything good. I'd bring it to Pele or Kaysea and have them examine it to see if they could decipher what it could be.

"Why can't I just be rid of you already?" I muttered as I rolled the glass ball back and forth between my fingers.

I hissed as my finger brushed against a jagged section and blood smeared against the glass. The glass sphere glowed and grew warm. I swore and tried to drop it, but it disappeared in a flash of light. I shook my hand but could still feel the warmth on my fingers. It spread down my hand until it reached the first blue flower tattooed on my left arm.

I watched with wide eyes as the edges of the flower blurred. My skin heated and sweat formed. Blue sweat.

"What the fuck?" The blue ink faded from my skin as more sweat dripped off my arm. The heat spread up my arm and down my back. Without bothering to shift, I took off at a dead run towards the river two miles away. I was dripping in sweat as I dove into the cold water.

I pushed back up to the surface and brushed my hair back as I stared at my arms. The inky blue sweat had been washed away, and bare golden skin was all that remained. My fingers shook as I rubbed them up and down my arms. When the tattoos hadn't disappeared after Sebastian's death, I'd assumed they'd be with me for the rest of my life.

Why had he done it? Maybe part of him still remembered that cabin in the mountains. I didn't know.

But I was finally free of him. Relief and joy shot through me, and I shifted to my feline form. I bounded off into the woods, leaping over the forest undergrowth and pushing my body as fast as it could go.

I wasn't nearly free of all this. Emir and the rest of the Circle would try another method to entrap me. I had no idea of the identity of their mysterious friends, clearly helping them up their magic game. And the power I'd kept hidden my entire life was now known by multiple parties, which meant it was dangerously close to being brought out in the open completely.

In some ways, I had more problems now than a couple of years ago. But Sebastian's death had made me feel free for the first time in decades. And I was going to enjoy the hell out of that feeling while it lasted.

Miles and miles blurred by. A few startled rabbits and deer darted out, but I didn't bother chasing them. I wasn't hungry. I just wanted to run and not think about anything for a while. Eventually my pace slowed to a jog, but I kept going. I scoped out a few potential napping spots. Checked on the fae tree. And just explored the woods with no purpose in mind. It was glorious.

After a couple of hours, I made my way back to my clothes. My pace faltered as I approached. Andrei sat on the ground, back leaning against a tree.

"Hey, kitty cat."

I made a chuffing noise at him and shifted back to human form. His eyes turned yellow as they slowly traveled down my body.

"Hello, wolf." A smirk played across my lips while I pulled my clothes back on.

"Enjoy your run?" He got to his feet.

"I did. You could have joined me."

"Thought about it." The yellow in his eyes faded back to hazel. His gaze slid over my body once more. "Your tattoos are gone."

"Yeah," I said, the word catching in my throat. "It seems

I'm now finally and completely free of Sebastian. I can move on with my life."

"That's good." He gave me a genuinely warm smile, but something dark flickered in his eyes. "I'm happy for you."

"How's your sister?" I said carefully as I slid my weapons back on, ignoring the sharp pain I felt at what I'd seen in his eyes and what it likely meant.

Andrei tracked every movement but didn't say anything.

"Andrei?"

His eyes met mine, and we moved at the same time. His mouth was on mine in an instant. I pushed him back towards a tree, and he flipped me at the last second so my back was against it. He pinned me there, and I kissed him harder. I nipped his bottom lip, and he growled.

He pulled back after a moment, and I let him go.

"Sorry. I didn't mean to do that," Andrei said in a low voice.

He was staring at my lips, and I knew he was thinking all kinds of wicked things. He glanced up at me, and his eyes glowed yellow before I saw him pull the wolf back.

"It's been harder to keep the wolf under control." He took a deep breath. "I want to know more. About you. About magic. About everything. And I want us to figure out what we want to be. I just . . . need time."

"That's fair." Pain flashed through me, but I kept it off my face and out of my voice.

I'd known this was a possibility, that it was actually the most likely outcome. But even though I'd known this moment was likely coming, it still hurt like hell.

"Stela did not take the news of Jolie's death well. I didn't tell her that you . . . I didn't tell her exactly how she died. Stela doesn't believe Jolie was the bad guy in all this. She won't believe you had no choice." Andrei didn't believe I had no choice either, but he didn't say those words. We both knew how he felt. "I need some time to help her get through this and figure out how to keep my wolf under control. I don't ever want to lose it like I did when I attacked Stela."

"I understand." I reached out and touched his arm, enjoying the feel of his hard muscles beneath my fingers. "I'm here whenever you're ready. We're sticking around for a while."

"You and I are not done," he said roughly.

I took a step forward and kissed him lightly on the lips. "I know."

It was probably a mistake to give myself hope that he would come back. But I clung to it desperately, and it helped the ache in my chest.

We stood there for a minute with our heads bowed and foreheads touching before Andrei took a step back and grabbed a cardboard tube off the ground. He twisted the plastic lid off and tilted it until a rolled-up piece of paper slid out.

"Happy birthday, Nemain," he said and held the still rolled-up paper to me.

I gently took it out of his hand and unrolled it. My breath caught. "It's beautiful," I whispered as I looked at the water-color painting. He'd painted me leaning against the fae tree with Jinx watching me from one of the branches. It was serene and peaceful. I swallowed and looked up at him. "I thought you hadn't seen the fae tree?"

Andrei grinned. "I might have bribed Jinx to show me early this morning. Ever since you told me you'd napped against it, I wanted to see it. I thought it would make a good painting. Jinx insisted on being in it since he was the one to show me the tree."

"Thank you." I looked back at the painting and admired the swirling colors he'd managed to capture in the leaves. "I love it."

"Since you're sticking around, I figured you might want to

add more personal stuff to the apartment. Make it feel more like a home maybe?"

I raised a brow. "Weapons don't count?"

"It is possible to hang things other than weapons on the wall," he said wryly and then winced. "Maybe hang it away from that plant, though."

I laughed. "Probably a good idea. It's still mad about the beef."

He handed me the cardboard tube, and I carefully rolled up the painting and tucked it inside. "See you soon?" I asked lightly.

"You will." Andrei gave me one last smile and then walked off into the woods.

I watched him go into the darkening forest. The sun was setting. It was time to head back.

We'd promised the vampire kids we would take them out that night. The Council was still looking for them, so they weren't truly safe yet. But we couldn't keep them cooped up in that apartment forever.

I felt someone watching me but forced my body to remain loose. My fingers trailed down my thigh to the dagger I'd strapped there. The one I'd taken out of the vampire I'd missed last night. Fingers curling around the handle, I pulled it free and spun around. It flew towards a shadowy spot between a tight cluster of trees.

The faint mist that had been hovering in that area, barely visible, snapped tighter. Mikhail appeared and caught the knife an inch away from his face. Show-off.

"You could have just handed the knife back to me."

"Don't hang around in the woods like a creeper, and I won't throw knives at your face," I retorted.

He arched an eyebrow at me. "I'm pretty sure throwing knives at people's faces is a normal reaction for you."

"You more than most."

He rolled his eyes and looked the knife over, sliding it into the sheath he had strapped around his thigh. I decided ignoring him was the best course of action and walked back towards the road. He appeared by my side a moment later, and I sighed.

"Something I can help you with?" I asked, not bothering to keep the annoyance out of my voice.

"Definitely not relationship advice."

I stopped and closed my eyes. How mad would Magos be if I killed his nephew and left his body in the woods? I mean, they had barely spoken for the past few centuries. They weren't that close anymore despite the familial ties. I felt like it could be justified.

"You're thinking about killing me, aren't you?" Mikhail asked in a tone that said he wasn't worried, just curious.

I snapped my eyes open and glared at him. "Am not." I resumed walking. Big surprise, he followed.

"You definitely were. You're very quick to resort to violence. It's kind of funny the wolf has a problem with that. They're not exactly known for being pacifists."

"He's new to being a werewolf and didn't grow up in our world. He's still processing everything." I quickened my pace. "And why the hell am I explaining this to you? It's none of your damn business. Shouldn't you be leaving town anyway?"

He didn't reply, and we walked the rest of the way back to the road in silence.

I hopped on my bike and started it up but didn't pull away. Mikhail was just standing there. Hands clasped behind his back and a calm expression across his face. A hint of uncertainty shone in his eyes, but he didn't say anything.

The damn pull I felt towards him intensified. Mikhail was a complication that I didn't want or need. He was just hot, and my body was reacting to it, nothing more. My magic rippled beneath my skin, and I pointedly ignored it. Mikhail needed to get the hell out of my town, and hopefully I would never see him again.

For some insane reason, the words that came out of my mouth were the exact opposite of what I'd just told myself. "You don't have anywhere to go, do you?"

"I have plenty of places I can go," he said arrogantly.

I narrowed my eyes. He was such a liar.

"Let me rephrase. You don't have anywhere you *want* to go."

He looked away from me and stared down the road. I let out a long-suffering sigh.

"Are you done with the Council? Completely? No more hunting vampire kids for them?"

"I'm done." His eyes met mine once more, truth shining in them. "I've been done for a while."

"How hard will they come for you?" *How much trouble are you going to bring my way?* I didn't ask the last part, but he knew what I was getting at.

"They don't have anyone good enough to bring me in or kill me." His voice held no trace of arrogance. Simply stating the facts. "They might try. But it won't be anything I can't handle."

"If you betray us, I will break every bone in your body and dump you in a realm full of devourers," I promised.

"I have no doubt." He smiled at me, and a light danced in his twilight eyes.

I jerked my head in a quick nod over my shoulder. "Get on. Let's go home."

Epilogue

ON SILENT PAWS she stalked up the mountain path leading to the large stone home built into the mountainside. Seeing her son and being able to touch and speak to him had shaken her more than she'd ever thought possible.

She'd never doubted that she'd made the right decision in sending him to the child all those centuries ago.

But it still hurt.

When she reached the summit, she headed straight to the tall wooden doors of the home, and they opened for her immediately. She continued through the quiet house until coming upon the balcony that overlooked the valley below.

Two figures stood waiting for her.

The woman was watching the sunrise, but the man turned to look at her with his bottomless black eyes. She'd grown used to them centuries ago, but they still unnerved most people. A jarring reminder of what he was. What part of him was, anyway.

She leaped up onto the perch they'd built into the railing just for her. The woman tensed slightly. *When are you going to stop worrying about me falling to my death?* she asked the woman in amusement.

The woman turned and leaned back against the railing. Bright emerald-green eyes looked at her with warmth and a touch of exasperation. "It's a long way down. And last I checked, you don't have wings."

The man grunted in amusement. They'd been having this argument since the couple had moved into this house all those years ago. Been banished to this house. The price to leave was often more than they were willing to pay.

"You saw her yesterday?" the woman murmured. "In person?"

She twitched her tail as she looked out over the valley, not looking at any one thing in particular. *Yes. She is doing as well as can be expected. My son has guarded her well.*

"Oh, Nyx." The woman moved and stroked her back once in comfort and left her hand resting on the railing. Nyx leaned into it.

"How long do you think we have?" the man asked.

Nyx knew he was already thinking through multiple strategies for how to deal with the fallout soon to come.

Not long enough.

"Will she be ready?" the woman asked.

She'll have to be. We will all fall if she's not.

Want to Read More?

The next book in the series, A Shift in Fate is out now! Signed
paperbacks with character artwork are available on the Greymalkin
Press Shop at www.greymalkinpress.com.

Exclusive Bonus POV

***Want to know what Mikhail was thinking when
Nemain got a little stabby in Chapter 11?***

Read the chapter from his perspective! Join the newsletter on
https://maddoxgreyauthor.com/newsletter-signup/ to get this
bonus chapter and others!

Lost Legacies Guide

<u>CHARACTERS:</u>

Andrei - local werewolf, in a casual relationship with Nemain
Cian - feline shifter with necromantic magic; twin brother of Nemain; has a strained relationship with her but still loves her fiercely
Damon - teenage vampire on the run from the Vampire Council
Dante - necromancer, incredibly powerful and in a long-term relationship with Nemain's brother Cian
Eddie - local who owns and runs a shop of magical oddities and supplies, nobody knows what he is
Elisa - oldest of the teenage vampire runaways
Isabeau - child vampire that the teenage vampires take care of and treat as a younger sister
Jinx - a fae cat known as a grimalkin, him and Nemain have been together since she was born; he's grumpy and has the ability to inflict bad luck on others
Jolie - human with a small amount of magic, dating Andrei's sister Stela

Kaysea - mermaid princess and bestie of Nemain; Myrna was her twin sister; older brother Connor is very protective of her

Luna - another grimalkin (because the only thing better than one cat is two cats); unlike Jinx she is sweet and cuddly; has no memories of her life prior to a year ago

Magos - old vampire warrior, his past is a bit of a mystery but he's loyal to Nemain and their relationship is similar to that of a an uncle/niece despite not being related

Mikhail - vampire assassin of the Vampire Council; nephew of Magos

Misha - part of the teenage vampire group, looks very similar to Elisa but they don't know for sure if they're actually related, either way they consider each other brother & sister

Myrna - Nemain's mermaid lover who was killed by Sebastian, twin sister of Kaysea and younger sister of Connor

Nemain - feline shifter with dark magic that she shouldn't have and will get her killed if others find out; on the run from her ex-lover Sebastian while she figures out how to get her revenge

Pele - daemon who runs the local tavern, The Inferno; close friends with Nemain who she has been in an ongoing casual poly relationship with for centuries

Sebastian - warlock who was in a relationship with Nemain for decades before she realized he was using her and left him; he killed Myrna in retaliation and has continued to stalk and torment Nemain

Stela - werewolf, younger sister of Andrei and currently dating the human Jolie

<u>REALMS:</u>

*Note, this is not an extensive list of all the realms because there are many. Only those relevant to the story are mentioned.

Human Realm - the modern world that humans are familiar

with; most humans are completely unaware that their realm is one of many or that magical beings walk amongst them

Kanima - former realm of the feline shifters; this is where Nemain's parents were born; it fell to devourers and the survivors fled to the human realm

Cerulle - former realm of Magos and Mikhail; also fell to devourers; survivors fled to the human realm and were later killed during the vampire and werewolf war

Tír fo Thuinn - despite being referred to as a realm, this is actually a territory that stretches across all the fae realms, it is the dominion of the sea fae, all the oceans and seas belong to them

Mag Ildathach - fae realm, belongs to the Seelie Court; name means multi-colored plains

Mag Mell - fae death realm, belongs to neither the Seelie or the Unseelie; like all death realms it is difficult to fully comprehend or travel in without necromantic magic; currently where Dante & Cian call home

Acknowledgments

Publishing this book is one of the most terrifying things I've ever done in my life. Easily in the top five. The other four involve heights and the one time I had to play the piano in front of two thousand people. I'm the type of person who has a difficult time being satisfied with their own work and has a hard time letting something go. So publishing a book was incredibly stressful for me. Once it's out there, it's out there and there's no taking it back.

When I closed my eyes and clicked the publish button, I knew the book wasn't perfect. I knew it could be better. Writing is both an art and a skill, and it's something that you get better at with time and practice. So I had to accept that I did the absolute best I could and each book would be a little bit better.

I can't thank my editing team, Sara LaPolla and Karen Robinson, and my beta reading team enough. I learned so much from all of them while working on A Shift in Shadows, and they truly helped me realize what I wanted this story to be and supported me in getting there.

Thanks to all my friends and family for supporting me throughout this entire process. Danny for agreeing with me on how to pluralize loki. Diana, for last-minute sanity checks on grammar rules and style changes. And of course, my furry companions Dahlia and Clio for looking adorable, while I have completely one-sided conversations with them about problems with a scene.

And last but not least. Thank you so, so much to all the

readers who took a chance on an unknown, new author and picked up this book. I hope you stick around to see what Nemain and the crew get up to. It's gonna be a fun ride.

Y'all are the absolute best.

About the Author

After earning a degree in history and political science, Maddox was pulled kicking and screaming from the world of academia and thrust into the tech industry. Because they had bills to pay and nerd muscles to flex.

Whenever possible, they leave reality behind to build fantasy worlds filled with snarky morally grey characters and hot but devious love interests. Maddox currently resides in the northeast, but they'll always consider themselves Californian at heart. They live with their partner and faithful, but often stinky, furry companions.

To get regular email updates about new releases and other announcements, be sure to sign up for the newsletter on maddoxgreyauthor.com

facebook.com/maddoxgrey.author
instagram.com/maddoxgrey.author
tiktok.com/@greymalkinpress